This was going to be a long day, Ryan thought wearily. But if he could just keep Christine talking…

He didn't know anything about her, didn't know whether or not to believe her story about kidnappers, but he knew she was involved in *something* unsavoury.

The truth was, she fascinated him. He couldn't escape the feeling that she was a very complicated person and he was only scratching the surface.

But then he looked around. Right now, he had a bigger problem than his growing obsession with Christine Greenlow. They were being followed again…

Dear Reader,

It's a new year, a fresh start, and we have plenty of fantastic reading material from fabulous writers to keep you enthralled all year long.

Aimée Thurlo brings us another of her sexy Navajo heroes in *Redhawk's Return*, the second book about a Redhawk brother, and Laura Gordon gives us a strong McQuaid lawman hero in *A Cowboy's Honour*. There's a third McQuaid man to come in March, so keep your eyes peeled.

Karen Leabo's *Ryan's Rescue* is a classic woman-in-jeopardy tale of adventure and suspense, when all we really know is that our hero is not what he seems...

Jackson's Woman is an unusual **Her Protector** story from Judi Lind, and those of you who enjoy tales of the old West will adore it—Jericho Jackson's the kind of man we'd all travel through time for.

Enjoy them all and have a happy 2000!

The Editors

Ryan's Rescue
KAREN LEABO

*First published in Great Britain 2000
Silhouette Books, Eton House, 18-24 Paradise Road,
Richmond, Surrey TW9 1SR*

© Karen Leabo 1998

ISBN 0 373 07832 3

46-0001

*Printed and bound in Spain
by Litografía Rosés S.A., Barcelona*

KAREN LEABO

credits one of her teachers with initially sparking her interest in creative writing. She was determined at an early age to have her work published. When she was still at school she wrote a children's book and convinced a publisher to put it in print.

Karen was born and raised in Dallas. She has worked as a magazine art director, a freelance writer and a textbook editor, but now she keeps herself busy writing full-time about romance.

Chapter 1

They were coming for her soon.

Christine Greenlow, who forty-eight hours ago had been dressing for her father's campaign dinner and worrying about seating arrangements and floral centerpieces, now sat on a filthy mattress in a hot, rat-infested tenement, worrying about whether she would live to tell about it.

So far, she'd managed to avoid serious harm, but only because the radicals who'd kidnapped her were more interested in the money they would get out of her father than anything else. Also, several of the radicals were women. None of them had shown her the slightest kindness, but their mere presence had provided some measure of safety from the men's more prurient interests.

Now, however, it appeared that no ransom would be forthcoming, at least not immediately. The group that had been milling around in the other room, drinking and boasting and spending the ransom money ten times over, had thinned out. The women had gone home, and only two of the men—the meanest and ugliest, Christine feared—remained. They were restless, impatient and angry.

Christine could hear them talking though the paper-thin door that separated her room from the rest of the apartment, and their ideas regarding her fate had gotten more suggestive and crude with each passing hour and each beer they drank.

She had to do something. Thus far, she'd been as quiet and cooperative as possible, because she believed her father would ransom her quickly and she would be freed. But that faith had gradually shriveled. She didn't know what had happened, but her captors hadn't received the money. If they couldn't get the money they were counting on, then her life wasn't worth much. That was why she had to act.

A man entered her room and flipped on the light. He was tall, gaunt, with greasy hair and a ravaged face. Not that she should criticize grooming at the moment. She hadn't had a bath in two days.

"You still with us?" the man asked.

"No, I left for a fancy-dress ball," she retorted. She was real tired of acting like a good girl.

"Oho, getting cheeky on us," he said with a toothy smile. "'Bout time you found some vocal cords. Hey, how about talking dirty to me?"

"Go to hell!"

"Well, that's a start, though not exactly what I had in mind." He pulled up a metal folding chair and sat down. "We need your help, sweetcakes."

Christine sat leaning against the wall, her wrists tied behind her to a pipe. She kept her back erect, putting as little of her body as possible in contact with the disgusting mattress. Somehow she'd managed to sleep in that position, but only a couple of hours at a time. She stared up at the man, saying nothing.

"Doesn't look like your old man's coming through for you," he began. He pulled a Camel filter out of his T-shirt pocket and lit it with a match.

Christine shrugged. "He's not the type to kowtow to people like you." And he wasn't the type to part easily with a million dollars, either. That was the amount she'd overheard.

"Kowtow, huh? Nice word. Bet you learned all kinds of big words at that finishing school he sent you to, huh?"

She didn't respond.

"So what's it gonna take? What'll send Daddy running for his checkbook? You know him best. Been like a wife to him since your mama died—that's what they say."

"I don't think anything will make him pay you a million dollars," she said, fervently hoping she was wrong. "He's a man of principle."

"Principle? He poisons our waters, our wildlife, our *children,* and you call that principle?"

Christine had heard these shopworn arguments before. Her father had initiated a piece of legislation that lifted restrictions on certain kinds of chemical-waste disposal. The bill, signed into law a year ago, had applied only to a particular class of inert waste materials deemed harmless by the FDA. But that didn't stop some of these left-wing environmental radicals from blaming every pollution problem on the law, including spills and waste disposal that had taken place a generation ago.

"He'll never give in to you," Christine said calmly, "no matter what you do to me, no matter what I say to him." Maybe if they thought it was a lost cause, they would let her go.

"That so?"

Christine stifled a gasp as he pulled a switchblade out of his back pocket and flicked it open. It made a deadly sort of *snick* that brought her stomach into her throat.

"What if we started sending him body parts, one at a time?"

Suddenly Christine didn't feel calm anymore. She'd known these radicals were out in left field, borderline violent, but she'd never thought of environmental activists as vicious or bloodthirsty.

"Or, even better, what if we sent him some pictures of

his little girl having a good time with ol' Denny, here? A real good time. You know what I mean, don't you?"

Yes, she was afraid she did, and he wasn't talking about dancing the hokeypokey. The man rose slowly from his chair and sauntered over with the knife. She gasped as he brought it close to her face, but in the end he used it to cut the bindings at her wrists.

With a sigh of relief, she brought her hands in front of her and rubbed her bruised wrists. That felt so much better. But her relief was short-lived, because she realized the man wasn't going away. He hovered over her, looking down the front of her torn, dirty dress.

That was when she knew her time was up. She was about to enter hell. No sense going quietly.

Without warning, she screamed—a long, loud, ear-piercing shriek of fury that caused her captor to cuff her hard on the side of the head.

"Shut up, woman!" he yelled at her.

She screamed again, louder, and when he tried to hit her again, she grabbed his hand and bit him.

He yowled in pain. While he was still off balance, she kicked one foot into his groin, hard. She was on her feet in a flash, heading for the window. She intended to break it with the folding chair. Then, if she couldn't climb out and escape, she could at least call for help. They were in an urban area. She'd heard the sounds of cars and sirens outside. Someone would hear her.

But the man grabbed her by the ankle and she fell down on her elbows.

"What's going on in here?" The other man, short and stocky, with a blond buzz haircut, burst into the room. "Denny?"

"She's outa control, man," the tall one said in a wheezy, pain-riddled voice. "Get her. Do something with her. I'm hurt."

Christine screamed again. "Help! Help! Fire! Call 911!" She remembered hearing somewhere that to yell, "Fire!" would bring more attention than just yelling for help. She struggled to free herself from the steel grip around her ankle, kicking and clawing.

"Shut up, shut *up!*" the tall one yelled. "Pete, do something! Shut her up before someone calls the cops!"

She should have done this two days ago, Christine realized. She screamed until her throat was raw. The second man ran from the room. The tall man—Denny—recovering somewhat from her assault, dragged her by the ankle until he could reach her throat. He squeezed until she was forced to stop screaming.

"Here, give her this," said the shorter man as he raced back into the room holding a syringe.

No, not again! Christine shook her head frantically, but it was no use. They were going to drug her again, as they'd done when they grabbed her at the front door of her father's house. They'd posed as deliverymen to get through the front gates. She'd okayed it, because she'd been routinely accepting packages for weeks now—wedding presents. She couldn't believe she'd been so stupid.

The needle plunged into her arm. She had about ten minutes of fight left in her, she figured, before the drug took full effect and she became a drowsy, complacent idiot.

Instead of continuing to fight, which she knew was useless, she went completely limp, letting her eyes roll back in her head.

"Damn, that worked fast," Denny said. He loosened his hold on her throat.

"What'd you untie her for?" the second man complained. And he proceeded to remind Denny, in great detail, what his girlfriend would do if she found out her man had been messing with the hostage.

Christine kept her eyes closed and forced herself to slow her breathing.

"Tie her up again," the man called Pete said. "There's some more rope in here."

Denny stood. Christine watched him through her lashes. He nudged her with his foot, shrugged, and walked out of the room.

She was on her feet in an instant. The room's single window opened with only a whisper of noise. Christine looked down. They were on the second floor. She could do it, she told herself. Now or never. Do or die, perhaps literally. She climbed out, dangling from the sill for a heart-stopping minute before she let go and plunged fifteen feet into a huge bush.

She was scratched and bruised, but otherwise unhurt. Clambering to her feet, she picked a direction and ran as fast as she could. She had perhaps another seven minutes before she lost control of her senses.

She was in a run-down block of apartment buildings and boarded-up stores—not the sort of place a woman wanted to find herself after dark, or in broad daylight, for that matter. She ran. Two blocks up, she encountered an old man leaning against a wall, holding a bottle in a paper sack.

He looked at her suspiciously as she approached him.

"Excuse me, sir," she said, breathing heavily. Her vision was getting a little blurry. "I need a phone. A phone? Telephone?" She mimed her request, in case he didn't speak English.

He shook his head in disgust. "Get away from me, girlie. Damn crack addicts get weirder every day." He looked down at her feet, and she realized she wasn't wearing any shoes. How strange that she hadn't noticed until now.

When the man made a threatening gesture, she started running again. Arbitrarily she turned left at the next corner. She saw lights up ahead, a few cars. Thank God! She was starting to feel dizzy. She slowed to a trot, then a walk. She couldn't seem to get enough oxygen into her lungs. She had to hold on a little longer, just a little.

She kept walking. A delicious languor began to invade her muscles. Neon lights flashed, forming brilliant patterns. She stopped and stared.

"Hey, sister, wanna share some of that?"

Horrified, she realized the comment was directed at her. Staring straight ahead, as if she hadn't heard, she resumed her walk. A phone. She had to find a... Ah, something smelled good. Barbecue. She was starving.

She wandered through a doorway. A sea of faces turned and stared at her. "Ah, I'm looking for a..." What was she looking for?

"Hey, you can't come in here without shoes," a burly man informed her as he took her by the arm and turned her around. Under his breath he added, "Jeez, honey, what are you flying on?"

Oh, well. It was a beautiful spring night, with just a hint of chill in the air. At least she thought it was spring. She felt good. No worries. She couldn't remember the last time she hadn't been worried about *something*. Maybe before her mother died, and that was a long time ago.

Shouldn't she be somewhere? It seemed like she always had to be somewhere, meeting with caterers or fund-raisers or maintenance people, changing clothes, rushing to this function or that, putting a good word in this man's ear or charming his wife. But for the life of her, she couldn't remember where she was supposed to be right now.

And she didn't much care.

A man began walking beside her down the cracked sidewalk. "Going my way, sweetheart?"

She stopped and looked at him. He was just a teenager, but he was dressed all in black leather and had a ring in his nose, which gave her pause. "I don't think so. You're a little young for me, don't you think?" She smiled.

He laughed, not pleasantly. "Does that matter? Long as I got your price." He grabbed her by the arm. "C'mon, I got a van parked a couple of blocks away."

Why did men keep grabbing her? she wondered blearily. "No, let go," she pleaded ineffectually. "Don't want to go wif you."

"I got drugs," he whispered. "You know, coke? How 'bout ecstasy? I hear the girls love that stuff."

A couple of other young toughs came up.

"What we got here?" one of them asked. The others whistled and jeered. Christine didn't know what to do.

These young men were ruining her cheerful mood. She
crossed her arms, feeling suddenly chilled. ''I'm not goin'
wif you,'' she said, wondering why her words were so
slurry, so hard to get out. She thought maybe she should
be afraid, should scream, but when she opened her mouth,
only a squeak came out. The teenagers around her closed
ranks, smiling, showing bad teeth.

''Would ya look at that.''

Ryan Mulvaney glanced up from the early edition of
tomorrow's paper without much interest. He'd just spent a
fruitless day trying to track down a certain prostitute who
allegedly had an ongoing relationship with a certain well-
known police official. But the prostitute, if she really existed, was more slippery than any politician he'd ever interviewed. Everyone on the street had heard of her, a few
claimed to have met her or said things like ''She's a good
friend of my friend Angie.'' But no one could tell Ryan
where to find her.

Exhausted, frustrated, he'd stopped in the first beer joint
he saw, to knock down a cold one before heading home.
Not a pretty place. Johnny's was the type of bar that didn't
look too kindly on strangers.

But he wasn't in the mood to be challenged, either. The
regulars threw him a few suspicious looks, but when he
glared right back at them, they kept their distance.

The man who'd spoken was standing in the open doorway, watching something in the street. Ryan dismissed him,
resuming his perusal of the paper, grinning slightly as he
skimmed over his own story. He loved that byline: Ryan
Mulvaney, Special to the *Guardian.* Resigning his staff reporter's job had seemed a difficult decision at the time, but
freelancing was actually a lot more fun than being a staffer,
even if the income was slightly…unpredictable.

Four guys had gathered at the doorway. They were all
watching something in the street, adding their whistles and
jeers.

Curiosity piqued, Ryan stood and sauntered to the door.

He edged his way in front of the other men. And what he saw made him look twice.

An extraordinary-looking woman in a torn, soiled red cocktail dress was fighting off what looked like an entire gang. The teenagers wore Pit Bull colors—Ryan's gut immediately tightened with an instinctual reaction—but by the looks of them they were junior members. The woman was barefoot, and she swayed on her feet like she was drunk.

A prostitute who'd bitten off more than she could chew. That was Ryan's first thought. But something was out of kilter. That dress…and she certainly didn't have the hard-bitten look that a hooker in these parts would have.

Without considering the consequences of his actions, he strode out into the street, right up to the woman.

The gangbangers looked at him, surprised.

"You having problems, honey?"

"Sure am." She dragged those two words out into several syllables. "They won' let me leave. I di'n *ask* 'em to walk with me." She considered him with bleary blue eyes. Then she smiled. "Oh, hi, Sam."

He put his arm around her shoulder. She immediately plunked her head against his chest. "C'mon, honey," he said. "Time to take you home. You've had a little too much to drink."

The biggest of the thugs walked up to Ryan, chest puffed out. "She yours, man?"

"Ah, yeah." For the moment.

"Wanta sell her?"

Ryan tried not to let his revulsion show. He knew all about the sexual habits of the Pit Bulls, but it never ceased to shock him that such things went on, mostly unchallenged. His own sister… But he wouldn't think about that, now. It always angered him to think about her wasted life, and he needed a cool head.

Knowing these guys probably had weapons—knives, if not guns—he put on a brave front. "I've been tempted from time to time, but no, I think I'll keep her." He stared at the others one at a time, daring them to contradict him, praying they wouldn't recognize him. Not much chance of that, really; these guys had still been in nursery school when Ryan raked the Pit Bulls over the coals in a series of shocking articles.

"That's nice of you, Sam," the woman murmured. "To keep me, that is."

One by one, the gang members drifted away, with hard, parting stares. His arm still around the woman's shoulders, Ryan turned and started down the sidewalk. She stumbled along with him. She didn't smell too good, he noticed, but she also didn't smell like booze.

"What're you on, honey?"

She shrugged. "I have no idea."

Great. "What's your name?"

"Ummmm, Chris—Chrissy."

"Do you have a last name?"

She mumbled something that sounded like "Green," but he couldn't be sure.

"Well, Chris-Chrissy, I think I should take you home before you get into real trouble. Where do you live?"

"One-three-five... Are you a p'liceman?"

"No. Why?"

"'Cause I'm not going to give my address to just anyone. I learned that in kindergarten."

"How about a general neighborhood, then?"

"Oh, that's easy. Capitol Heights."

Yeah, right. And he lived at the White House. They'd reached his car. He unlocked the passenger door of his ice blue Vette, relieved vandals hadn't bothered it. The car parked next to his had a flat tire and a broken headlight.

"In you go."

She more or less fell into the seat. He lifted her feet, which were encased in torn stockings, and tucked them in, noticing the firm muscles of her calves and her perfect pedicure. He touched the hem of the red dress. Silk. He would have bet her undies were Dior, too.

As he walked around to the driver's side, he noticed a scruffy-looking man standing several yards away, staring like he wished he could take a picture. He didn't look like a gang member—too old, too ragged—but he could be. Ryan shrugged. Who wouldn't stare at his newfound companion?

He slid behind the wheel and helped her with her seat belt. "What happened to you, lady?" he wondered aloud. "How in the hell did someone like you end up in this neighborhood? You could have been killed, you know. Raped, killed, thrown in the Potomac." He felt a sudden surge of protectiveness toward her, mixed with anger. "If you're going to do drugs, at least do them with people you trust, in a place that's safe."

"I don't do drugs," she said, sounding bewildered. "If you're going to yell at me, I'm leaving." She reached for the door handle, but he'd locked the door, and she couldn't figure that out. Neither could she unfasten the seat belt.

She was sound asleep within three blocks. He should take her to a hospital, he decided. Turn her over to the authorities and be done with it. But his reporter's instincts were kicking in. Who was this mystery woman, and how had she landed in such a predicament?

Ryan could already see a fuzzy headline: The Decadent Underworld: Washington's Rich Risk Their Lives Living in the Fast Lane.

At a stoplight, he reached over and felt for the woman's pulse. Her skin was smooth, the heartbeat strong, if slightly accelerated. Her breathing was deep and even. He decided she wasn't in any immediate physical danger. He would take her home with him, wait for her to sleep off whatever she was on, then pump her for information.

Because of rush-hour traffic, it took him a full forty-five minutes to get home to his apartment in Georgetown. During that time, "Chrissy" stirred often, murmuring strange and intriguing phrases.

"And how much can we count on from you?"

"Not much, I assure you," Ryan responded dryly, "unless you give me something in return."

"Were you at the Swiss embassy party last Tuesday night?"

"Sure." Like any reporter had been allowed into that bash. "Were you there?"

But she wasn't hearing him. She was carrying on some imaginary conversation with someone in her head. "I thought so. I remember that darling mustache. So, tell me, who do you favor among the Republicans?"

Ryan rubbed his bare upper lip. She definitely wasn't talking to him. "Personally, I like Adlai Stevenson."

She giggled. Her eyes were firmly closed. "You're so funny. But I'm engaged, you know. You shouldn't stand so close to me, or people will talk."

Engaged, huh? Figured. Probably had a rich fiancé who supplied her with all the dope she wanted. Bastard. She looked vaguely familiar, but he couldn't place her. But the political beat had never been his thing. He was a crime reporter. Occasionally he ran across dirt on the Washington crowd and dutifully reported it, but he certainly wasn't on a first-name basis with the D.C. glitterati.

As he pulled into the covered parking behind his apartment building, it suddenly occurred to him that he would have to sneak Chrissy past his landlady, Mrs. Reiser. He loved his old brownstone apartment, which had once been his aunt's. All his neighbors were elderly and quiet, and most of the time it didn't bother him that his landlady held certain rather antiquated ideas about houseguests of the opposite sex and the appropriate hours for entertaining. Actually, Mrs. Reiser's rules came in handy when he needed to get rid of some clinging woman who'd misinterpreted his flirtation.

But right now, those rules were a pain.

Ryan walked around to the other side of the car and opened the door. He intended to simply throw Chrissy over his shoulder, fireman-style, and carry her up the back stairs to his third-floor balcony. But the moment he opened the door, she woke up.

"Hi," she said with a ditzy smile.

"Good morning." He freed her from the seat belt and hauled her onto her unsteady feet.

She looked around at the encroaching darkness. "It's morning already? My, I never slept so fast."

He laughed. "It's evening. Time for all good girls to be fast asleep."

"Surely not before they eat. I don't think I've eaten in days."

Yeah? Too busy cramming stuff up your nose? He bit his tongue. Had to keep on the good side of Miss Manners here. He eyed the broken glass in the parking lot, then swept Chrissy and her bare feet up in his arms.

She wound her arms around his neck and buried her face against his shoulder in a trusting, childlike way that hit him right in his gut. Why should she trust him? He could be a sadistic rapist, for all she knew. Thank God he'd seen her when he did, or she'd be at the mercy of those punks right now. He'd seen the work they could do. He shivered.

All right, now to ease past Mrs. Reiser's first-floor apartment. He could have come up the front where there weren't as many windows, but the old lady was no doubt watching the front entrance. He couldn't come in that way without her pretending to walk into the hall for something and quizzing him about his day.

When he reached the bottom of the back stairs, he set Chrissy down. "Think you can walk a little farther?"

"Sure. Why shouldn't I?"

"Great." He took her by the hand and led her onward and upward. "Tiptoes, now."

Without warning, Chrissy broke into song, belting out "Everything's Coming Up Roses."

Ryan clamped a hand over her mouth. "Shh! You'll wake the neighbors."

"But I want to sing," she protested. "I can't remember the last time I did, but it sure feels good."

"Hey," Mrs. Reiser's thickly accented voice boomed from behind French doors, "who's out dere?"

"Oh, now you've done it." Ryan grabbed Chrissy

around the hips and hoisted her over his shoulder, then took the stairs two at a time.

"What—" she started to protest.

"Quiet. We're almost there." He was panting like a dog by the time he reached his own balcony. Thank God he hadn't thought to fasten the dead bolt. He opened the French doors with his key and carried Chrissy safely inside, where he dumped her on his sofa with a sigh of relief. She was a slender woman, but she had to be at least five-foot-eight, and he didn't have the stamina he used to when he was a young reporter, chasing thugs down alleys and over fences.

"Would you like to lie down and take a nap?" he asked his guest.

"Mmm…" Her eyes were already closed. "Where's the bedroom?"

"I, um, thought you wouldn't mind sleeping on the couch." After all, a few minutes ago she'd been snoozing just fine in a bucket seat.

"Okay." But she opened her eyes. "Bathroom?"

Lord, he hoped she wasn't going to get sick. "This way," he said on a sigh, leading her to his old-fashioned bathroom, with its ball-and-claw-footed tub. While she was busy, he went for the white pages. A quick perusal yielded no Chrissy or Christine Green, especially not in Capitol Heights. She probably had an unlisted number, he reasoned.

He gave her ten minutes in the bathroom. When she didn't reappear, he went looking for her. Water was running. He rapped sharply on the door. "Chrissy?"

No answer.

She hadn't locked the door. He cracked it open. She was in the tub, her hair piled up in a sudsy bouffant. And she was fast asleep. Another couple of minutes and the tub would overflow. Or she would slip below the surface and contentedly drown.

He stepped inside and shut off the water, trying to peer between the bubbles at the languid form beneath the water. All right, not very gentlemanly. But what guy wouldn't, especially after feeling her softness pressed against him as he carried her upstairs?

He grasped her bare shoulder and shook. "Chrissy? You have to wake up now." But she was out, this time for good.

With a sigh, he began rinsing the shampoo out of her hair, tipping her head back so that the soap wouldn't get in her eyes. As he held her, his hand at the back of her slender neck, he couldn't help but be affected by her with a certain tightness in his nether regions.

The response got worse when he emptied the tub and pulled her naked body into his arms. He felt horribly guilty, getting hard for an inert woman. But she was gorgeous, perfectly formed in every respect, from her scalp to her polished toenails and everything in between. Probably kept in shape by constant trips to the health club, he reasoned. Aerobics and juice bars by day, coke and booze by night.

He carried her, dripping wet, to the bedroom, where he'd laid out several towels on the bed. He laid her down, then rubbed her dry, enjoying the rosy glow her skin took on. She looked healthy. Couldn't deny that. Her pulse and her breathing were still within acceptable margins.

With a sigh of regret, he yanked the covers out from underneath her and covered her up. He even pushed a pillow under her head, though he doubted she knew the difference.

"Mmm, thank you. This champagne is delicious. Imported?"

"Yeah, imported," he murmured. He was sorry to say he didn't have anything in the refrigerator fancier than plain ol' American beer. Boy, was this little rich girl in for a surprise when she found out how far she'd come down in the world.

Chapter 2

Christine woke up to the delicious smell of clean sheets and fresh coffee. She inhaled deeply, stretched…and then her eyes flew open and she gasped as memories of the kidnapping flooded her consciousness.

Where was she? What had happened to her bug-infested mattress and the rope around her wrists and…for heaven's sake, what had happened to her *clothes?*

Think, Christine, think. Okay. She remembered the guy with the knife. She remembered the syringe, and her drop into the bushes from the second-story window. She remembered running, and talking to a wino. But after that, it all became a blur, then a blank.

God only knew where she'd gone or what she'd done after the drug took effect. She might have landed herself in a situation as bad as or worse than the one before, although, she thought as she gazed up at the gently turning ceiling fan, she certainly couldn't fault the sleeping accommodations. She was in a queen-size bed with feather pillows and a down comforter. Her lack of clothing bothered her, but at least she was…she paused and smelled the skin on her arm, and a handful of her hair. Yes, she was clean!

And if she'd been violated, she didn't remember. She didn't feel any soreness, except for her jaw where the kidnapper had hit her, and her elbows where she'd fallen. She examined her body, finding no other new bruises. In fact, she felt pretty good. She wondered how long she'd slept.

If she could just find some clothes, now, she'd be out the first door she saw and on her way straight to the police. Dragging a sheet with her, she wiggled off the side of the bed and tiptoed to a closet door. When she opened it, a variety of long-sleeved shirts greeted her. They were large—a man's closet. She grabbed the closest shirt, a pale blue number with minuscule pinstripes, and shoved her arms into it. It reached midthigh. She fumbled with the buttons, rolled up the sleeves, then began looking for something she could cover up her bottom half with.

Abandoning the closet, she decided to investigate the chest of drawers. The top drawer yielded briefs and socks. She appropriated a pair of each and quickly donned them. It felt funny to put on men's underwear, but hey, it did the job. She rummaged around in the other drawers until she found a pair of denim shorts. The fit wasn't too bad. The guy who lived here must be pretty slim, she deduced. But with wide shoulders.

She was searching the closet again for a belt when she saw, in the mirror on the inside of the closet door, a face behind her. And what a face. The enormously attractive man was watching, looking faintly amused, as she rifled what were presumably his things.

She caught his gaze in the mirror, and her breath whooshed out of her lungs. "Hi."

"You're awake, I see."

Mmm, his voice was like warm whiskey, deep and—Jeez, what was she thinking? This guy could be some hood off the street. She had a fuzzy memory of talking with some young men in leather jackets. "Where am I?" she asked, turning around to face him. He was wearing jeans and a sleeveless ribbed undershirt that clung to him as if it were painted on. Yum. Like some primitive construction worker or… Egad, she was doing it again.

"You're at my house. You were pretty out of it last night."

"And you are…?"

"Ryan Mulvaney. You were wandering the streets last night, in a real bad part of town. You're lucky I found you. There were other…interested parties."

She shivered, imagining. "Well, thank you, then."

He acknowledged her gratitude with a nod. "There's coffee ready in the kitchen. Don't have much in the way of breakfast, but I could fix you some toast."

"That sounds divine." She looked down at herself. "I guess I should have asked before I borrowed your clothes, but frankly, I was a little disoriented when I woke up. I wasn't sure I was safe."

"And are you sure now?"

Looking at him, at his wicked brown eyes and his thick, rich black hair, and that day's growth of beard that shadowed his prominent jaw, no, she wasn't sure at all. "Should I be frightened?"

He smiled, revealing beautiful white teeth. Instead of calming her, the smile caused her heartbeat to kick in to overdrive. "I'm not in the habit of ravishing young women off the street, but there's always a first time. As for my clothes…" He gave her body a leisurely perusal from shoulders to knees. "They never looked better."

She cleared her throat. "Yes, well, do you have a phone?"

"There's one in the kitchen. This way."

She followed, confused as to why she didn't simply blurt out the whole sordid story to her rescuer. Something was holding her back. Before she volunteered anything, she'd better find out exactly who he was, she decided. He could be one of the kidnappers, toying with her. They weren't all poor scum. Some of them had money, connections. Once they found her missing, they would have called in all the reinforcements to locate her.

The smell of coffee sidetracked her from her intention to call the police, making her realize how hungry she was. Dizzy, in fact. She paused as they entered the kitchen, grabbing her host for support.

He steadied her. "You okay?"

"I haven't eaten in a while. If it's not putting you out too much, I really would like that toast," she said as he sat her down in an ice cream parlor chair pulled up to a tiny round marble table.

"Coming right up."

She saw the phone on the wall, several feet from her reach. The police... But her resolve vanished when Ryan set a mug of fragrant coffee in front of her, along with a gallon jug of two-percent milk and an empty glass.

"Get some of that milk in your stomach," he ordered.

She was happy to comply. She poured half a glass and drained it, thinking that plain milk had never tasted so good. The coffee, too, was heavenly. "Thank you so much. It's delicious."

"You're welcome. Sorry I'm all out of caviar for the toast."

He was making fun of her, she realized belatedly. All right, so perhaps this wasn't a situation that called for finishing-school manners. She couldn't help it. Politeness came naturally to her. She'd been very polite with her captors, even thanking them when they opened doors and shoved her through them. Whenever she was upset or unsettled—which seemed to be happening a lot lately—she fell back on the comfortable rituals pounded into her head by her parents, various nannies and a very expensive Swiss boarding school.

"I could help you butter the toast," she offered after a long sip of coffee.

"You stay where you are. I don't want you fainting on my kitchen floor."

A short while later, a stack of whole-wheat toast ap-

peared in front of her. She dived into it with relish. Ryan
returned to the refrigerator and began rummaging around.

The Sunday *Guardian* sat next to her, freed from its
rubber band but still curled up, apparently unread. Christine
glanced surreptitiously at the front page. She started when
she saw her own picture staring back at her.

Munching toast, she spread the paper out and scanned
the story of her disappearance. Her father was quoted ex-
tensively, and boy, did he come off like a tragic hero. There
was even a picture of him, alongside hers, dabbing his eyes
with a handkerchief.

Then a particular paragraph caught Christine's attention:

No one has yet claimed responsibility for Ms. Greenlow's abduction. No demands for ransom have been
made. The police have no evidence of foul play.

What? Excuse me? She'd heard every word of the phone
call made to her father's house. She'd heard the radicals'
leader explain to her father exactly who the kidnappers
were—they had some complicated name that spelled out
NATURE as an acronym—and she'd heard the demand for
ransom. One million dollars.

Why, then, was the press denying the phone call existed?

There could be a couple of reasons, she realized before
she could fly off the handle. Maybe the police hadn't di-
vulged that information to the newspaper. If this group of
crazies was seeking publicity, which they clearly were, perhaps the cops didn't want to give it to them.

The other possibility was that her father hadn't told the
police about the phone call. Maybe he feared that revealing
too much to the police would endanger her. Or…maybe he
didn't want anyone to know about the ransom demand because he had no intention of paying it or mounting any
type of rescue attempt. She had to admit, having her out of
the picture would be very convenient for him right now,

and the sympathy he was milking from this story would buy him millions of votes come November.

She was horrified at the turn her thoughts had taken. Did she really believe her own father would sacrifice her for the sake of his campaign?

Not the Stan Greenlow she'd grown up with. But the man he'd become during the past two years, as his drug addiction took over his life? She wasn't sure. Honestly. When it came to his pills, he would lie, steal, fake illness—whatever it took. And she had put him in a very uncomfortable position several days ago, when she threatened to go public with his problem if he didn't get professional help.

Yes, having her out of the way was very convenient.

"I have some jam and marmalade here," Ryan said as he placed a couple of jars on the table. "And some honey—what happened to the toast?"

She looked down at the empty plate. "I guess I ate it." And she was still hungry. "Did I eat yours, too? I'm sorry. I wasn't paying attention. I'll make you some more."

She started to rise, intending to take the newspaper with her and shove it out of the way someplace, but Ryan stopped her with a hand to her shoulder. The warm feel of his touch sent a jolt through her, boosting her awareness and her apprehension. With those muscles, he could overpower her in a heartbeat.

But he quickly withdrew his hand. The touch had been a gentle nudge, not a gesture of force. She tried to relax. If he was going to harm her, wouldn't he have done it by now?

"That was the last of the bread," he said. "Don't worry, I'll find something." Seemingly unconcerned, he picked up the jellies and returned to the fridge. While his back was turned, Christine opened the front section to a random page and folded it back, hiding her picture. If she was lucky, Ryan was the type who only read the sports section.

When he finally sat down in the chair opposite hers with his own cup of coffee, he was munching on a banana. She didn't realize she was staring until he broke off half and offered it to her.

"Oh, no, um, I—"

"C'mon, take it. You were almost drooling."

She did, and devoured it in three bites. "Thank you," she said after wiping her mouth with the paper napkin he'd thoughtfully provided. "I don't mean to be such a hog. I haven't eaten in…well, a long time."

He eyed her speculatively, and she realized she was going to have to offer him some kind of explanation for her dire circumstances. But she resisted the idea of telling him about the kidnapping, about the fact that her father had refused to pay the ransom. Even if his refusal had been motivated by the best intentions—like maybe he refused, on principle, to give in to terrorist demands—she couldn't bear to admit that her own father hadn't moved heaven and earth to get her back, maybe save her life.

"So," Ryan said, "what's your story, Chrissy Green?"

Where had he come up with that name? She must have given it to him last night during her delirium. She shrugged uneasily. "No story. I just had too much to drink last night. I don't normally drink except an occasional glass of champagne, but I was at this party, and the host was serving a liqueur of some sort. I had no idea how strong it was.…" She could see he didn't believe her. She would have to come up with something a bit more dramatic.

"How did you get the bruise on your face?" Ryan asked, softly touching her cheek with his fingertips. "I didn't notice it last night, but it sure came up pretty and purple this morning."

She gingerly felt where his hand touched her.

"Yeah, that's it."

"My…my boyfriend hit me." It was almost comical, referring to that greasy, disgusting man who'd knocked her in the face as her boyfriend. "He gets ugly sometimes, when he drinks too much. I ran away from him. That's how I ended up where you found me. I jumped out of the car just to get away from him—didn't realize what a bad neighborhood we were driving through.''

This story appeared to sit better with Ryan. Although his outrage over her battery was apparent, he seemed to believe her this time.

"I'm going to leave him for good," she said, to put his mind at ease. She didn't want Ryan thinking she was some mealy-mouthed perennial victim who put up with her boyfriend beating her up. "I told him if he ever hit me, that was it."

"Will he let you?" Ryan asked. "Leave, that is? My experience with this type of guy is they don't just meekly stand by and accept rejection. You won't be safe."

"Oh, he wouldn't dare touch me again," Christine said, draining the last of her coffee. "He knows I'd file charges."

"Exactly!" Ryan said triumphantly. "You shouldn't let some jerk get away with hitting a woman. I'll go with you to the police, if you want, and—"

"No," she said quickly. "No, I really don't want to involve the police."

He looked disappointed at that.

"I was thinking of just…going away for a while," she said. "I have a…friend down in Raleigh who's been wanting me to visit." Actually, a half sister—another of the senator's little secrets. He'd fathered a child out of wedlock when he was in college. His own father had paid off the pregnant woman, but Stan had secretly kept track of her. Michelle Potter, Christine's half sister, had even come to visit a few times, posing as a cousin. No one had ever questioned it.

Christine had been drawn to Michelle, the "big sister" she'd always wanted. The invitation from Michelle to visit her in Raleigh was genuine, even if the rest of Christine's story to Ryan was pure invention.

"I think that's an excellent idea," Ryan was saying. "Get away from the jerk, give things a chance to cool down.'' He glanced at his watch. ''If you're done with breakfast, I'll take you home.''

''Oh, I can't go home,'' she said with genuine alarm. No way could she face her father, knowing what he'd done, or hadn't done. ''I mean, I live with him.''

''The jerk?''

''Yeah.''

''Won't he be at work or something? Oh, it's Sunday. Guess not.''

''Especially not the way he was drinking last night. He'd be too hungover. And mean,'' she added. Maybe she was laying it on pretty thick, but she wanted Ryan to believe she had nowhere to go. Otherwise, how could she expect him to help her reach her half sister?

''All right, but what do you intend to do?''

She shrugged. ''Couldn't I just—''

''Nuh-uh, no way. You're not hanging out here. I've got work to do. I mean, you seem like a nice lady, but how do I know?''

''What kind of work do you do?'' she asked, seeking to deflect the conversation away from her.

''I'm a, um, mechanic. Unemployed at the moment.''

Oh, yeah, she thought, looking around at the expensive furnishings. The one-bedroom apartment wasn't large, but the lush decor screamed, ''Designer!'' Everything was first-rate.

''I inherited these digs from my aunt, all right?'' he said, obviously reading her skepticism. ''Besides, you think mechanics can't make some decent dough?''

She looked at his fingernails. Clean and pristine, neatly trimmed. No sign of grease. ''I didn't say a thing.'' But she knew he was lying. Maybe he'd been preyed upon by gold diggers in the past, and hid behind a poor-mechanic facade. That explanation made as much sense as her lies to him. ''Well, if I can't stay here, think you could get me a plane ticket to Raleigh? I could pay you back as soon as I get there—wire you the money or something.''

''You don't have access to money?''

"Not on a Sunday morning. No ATM card. I guess I left my purse in my boyfriend's car." Boy, this lying stuff was difficult. All these little details cropping up. "Tomorrow I could go to the bank and make a withdrawal, I suppose. But since you'd like to get rid of me today…"

He stood decisively. "I can lend you the money. Let me go make a phone call to my travel agent and see what a ticket to Raleigh costs."

"Thanks, that's awfully nice of you."

He shrugged. "That's me, nice-guy Ryan."

She doubted anyone called him that. He wasn't some kind of sucker. The only reason he was making a very risky loan to buy her a plane ticket was that he wanted to be rid of her that badly. She didn't know why that thought made her feel so glum.

Ryan retreated to his bedroom office, feeling ambivalent about his houseguest. She was trouble, that much was certain. Abusive boyfriend, drinking and/or drugs…and beautiful enough to take his breath away, even wearing his clothes. He never should have gotten mixed up with her in the first place, never mind his story idea about life in the fast lane.

He was glad he'd rescued her. The state she'd been in last night, she could easily have gotten herself killed. But now that he'd brought her home, where did his responsibility end? *I mean, lending her money for a plane ticket?* If anyone else was contemplating such a foolish gesture, he would be calling him a sucker. But somehow he didn't have the heart to just dump Chrissy out in the street. With nowhere else to go, she might go straight back to the jerk who'd abused her.

He couldn't have that on his conscience, could he?

He sat down at his desk, flipped open his Rolodex until he found his twenty-four-hour travel agent's number, and dialed. He was immediately put on hold. While he waited, he flipped on the portable TV that sat on his desk, hoping to catch some news. He'd been working on a piece about a possible serial killer, and each morning when he turned on the TV he waited with a mixture of anticipation and dread for the news that another homeless person had become a victim.

Not this morning, thank God. The top story, though, caught his attention in a hurry. Instead of giving the usual rundown on budget deficits and the latest foreign civil war, the earnest anchorwoman told of a Pennsylvania senator's daughter being kidnapped from her father's home in Capitol Heights.

Ryan's head snapped toward the tiny television screen when they flashed a picture of the stunning blond victim. He squinted, drew closer, pulled back.

Had to be. Good God almighty, the kidnap victim was sitting in his kitchen! What in the hell was she doing here, using a phony name? A kidnapping would explain the state of her clothing when he'd found her, and the bruise on her cheek. But if she'd escaped or been released, why wasn't she at home? Why hadn't she gone to the police?

One possible answer came to him. She'd never been kidnapped at all. She'd disappeared, gone on a bender, and her father had invented the abduction story to explain her absence and get himself some publicity. Senator Greenlow had narrowly defeated his opponent in the recent Pennsylvania primary, Ryan recalled, and he faced a tough battle in the fall against his flashy Democratic opponent. Greenlow's sudden lack of popularity stemmed from some unfavorable press he'd garnered—something having to do with antienvironmental legislation. He would have to shake that off if he wanted to win in November—or if he wanted to make another run for the presidency in a couple of years, which everyone expected him to do. He was a perennial presidential hopeful, had been for the past three elections.

If the kidnapping was a fake, Ryan was sitting on one of the best stories of his career.

A woman's voice came on the telephone line. "Thank you for holding. How may I help you with your travel plans?"

Ryan didn't answer. His mind was churning with possibilities, plans drawn up and rejected, approaches that would yield the most interesting copy.

"Hello? Anyone there?"

"Oh, um, sorry, wrong number." He hung up on the travel agent, flipped to a different card in his Rolodex and dialed again. Fran Renner was the best freelance photographer he knew—or at least the only decent one who would work on spec at a moment's notice. She'd been a little cool toward him since their brief, ill-fated affair last year, but she was a sensible woman. She wouldn't let personal feelings get in the way of a blockbuster story like this.

"Hello?"

"Franny, glad I caught you at home," he said in almost a whisper. "I've got something going, and I need your help. It's big, Fran, real big."

"Ryan? For heaven's sake, Ryan Mulvaney, it's nine o'clock on a Sunday morning. You've got your nerve. I don't suppose you have a client for your story?"

"How does *Primus* magazine sound?"

"You don't have a deal with *Primus,*" she said flatly.

"But I will. You'll have to trust me on this one. Meet me at Costello's Café at—"

"I'm not meeting you anywhere until you tell me what this is about. You and your cloak-and-dagger sneaking around. And I want money up front, whether you sell the story or not."

Naturally. Fran was the skeptical type. "I can't go into explanations right now. And, yes, I'll guarantee you the money, if you want, although you'd be smarter to take a percentage on spec."

"I'll take the up-front money, thanks just the same. How much?"

He sighed. "Five hundred dollars."

"Make it seven, and I want to see green money before I shoot a single frame."

"Six. And I'll pay you next week. You know damn well I'm good for it."

There was a long pregnant pause. "True," she finally said. "You're a driven son of a bitch, Ryan, but you've never been a chiseler. Deal. Meet you where?"

He tried not to let her criticism bother him. "Costello's, over on Richmond. Don't come up to the table, and keep your camera out of sight. I don't want my friend to know you're there. Just sit down at the café. I'll find you."

After he ended his call with Fran, he went through all his pants pockets, including the ones in his closet, and came up with ten dollars and change. Not enough to pamper a society girl like Christine Greenlow, even for an hour. Looked like he'd have to resort to plastic.

Christine looked up when her host reentered the kitchen, and she had to take a deep breath to counter light-headedness. He'd covered up the undershirt with a crisp cotton shirt similar to the one she was wearing, except that it fit, pale yellow in color. He'd also combed his hair and shaved. *GQ*-perfect, but still with a rough edge. Why did he seem so exciting to her?

Maybe it was simply the adrenaline in her system. She was having an adventure—the only adventure of her boring life, she realized—and that made everything seem exciting.

Funny, she'd never thought of her previous life as boring until she was kidnapped. She'd thought of herself as content, settled, and had even been slightly contemptuous of those who always lived on the edge. Her father's addiction had been the only fly in the ointment, and she'd felt confident that Stan Greenlow would see the light, get some confidential counseling, and everything would be as it had been.

Even her impending marriage to Robert Warner hadn't worried or upset her too much. Her father had introduced them two years ago, and it had seemed like a natural extension of the life she'd chosen that she should marry a man in politics—a congressional aide for one of her father's cronies—and life would go on.

Why did it suddenly seem that her life had been empty, shallow?

"Bad news," Ryan said as he claimed the chair across from her. "All the seats on all the flights to Raleigh are booked until Tuesday."

Christine sagged with disappointment. She was anxious to get out of town, to confer with her half sister. Practical, solidly middle-class Michelle could look at things with a perspective Christine didn't have. She was unsentimental, and she had once lightly rebuked Christine for not "getting a life" of her own, though Christine had dismissed the gentle chiding at the time.

Now it seemed that Michelle might have some answers for her. And she would have to wait until Tuesday to meet with her. Meanwhile, what would she do with herself? Ryan had already said he didn't want her taking up space in his apartment for any length of time.

"The good news," Ryan said, "is that I have some business in Raleigh. Nothing urgent, and I'd planned to take care of it later in the month, but I could do it tomorrow as well as any day. In fact, my sister lives in Emporia, which is on the way. I'm overdue to visit her."

"You mean you'll drive me?" Hope flared.

"Sure. It's only, what, five hours?"

"About that, I guess."

"Then we'll leave first thing tomorrow morning."

"And what about today?"

Ryan looked resigned. "I guess you can hang out with me."

Well, it wasn't the most gracious invitation she'd ever had, but she'd take it. Suddenly she giggled. The sound of her own voice making such a weird noise surprised her, and she realized she didn't often laugh, or giggle. Or maybe even smile.

"What's so funny?"

She shrugged, in love with the idea of having a whole day, almost twenty-four hours, to kill. No meetings, no telephone or beeper, no worries. The best part was that she got to spend it with her handsome knight in shining armor.

She thought again about the police. She should let someone know she was out of danger. But there would be questions, hundreds of them. Her father would be notified, of course. She would have to talk to him.

She sighed. She simply couldn't face such an ordeal right now. Maybe it was the drug she'd been given, but something was wrong with her. For the first time in her life, she was unable to face responsibility.

For a whole day, she could be someone else. Not the senator's staid daughter or the congressional aide's demure fiancée, but someone named Chrissy, whose main concern right now was the fact that she had no shoes.

Chapter 3

"**W**here are we going again?" Christine asked as she watched Ryan putting on his Nikes. They looked well-worn, as if perhaps he actually ran in them, as opposed to making a fashion statement. She thought longingly to that one year she'd spent at Radcliffe, when she adopted the habit of running three miles every morning before classes. She'd wanted to continue after her father called her back home, but he'd insisted it was too dangerous for her—the daughter of a public figure—to run amok on the public streets of Washington without protection.

Ironically, it had turned out that his own front porch was the most dangerous place for her, but, of course, he couldn't have anticipated that.

"We're going to a cappuccino bar," Ryan said casually.

"We just had coffee."

"Yeah, but this place has really good coffee. And cinnamon rolls. I get the feeling you're still hungry."

She was, though she was too embarrassed by her unlady-like appetite to agree with him out loud. The thought of a gooey, fat-laden cinnamon roll made her mouth water and her stomach rumble. "We'll have to do something about my bare feet," she said. "I can borrow your shirts and shorts without that much trouble, but I'm guessing your shoes would be less than a neat fit." She felt silly even asking; she'd never in her life been unable to walk into any store in the city and purchase what she needed. "I'll pay you back if you buy me some shoes. Some cheap canvas ones would be fine."

"Okay. First stop, Target," he said, giving the discount store's name a French pronunciation: Tar-*zhay*. "Is there anything else you need?"

"A toothbrush," she said, a little desperately.

"Okay. How about…underwear?" He raised one eyebrow and waited for her to answer.

"If you must know, I'm wearing a pair of yours, and they're pretty darn comfortable. I don't think I've worn plain cotton undies since I outgrew my Carters."

Maybe he'd intended to embarrass her by mentioning underwear, but he was the one who looked away a bit nervously. "Target, I'm pretty sure, sells the all-cotton variety for ladies," he mumbled. "Anything else?"

She wondered if she would be recognized in the street. Not that she looked a lot like the photo in the newspaper, which had been taken a couple of years ago, when her hair was shorter. Plus, she'd been glammed up for the camera. Nonetheless, her face was a familiar one in certain Washington circles. "Sunglasses and a hat," she said. "And that's all, I promise."

"So none of your friends will spot you slumming with a mechanic, I presume," he said matter-of-factly as he stood and walked back into the kitchen. She followed, curious, to find him rummaging around in a drawer. He came up with a pair of aviator sunglasses. "These never fit my face right. Try 'em on for size." While she did just that, he disappeared into the bedroom, returning shortly with a Baltimore Orioles baseball cap.

Surprising her, he grabbed her hair, twisted it up at the

crown of her head and plopped the cap on top. She shivered as his fingertips brushed her nape.

"There, your own mother wouldn't recognize you."

She must have flinched or looked surprised, because he immediately said, "Sorry, did I say something wrong?"

She smiled reassuringly. "I shouldn't be so sensitive, or so transparent. My mother died a few years ago."

"Now I really am sorry," he said again.

"Don't be, not for using a common expression." Although privately she had to admit that not a week went by that she didn't fervently wish her mother hadn't left her to deal with her father alone. Stan Greenlow would never have made the life-threatening decisions he'd made if his wife was beside him, to temper his melodramatic nature.

"I'm ready if you are," she said, anxious to be off the subject of her mother. If she wasn't careful, she would give him all the clues he needed to figure out her identity, with or without seeing a picture. Chrissy Green? Was that the name she'd given him last night? Well, she never had been much of a liar.

Ryan nodded, and they were off.

They tiptoed down the front stairs. "You probably don't remember me telling you this last night, but my landlady's a dragon," Ryan whispered as they descended. "If she finds out a woman slept in my apartment, she'll throw me out."

"You've got to be kidding. What century was she born in?"

"Deadly serious. It's in the lease. I thought she was a bit Victorian when I read the terms, but the rent is pretty low, too, so I couldn't pass up the opportunity."

"How do you manage?" she asked, imagining that he probably had a slew of sleep-over girlfriends. No man with his looks didn't at least have the opportunity.

"I abide by the terms. Guess I'm old-fashioned."

"What about me?"

"You're the exception. I tried to take you home last night, but you wouldn't give me an address. I didn't have much choice but to take you in. Quiet, now,'' he said as they reached the first floor landing. With cautious glances over his right shoulder toward apartment 1, he tiptoed to the front door and pulled it open noiselessly. Only someone with an inverted glass against the wall would have heard the slight noise.

The door to apartment 1 flew open, and a formidable-looking woman in curlers and a pale green housecoat accelerated into the foyer. "Mr. Mulvaney!" she boomed.

Ryan jumped at least a foot. "Mrs. Reiser, good morning. I'd like you to meet my, um, cousin Chrissy from New Jersey."

New Jersey? Calling upon her negligible dramatic skills, Christine summoned what she thought was a Jersey accent. "Pleased ta meetcha." She extended her hand, and Mrs. Dreiser shook it gingerly in her own big, blunt one.

"Yes, well. Here for a long visit?" Her nose almost twitched with curiosity and suspicion, as if she were trying to ferret out a moldy piece of cheese from the refrigerator.

"Just till tomorrow," Christine said.

"Just for breakfast," Ryan said at the same time, then quickly added, "Well, she'll be in town till tomorrow, but we're just having breakfast. She has other people to visit."

"I see," Mrs. Reiser said, in a tone of voice that indicated that she didn't see at all. She stooped down to retrieve her paper, gave Ryan a hard look that seemed to say, *Watch your step,* then retreated into her apartment.

Ryan hurried out the front door. "C'mon, before she decides to do a full interrogation."

"You're actually afraid of her," Christine said, amazed. "Last night you rescued me from some gang in a terrible neighborhood, and today you're afraid of a little old lady wearing sponge rollers in her hair?"

"She terrifies me," he explained as they walked around the building, toward the carports in back. "I mean, what's the worst some knife-wielding thugs can do to me, carve me up? Mrs. Reiser can throw me out in the street. Even worse, she can tell my mother. They're good friends. And, believe me, when she's mad, my mother makes Mrs. Reiser look like Tinker Bell.''

Christine laughed at that. Ryan Mulvaney had a way with words, not to mention a way with her hormones. It felt good to laugh, she realized. The sun was warm on her face and arms. She wanted badly to indulge in those simple pleasures. But then she thought about her father, and she immediately felt melancholy again. She was going to have to talk to him, and soon. It wasn't fair to continue to let him think she was being held hostage.

If he even cares, she thought with a grimace. Her throat tightened, and she determinedly swallowed the rising lump. It had to be a misunderstanding, a miscommunication of some sort. Her father might be angry with her, but he wouldn't abandon her to a bunch of bloodthirsty terrorists.

She started to step out into the alley behind the brownstone, but Ryan grabbed her arm, halting her. "Broken glass. I'll carry you."

"But—"

Ryan ignored her objection, scooping her effortlessly up into his arms. "This is how we did it last night."

She had a vague memory of having been in this position before. She also remembered that she'd liked it. She felt her face warming, and was glad for the baseball cap, which shielded her from Ryan's view. She couldn't allow him to know how he affected her, no matter how novel and exciting the sensations. If she really wanted to become her own woman, it didn't make sense to start out pinning her yearnings on a man, any man.

She fully intended to live life on her own terms as soon as she could manage it. That meant no men, at least for a while. Men always expected a lot from her if she gave them the least little part of herself, and she was good and tired of it.

Even as that thought crossed her mind, Ryan set her down beside a blue Corvette, and she found herself thrilled at the idea of riding around in such an exciting car. That made no sense. She could have bought herself her own

Corvette, if she wanted. But somehow, Ryan's was much more appealing.

The discount store in nearby Arlington was mind-boggling. Christine expected someone to stop her from entering the store in stocking feet, but either nobody noticed or nobody cared. She hadn't been in such a store in years. She and her father had servants to do all the shopping. It felt weird to be bombarded with so much merchandise, so many signs.

Ryan took her hand to lead her through the crowd of Sunday shoppers to the shoe section. She quickly found a pair of crepe-soled canvas flats—with yellow stripes, no less—for $9.99. She thought of how shocked Connie, her maid, would be when she saw them, and smiled. Constance, pushing seventy, had been working for the Greenlow family since her teens, and she'd absorbed an uncanny snobbishness—through osmosis, Christine liked to think. Constance would get the vapors at the thought of any Greenlow entering a discount store, much less wearing apparel purchased there.

Christine took a quick tour of the underwear section and picked up some panties, T-shirts and socks—enough to last a couple of days. She pulled off her socks and slipped the shoes on the moment they were outside. "Very comfy." She made Ryan stop in the first gas station they saw so that she could brush her teeth in the rest room with the toothbrush and toothpaste he'd bought for her. Now she was ready to face the day.

While waiting for Chrissy to finish her morning ablutions, Ryan filled his car with gas and used his mobile phone to call Fran's voice pager, all the while keeping a sharp eye on the ladies' room door. He didn't think Chrissy had any plans to slip away. In fact, she'd seemed eager to hang out with him, a fact that stroked annoyingly on his ego. But he couldn't be too careful.

He listened to Fran's voice mail recording, then the beep. "It's Ryan. We're running late, but please wait for us at Costello's," he said. He was up the creek if he couldn't connect with Fran. His story would be too easily discounted without good pictures.

"I feel so much better," Chrissy said as she bounced back into the car. "There's a restaurant right next door. We could go there for coffee."

Ryan tamped down his alarm. He had to get them to Costello's without arousing Chrissy's suspicions. "And what about the cinnamon rolls?"

"Oh, yeah, how could I forget? Drive on."

Relaxing, Ryan put the Vette in gear and headed back toward Georgetown.

Parking was a near impossibility in Georgetown, especially on weekends. Christine wondered why they didn't simply park in Ryan's apartment carport and walk from there—she thought it was only a few blocks. But then he lucked into a spot on a side street. They walked three blocks to Costello's.

Christine suspected the café was one of those places that was almost too trendy for its own good. Her suspicions were confirmed when she saw the crowd waiting to be seated. The people she socialized with eschewed scenes like this. They usually went to staid, established, even stuffy restaurants where their mere names were enough to immediately get them a table. Often they managed a private room.

This place was so rough-and-tumble that Christine had to watch that her toes didn't get stepped on as people milled around her. She loved it. The variety of humanity surrounding her took her breath away—everyone from blue-haired after-church ladies to goateed musician or artist types here to treat their hangovers with heavy doses of caffeine.

She stepped closer to Ryan to let an exiting group pass. He put an arm around her shoulders. The protective gesture seemed perfectly natural, and Christine leaned in a little bit, reveling in the warmth emanating from his body and the clean, male scent she could barely detect.

She remembered this feeling. She'd had a boyfriend her

freshman year in college, Doug Vega, a friend's older
brother who'd escorted her to some silly sorority parties,
groped with her in the back seat of his car, and finally taken
her virginity in a hotel room he'd rented for the occasion.
The whole affair had lasted only a couple of months, ending
abruptly when her father pulled her back to Washington.
He'd needed her, he claimed, and, as always she'd come
running.

She'd realized later that she hadn't really been in love
with the boy, but she remembered her fling with him as an
exciting, heady time. They'd been wildly attracted to each
other, and their few brief liaisons had given Christine an
exquisite taste of the forbidden.

Later, she'd talked herself into believing that mature relationships were based on things more important than hormones. In fact, she'd convinced herself that the intensity of
her physical feelings for Doug had been a result of her
youth and the fact that he was her first.

Suddenly she wasn't so sure that was a correct assump-
tion. She'd felt a calm acceptance toward the physical aspects of her relationship to Robert, her fiancé, and believed
that was the way things were for adult couples contemplating a lifetime together—pleasant interludes on infre-
quent occasions.

Now, feeling that quivering in her abdomen that she remembered from years ago, she realized she'd been dead
wrong. And she was furious with herself that she'd come
so close to throwing her womanhood away in a marriage
that was merely "pleasant." What on earth had made her
think it was okay to marry a man because he was a good
social match for her and she didn't find him repulsive?

She'd been way too sheltered, too saturated with her father's views and opinions, to realize she'd never learned to
think for herself or make her own decisions. This was quite
a revelation. She'd always believed herself to be a fairly
intelligent person. But her ignorance was staggering.

"Ryan, party of two," a voice called out over a loudspeaker.

Ryan acknowledged the page and guided Christine toward the hostess with a hand at the small of her back. The hostess grabbed two menus and led them toward a table by a window, where they could see all the shoppers patronizing the little stores across the street. Christine couldn't get enough of watching. She might have been a visitor from another planet, for all she knew about what real people did in Washington, D.C.

"Your server will be here shortly," the hostess said. She poured them both coffee and disappeared.

Christine eyed the tip left by the previous diners. With a silent apology to the server, she flattened her menu out on the table, slid her hand underneath and raked a quarter into her lap. She needed to call her father, but not under Ryan's watchful eye.

When the waitress came, Christine promptly closed the menu. "I'd like a cinnamon roll, please." She could already smell the cinnamon in the air, and her mouth was watering. "And a bowl of oatmeal with bananas?" She looked at Ryan.

He rolled his eyes and nodded. "I'll just have coffee. Man, for a little thing, you sure can pack it away."

"I'm not so little. Five-foot-eight. And I told you, I haven't eaten much the past couple of days."

"Why not?"

She squirmed. "Worry, I guess."

"About your boyfriend?"

She seized on the explanation. "Yes, that's it. I've been wanting to leave him, but I was scared." Keep your explanations simple, she warned herself. Even practiced liars could trip themselves up, and she was anything but practiced. She was already nervous about the skeptical looks Ryan kept giving her. She needed his help in getting to her half sister's house in Raleigh. With Michelle's moral support, she was sure, she could pull herself together enough to break free from her father's domination.

But Ryan didn't seem intent on quizzing her. His eyes constantly scanned the crowd.

"Looking for someone?" she asked innocently.

"Oh, sorry. I thought I saw someone I know, but I was wrong."

Christine didn't doubt him aloud, but she knew he wasn't telling her the whole truth. What if he really was somehow involved with the radicals who'd kidnapped her? Maybe he'd contacted one of the leaders and told him to come take her off his hands?

No, that was ridiculous. Anyway, no one could take her against her will, so long as they were in a public place. She resolved to stay out in the open, in full view of people, until she could figure out what Ryan Mulvaney was up to.

In fact, maybe she'd shake him loose. With one phone call, she could have her father's limousine here to pick her up. She could go home, collect a few things—including her checkbook—and simply move out of her father's house. Go to Michelle's, stay in a hotel, whatever she wanted, and her father couldn't stop her.

Except she was afraid he could. He had a way of manipulating her that was nothing short of a true art form. It had begun when her mother died. Stan had taken it so hard, Christine had feared that he would simply expire from grief, and she'd turned cartwheels to make him smile. He'd soon learned that if he could make her feel sorry for him, she'd be putty in his hands.

Only now was she beginning to see how unfairly she'd been treated, how naive about her father she'd been. But she was afraid that open revolt against him was still beyond her abilities. She had to exercise her "independence muscles," work out a sensible plan, before facing him head-on.

Her food arrived, and for a few minutes, at least, Christine turned off her brain and indulged herself with the gooey-sweet cinnamon roll. Ryan watched her, seemingly fascinated. She was too hungry to be self-conscious about his interest. She savored every bite, then moved on to the oatmeal. When the bowl was clean, she finally felt full.

"Thank you so much for breakfast," she said after daintily wiping her mouth with her napkin. "I haven't felt this good in a long time." Oddly, despite her circumstances, she meant that. She would feel even better after she got the phone call to her father over with. She'd seen both rest rooms and phones at the front of the restaurant. She stood, surreptitiously transferring the quarter from her lap to her shorts pocket. "Excuse me, I need to make a trip to the ladies' room."

The crowd in the lobby was easing up, but a man was using the phone. Christine tapped her foot nervously as she waited for the phone to become available. She couldn't stay gone all day, or Ryan would come looking for her.

At last the caller in front of her hung up. Christine seized the receiver and dialed her father's private line. His personal secretary, Jerome Jenkins, answered, sounding nervous.

"This is Christine," she said without preamble. "I need to speak to my father immediately."

"Christine? Gosh, is it really—"

"Now, Jerome," she said in her most commanding voice. "It's urgent."

"Yes, ma'am."

Moments later she heard her father's voice. "Chrissss-tine? Honey?"

"Yes, it's me." She winced. Her father's voice was slurred, which meant he'd taken too many tranquilizers again. Damn him! How did he expect to run a nation, if he didn't even have control over his own behavior, his own addictions?

"Where are you?" Stan demanded.

"I'm safe," she assured him, then lowered her voice to a whisper. "I got away from the kidnappers. Daddy, why didn't you pay the ransom?" She closed her eyes and prayed that he would have some logical explanation. *The FBI was running things. I had no choice but to follow their directions....*

"A million dollars—tha's a lot of money," he said, the

words slow and laborious. "I was trying to pull it together. I told those slimeball terrorists that I was working on it."

His words were like knives in her heart. He was lying. She knew more about his finances than he did, and Stanley Greenlow could have snapped his fingers and had a million in cash within thirty minutes.

"Christine, where are you?"

"I'm safe," she repeated. "And I'm not coming home for a while."

"Not coming— What are you talking about? Where would you go, for God's sake? Don't tell me you're hiding out at Robert's house. He would have told me—"

"No, not Robert's."

"What am I supposed to tell the media?"

Was that all he was worried about? "Tell them whatever story you think will keep you in the public's good graces," she said harshly. She'd never spoken like that to her father, but maybe it was time to shake him up a bit. It seemed as if his priorities had gotten skewed.

"Christine, I demand that you come home this minute. Where are you? I'll send the limo."

"I'm not listening to your demands anymore, Daddy." Since he hadn't listened to hers in a very long time. She hung up before he could argue further.

The moment Chrissy turned her back, Ryan had motioned to Fran, whom he'd spotted a few minutes earlier at a table across the room. He'd stood and followed Chrissy at a discreet distance, indicating that Fran should come, too. Then, as they leaned on the bar, shielded from Chrissy's view by a huge ficus tree, he'd told Fran what was going on.

"Are you sure that's Christine Greenlow?" Fran asked as she and Ryan watched the tall, slim woman talking on the pay phone. "Doesn't look like her."

"I'm sure."

"Who's she calling?"

"I don't know," Ryan said anxiously. "She said she was

going to the ladies' room. But take my word for it, it's her. Are you in?''

"Hell, yes," Fran said. "I've been waiting for a story like this for a long time. Got to hand it to you, Mulvaney, if this is for real, you came through."

He bussed her on the cheek. "I knew I could count on you."

"Oh, cut it out," she groused, rubbing peevishly at her face. "We gave up all that mushy stuff months ago."

"Hey, what's a peck on the cheek between friends?"

Fran rolled her eyes. "I never know with you, Mulvaney."

"If I were putting the moves on you, you'd know," he said, teasing. "Now why don't you mosey on over there to the telephones and see if you can hear what she's saying?"

"I'm a photographer, not a reporter."

"I'm not asking you to quote her. I just want to know what she's up to, so I'll be prepared. She could be calling the cops, her fiancé, her pusher. Who knows?"

"You really think she could be using?" Fran said. "She looks awfully healthy from this angle."

With his eyes taking in the lush curves of her derriere, Ryan had to agree; in fact, he'd been thinking that very thing last night when he toweled off her nude body. Now she stood with one long leg propped on the edge of a potted plant and was idly rubbing her thigh. He could almost feel *his* hands doing the same thing. "I don't know. But there's something really fishy going on, or else why would she be hiding her identity? People don't take up aliases if they're not into *something* illegal."

"I agree. Let's stick to her like Velcro," Fran said. "I'm willing to bet she'll lead us somewhere interesting."

And, Ryan admitted silently, he was looking forward to the trip.

"You've got the hots for her," Fran declared.

"What? Who, me?"

"I've seen that look on your face before. At one time, you were looking at me with that gleam in your eye."

Ryan frowned. "I'm sure you're mistaken," he said, in a tone of voice that invited no further discussion on the subject. "Just follow us, okay? Don't let her spot you."

"I'll do my best. But don't drive too fast. My Isuzu can't keep up with your Vette if you drive like you normally do."

"I'll keep it under ninety. Oh, can I borrow some money?"

"What?"

"I need cash. My credit cards are tapped out." A huge payment for an editing job he'd done was overdue, and until the check arrived, he was fiscally handicapped.

"Fine." Fran huffed, handing Ryan a couple of twenties. "You're lucky I went to the bank yesterday. And I want it back with interest."

Ryan nodded as he stuffed the bills in his pocket. "Uh-oh, here she comes." Ryan slunk guiltily back to his table, leaving Fran to her own devices. He slid back into his chair, slouching a bit, as if he'd been there all along. The waitress came by, and he paid the check just as Chrissy returned.

"I was beginning to think you'd ditched me," he said, only half kidding. He'd actually been worried that she was calling a cab and was planning to disappear, and the notion had caused him considerable anxiety. Was Fran right? Had he been looking at Chrissy with something other than professional interest? Surely he wasn't lusting after so unreachable a woman. Of course, he did vividly remember what she'd looked like when he pulled her out of the bathtub last night, her skin flushed and slick from the warm water. And, yes, he remembered how that body had felt against his when he carried her into the bedroom and tucked her under the covers, aching to do something more.

But that was last night. Now that he knew who she was, he'd ceased thinking of her in those terms. Lust was one of those things that could be controlled, turned on and off like a faucet. He would never let desire interfere with his work. Never.

Fran was just yanking his chain, he decided. She was like that. He couldn't imagine why he'd been so enamored of her a while back.

"Long line in the bathroom," Chrissy explained, not meeting his gaze.

Another lie. He'd watched her from the time she left the table until she returned, and she hadn't even entered the bathroom.

"This place is getting on my nerves," Ryan said irritably, pocketing his receipt. "Let's get out of here."

"Fine by me."

It wasn't until they were out in the clear April sunshine that he regained his former, more relaxed mood. Everything was going according to plan. In companionable silence, they walked at a leisurely pace toward his car.

When they were almost a block away, Ryan heard something—screeching brakes, the roar of powerful engines. Normally such noises wouldn't have alerted him. They were in an urban area, after all, and traffic noises were the norm. But perhaps his senses were more keenly alert today, because he turned around to look back in the direction they'd come from.

Four cop cars—unmarked, but obviously cop cars—had pulled to a stop in front of Costello's, parked about as illegally as they could get. Men in suits were jumping out, leaving doors open, shouting orders to each other, about as subtle as the G-men in an old gangster movie. The only thing they didn't do was flash guns, but Ryan imagined the guns were there.

Chrissy turned and stared. Her hand flew to her mouth. "Oh, my word," she murmured through her fingers.

Other phrases came to Ryan's mind. Unless he missed his guess, a slew of FBI agents and/or plainclothes detectives weren't descending on Costello's because someone had walked out on his bill.

Chapter 4

Christine could have kicked herself. That phone call to her father had been traced, no doubt about it.

That meant the police were directly involved. The knowledge gave her small comfort. Connie could have notified the police. The wizened little maid always got bent out of shape if she didn't know exactly where Christine was.

"Wonder what that's about?" Christine asked casually, continuing to walk toward Ryan's car.

Ryan shrugged. "Who knows? It probably boils down to drugs. Almost everything does these days."

She felt him watching her, as if gauging her for a reaction. How was she supposed to react? Did he think she was some sort of junkie? After her performance last night, she wouldn't blame him.

A few moments later, he seemed to have dismissed the excitement at Costello's. "So, we have the rest of the day to kill. What would you like to do?"

"You don't have to entertain me," Christine said. "If you have things to do, I can tag along, or you can leave

me at your apartment. I saw you have a wallful of books."
Reading. She hadn't done much of that lately. She loved
to read, especially historical novels that took her away to
another world.

"I don't have an agenda," he said. "Anyway, the
weather's too nice to spend it with my head under the hood
of a car. C'mon, it's your call. I'm game for anything."

"Well..." She hesitated, glancing up at a billboard to
collect her thoughts. The billboard depicted a zebra wearing
hiking boots, and the image inspired her. She blurted out,
"The zoo?"

"You're kidding."

"I haven't been to the National Zoo for probably fifteen
or twenty years," she explained, warming to the idea. "I
read somewhere that they have this new penguin exhibit—"

He laughed, the sound sending waves of pleasure down
Christine's spine. "All right, all right, the zoo it is. Haven't
been there myself in a while. They don't put the animals
in cages anymore, you know. They're mostly in natural
habitats."

"Oh, I've heard all about that. In fact, I helped out with
this fund-raiser for the lions—" She stopped herself. Darn.
How smart did Ryan have to be to figure out who she was?
She cleared her throat, then continued. "Do they have one
of those rain-forest places where the birds fly all around
you?"

"I think so."

"Great. Let's do it." Christine felt like a little kid again.
How long had it been since she felt such a surge of anticipation flowing through her? The giddy feeling made her
all the more certain that her emotional life was crippled, in
sad need of rehabilitation. How had she let things get so
bad?

A little at a time, she supposed.

They'd reached Ryan's car. He unlocked the passenger
door, opened it, then froze, peering off down the street.

"What's wrong?" she asked, trying to see what he saw.

She felt a sudden chill. Were the terrorists back? Was she really safe with Ryan? Maybe she should abandon this crazy charade and just call the police, the way any normal, sensible woman would.

The only thing at the end of the street was a big Metro bus.

"Nothing's wrong," Ryan answered her. "I was just thinking that we won't be able to find a parking place at the zoo, not on a Sunday when the weather's so perfect. Why don't we take the Metro?"

"You mean, public transportation?"

"Uh, yeah, Chrissy. Buses and subways. That's how people in D.C. get around. I get the feeling you're not exactly from my side of the tracks, but surely you've ridden on the Metro."

"Oh, yeah, sure. Lots of times," she lied. How deliciously forbidden riding the subway seemed to her, exotic, maybe the way a limousine would seem to someone else. "How much does it cost?"

"I'll take care of it," he said, misinterpreting her question. She wasn't concerned about who would pay for their little jaunt to the zoo. Since she had no money, Ryan would have to pay. But she was genuinely curious as to how much it cost—for future reference. If she was going to change her life and live like a normal person, get a job, maybe commute every day, she would have to learn these things.

They walked downhill to the end of the block, toward the bus they'd seen. Christine paused every so often to duck into a shop that intrigued her. She lovingly caressed a wooden music box inlaid with mother-of-pearl, which she found tucked in a corner of an antiques shop. When she opened it, it played the French song "Alouette." The price tag was only a hundred and twenty-five dollars. If she'd had her charge cards with her, she would have bought it on the spot.

She supposed she'd better get used to suppressing impulse buys. In her future life, she wasn't going to be rich. She didn't kid herself that her father would support her in any way. She had a small trust fund from her grandmother's estate that was in her control, but she didn't think the interest was enough to live on.

As she reluctantly put the box back where she found it, she noticed Ryan studying her with undisguised interest. She smiled shyly, suddenly at a loss for words. He must find her an odd duck, she mused.

She thought they were heading for a bus stop, but Ryan waved down a cab. "This'll be easiest," he said as they climbed into the back seat. "Nearest subway station is in Foggy Bottom." He gave their destination to the driver.

Two blocks later, the cab stopped and picked up another couple. Christine looked at Ryan, raising her eyebrows in a silent question.

"What's wrong?" he asked, pulling her closer to allow the other couple room. She was almost in his lap. The enforced closeness made her short of breath. She found she couldn't muster an answer.

Ryan didn't seemed concerned about the extra passengers, so she supposed she shouldn't be, either. Cab sharing must be the norm, she decided, again realizing how ignorant she was about everyday life in the city.

The cab ride was short. Ryan paid the driver, then he and Christine went down into the subway station. Cool, fresh spring air gave way to stale underground mustiness as they descended a flight of stairs, but the station itself was clean and bright. Christine tried to see everything at once as Ryan put money in a machine for their fares.

The station was not very crowded. A few rowdy teenagers, a man dragging around a bag of aluminum cans, a young couple with two small children. She felt a sudden rush of compassion at the thought of how difficult it was for most people to make ends meet. The subway wasn't an adventure for them, just another part of the daily grind.

Her breath caught in her throat when she spotted a pathetic-looking man—he had no legs—meandering through the sparse crowd on a platform with wheels, begging for spare change. The teenagers threw some pennies at him, laughing as he scrambled around to collect the coins. His piteous expression tore at Christine's heart.

She nudged Ryan, who seemed to be studiedly ignoring the people around them. "Couldn't you give him something?" she asked, nodding toward the panhandler.

"Him? No way. You know who that is, don't you?"

"Should I?"

"Pitiful Pete. His part-time job is begging."

"Well, of course it is. What else would he do? He doesn't even have a proper wheelchair."

"Oh, yes he does. Right along with a proper house in Arlington, and a proper Jaguar specially outfitted so he can drive it."

Christine blinked a couple of times. "You're kidding. How do you know all that about him?"

"I, er, read it in the paper. Pete earned over a hundred thousand dollars—tax-free, mind you—last year. And when it's too cold for him to get out, he runs a successful mail-order lingerie business from his house."

Christine was really confused. "If he's not homeless, if he can drive a car…why does he do this?"

"Because he likes bilking people. It gives him a thrill, pretending to be poor." Ryan gave her a look that made her want to scramble for cover. "Everybody likes to pretend they're someone else occasionally. It's not so hard to understand."

"I suppose," she said noncommittally, refusing to meet his too-knowing gaze.

Then he smiled, and she felt okay again. He didn't know who she was. It was pure coincidence that he'd chosen to philosophize about something so close to home.

"C'mon, that's our train," he said as a distant roar grew louder and a subway car whizzed into view, stopping with uncanny precision.

The small crowd of people pushed together near the curb. Ryan's arm went around Christine's waist in a protective gesture. She grabbed his belt for added security, unable to bear the thought of getting lost. She hadn't experienced a press of flesh hemming her in like this since her last political rally, and it made her nervous. But as long as she had Ryan close by, she felt secure.

They were the last passengers to board, because Ryan stood back to let a woman with a bulky camera bag get on before them. Unlike the station, the train was packed. Christine found herself standing in the aisle, with Ryan practically in her pocket. It took her a few confused moments to figure out where she was supposed to hold on, during which she stumbled into Ryan, nearly knocking him over.

"Careful," he murmured, wrapping her hand around an overhead bar. But he didn't step away. "Normally it's not this crowded on a Sunday, but I think we're competing with a crowd of conventioneers."

Thank goodness for conventioneers, she found herself thinking. Ryan's nearness was intoxicating. Even given all the indelicate aromas around her, she could discern his clean, male fresh-laundry scent. She couldn't recall that Robert had ever smelled like this. In fact, she couldn't recall Robert smelling like anything, which amazed her. Perhaps her senses had been dead, and they were only now being resurrected.

Christine looked out the windows at the concrete tunnel walls flying by. It was a little bit oppressive, being underground. She would be glad to see daylight again.

The conventioneers got off a couple of stations later. Ryan slid into a seat and pulled Christine in after him. Their thighs brushed. Out of habit, she started to scoot away, but then she thought, *What the hell!* and stayed just where she was. After tomorrow, she probably would never see Ryan Mulvaney again. While she was still Chrissy Green, she would do just what she wanted—say outrageous things, eat unhealthy food. Flirt.

"Are you having fun?" Ryan asked suddenly.

"Sure."

"And we haven't even made it to the zoo yet," he murmured, studying her again.

* * *

Ryan wasn't sure what to make of Chrissy. The whole time she rode that crowded subway train—an experience most people would find unpleasant—she'd acted like a kid at an amusement park. Was her life really so sheltered?

When they arrived at the National Zoo, her exuberance could hardly be contained. "I remember those great big Z-O-O letters at the entrance," she said excitedly. "I couldn't have been more than five or six when my parents brought me here. We had a picture taken—the three of us—standing right by the *O*."

Ryan looked around for Fran. She'd done an admirable job of tailing them so far. Ah, there she was, pretending photographic interest in a sea of red and yellow tulips. As Chrissy removed her sunglasses and bent down to admire a solitary bloom, Ryan stood out of the way and Fran squeezed off a shot.

Perfect.

"So, did you have the proverbial happy childhood?" Ryan asked as they strolled toward a directional sign.

"You could say so," she answered thoughtfully donning the sunglasses again. "I was spoiled, I suppose. My parents lavished all their love and a considerable amount of material goods on me. Then Mom died, and the whole family thing came to a screeching halt."

"How old were you?"

"Fifteen."

"That's really young. It must have been hard." Ryan felt only a twinge of guilt, pumping Chrissy like this for his own selfish purposes. He wished he had a tape recorder, although his memory for quotes was almost uncannily accurate.

She shrugged, then glanced up at the sign. "Where to first? Let's see, hoofed animals, spectacled bears, beavers and otters... Oh, pandas! Remember Ling-Ling?"

"Yeah, sure." The whole country had watched as Ling-Ling and her mate tried to propagate their species. "She died a few years ago, if I recall."

"Yeah," Chrissy said sadly. Then she perked up. "Let's head toward the pandas. Then we can stop and see the zebras, and the elephants and giraffes and…ooooooh, Komodo dragons. Can't miss those."

Ryan flexed one foot against the concrete walkway. Apparently she wanted to see everything. This was going to be a long day. But if he could keep her talking about her family like he just had…

The guilt squeezed his conscience again. Normally it didn't bother him at all to gather information from an unwitting subject. But lying to someone as innocent as Chrissy made him feel like slime.

Wait a minute. Since when was she innocent? Last night she'd been drunk, or high, or both. He didn't know what to believe about kidnappers or an abusive boyfriend, but someone had socked her in the jaw. She was involved in *something* unsavory. He'd better watch his priorities.

He had to follow along at a trot to keep up with Chrissy as she flitted from one exhibit to the next, reading the information plaques and stumbling over the Latin names of the animals, laughing at the antics of the monkeys in the Great Ape House, wrinkling her nose at the smell of dung, getting all soft and teary at the sight of a female baboon cradling her week-old infant.

Ryan couldn't seem to get her talking about her family or her personal life for very long. She kept changing the subject—talking about the animals or, worse, turning his questions back on him.

Her ever-changing array of emotions fascinated him, yet he couldn't escape the feeling that she was a very complicated person and he was only scratching the surface.

When they reached Lion-Tiger Hill, Ryan turned to see if Fran was following, and he was startled to see a man in a leather jacket ambling along by himself. The man, in his mid-twenties, looked familiar. An aging Pit Bull, perhaps?

Ryan shivered involuntarily. Yesterday he hadn't scored any points with the gang by hustling Chrissy away from those young thugs. Was he being followed because of it?

Were the gangbangers planning revenge? He'd been the target of the gang's revenge before, and it hadn't been pretty. He'd had to disappear for a while until they lost interest. If the Pit Bulls had figured out who he was, their revenge could become revitalized.

But maybe he was imagining things. The leather-jacket guy didn't look very menacing. He was eating cotton candy, after all. Ryan pushed the stranger from his thoughts.

"Amazonia," Chrissy declared.

"Hmm?"

"That's the rain-forest place where the birds fly around free. Can we go there?"

"Sure, why not?"

They stopped on the way to Amazonia to get popcorn. Chrissy fed half of hers to the fat, greedy sparrows, giggling and pointing as they scuffled over each kernel she threw out.

When they entered Amazonia, Ryan immediately broke out in a sweat. It felt like ninety degrees inside the huge enclosed space, and it smelled of dank, growing things. Colorful birds darted from tree to tree all around them, screeching loud enough to burst eardrums. Chrissy was immediately taken with a blue-and-gold macaw, which sat on a branch invitingly close to the walkway.

"Hello, pretty bird," she cooed, holding out her hand. "You seem like a friendly guy."

"Um, Chrissy, the sign says not to touch the birds."

"I'm not touching him," she argued. "I'm making friends. Holding out an open hand is a friendly gesture in just about any culture. It ought to work with birds."

The macaw took one look at Chrissy's delicate pink hand and, apparently deciding it was edible, gave it a vicious bite.

Chrissy yelped and yanked her hand back. "The ingrate bit me!"

"Well, that's what happens when you disobey the

signs," he teased. But then, seeing that she was genuinely in distress, he sobered. "Here, let me see."

She offered him her hand. Her eyes looked so wounded and betrayed that he almost found it amusing. Almost.

"That damn bird drew blood," he said as he inspected her injury. There were two neat puncture wounds, one on her palm near her thumb, one on the back of her hand to match. Without thinking much about it, he drew her hand to his lips and pressed a light kiss on each of the lacerations, the way he would have for a child in similar circumstances. "There, is that better?"

When he looked up, he found no smile on her face, no gratitude for his small kindness. Her eyes had grown huge, and her expression could only have been described as hungry.

Suddenly he was hungry, too. He kissed her hand again, then folded it inside his and drew her closer. "Just what am I supposed to do with you?" He impulsively pulled off her baseball cap, wanting to see the tumble of blond silk. It cascaded to her shoulders, wildly out of control.

Just like the rest of her.

"Kiss me?" she asked in a tentative voice. Her breasts rose and fell with each breath, and he realized she wasn't wearing a bra.

Kiss her? Hell, yeah, and more. He lowered his head and claimed her moist pink lips with his.

If he'd expected the kiss to be tentative, he was disappointed. She took to it like a bird to the air, winding her arms around his neck, opening her mouth to him, teasing him with her tongue.

All right, so maybe she'd kissed one or two guys before. Was there anything wrong with that? he thought murkily.

The click of a camera shutter, and the whir of an autowinder brought him back to his senses. Fran! He opened his eyes, and from the corner of one of them he could see that his partner in crime had indeed recorded his passionate embrace with Chrissy.

That Fran was watching made him very uneasy. Not that

any romantic feelings remained between him and Fran. But he hadn't intended the kiss to be part of the story. That was private, and had nothing to do with the charade he was perpetrating on Chrissy.

He would have to tell Fran in no uncertain terms that she couldn't use *that* picture.

He gently broke the kiss. "I bet you forgot all about the parrot bite, huh?" he said inanely.

"I forgot all about a lot of things, including propriety," she said, nervously looking around to see if anyone was watching. Fran, thank goodness, had dropped out of sight. She was amazingly good at that. "I'm sorry. The whole thing was silly."

Ryan didn't think so. He touched his lips, remembering the feel of her. Hell of a kiss.

He plopped the cap back on her head. "Silly or not, I enjoyed it."

Chrissy's face was flushed and growing pinker. He found it charming that she could blush. He couldn't recall having seen a girl blush since high school.

"I need to find a rest room," she said abruptly. "I should, um, wash my hand to get the parrot germs off."

"I saw a ladies' room right by the entrance," he said. "I'll wait here for you."

"Okay."

He watched her walk away, her hips gently swaying beneath the borrowed denim shorts, her tumbled hair gleaming even in the dim rain-forest light.

"Well, that was interesting," Fran said close to his ear.

He jumped. The woman could melt in and out of sight like she had magic powers. "Ah. Fran. That wasn't supposed to be… That is, I didn't mean to kiss her. No more pictures with me in them, okay?"

"It's kind of hard, when you're sticking to her like duct tape. Look, stud, I have enough zoo pictures to fill a scrapbook. I thought she was meeting her pusher or something."

"I don't know what's going on, but stick with us awhile longer, okay? She's starting to trust me."

"I'll say," Fran said tartly.

Ryan ignored the gibe. "I want her to tell me what's really happening in her life right now. An abusive boyfriend? Maybe. But I have a hunch it's something more dramatic, or else why the faked kidnapping?"

"You've got a point," Fran said. "All right, a couple more hours. How much of this zoo stuff can one person stomach?" With that, Fran stalked away.

Ryan shook his head. He liked the zoo.

He decided he'd better go find Chrissy. He didn't imagine she would abandon him, but he couldn't vouch for her state of mind. He sauntered back toward the entrance of Amazonia, where the ladies' rest room was.

Chrissy blotted her face with a moist paper towel. She'd washed the parrot bite with soap and water, but that wasn't the real reason she'd retreated to the ladies' room. She'd needed some distance between her and Ryan. She'd spent half the day with him, and during that time she'd found him the most charming, fun, uninhibited guy she'd ever been around.

Not to mention sexy.

Where had that kiss come from? She'd started it, no doubt about that. At least he hadn't ridiculed her, or turned away in revulsion, when she asked him to kiss her. No, he'd done just what she asked, and more, kissing her until her toes curled and her skin broke out in goose bumps.

She hadn't felt like this since that giddy first love—that only love—in college.

She had to get a grip here. It was just the thrill of being on her own, of being free of the terrorists and her father's thumb. No reason to let that thrill take her to places she really shouldn't go.

Okay, she was sane now. She tucked her hair back under the cap, donned her sunglasses, and was ready to face Ryan again.

She turned toward the exit, surprised and not a little

frightened to see a man in a black leather jacket standing just inside the ladies' room door. He smiled, not pleasantly.

She tried for a smile of her own. "I think you have the wrong…" Oh, no. He was tall, gaunt, with greasy black hair and a ravaged face. Denny.

"I've got the right room, all right, Christine. And I've got a gun pointed right at your heart. You just come with me real quiet, and everything'll be okay." He crooked his finger at her.

"What do you want with me?" she asked, the question coming out in a squeaky whisper. "My father won't pay you the ransom."

"He would, if the right kind of pressure were applied. We did it all wrong before. No publicity. We were too afraid of getting caught. This time we'll get it right."

He closed the distance between them, took her arm. "C'mon now, Ms. Greenlow. Christine." On his lips, her name sounded obscene. "You and I are going for a little walk."

Not if she could help it. No way was she going quietly. What was the goon going to do, shoot her in the middle of a crowded zoo? He pulled her to the door, peeked outside to see that the coast was clear, then pulled her out with him. She stumbled and barely righted herself before falling.

He put his arm around her waist. The other hand remained in his jacket pocket, a grim reminder.

Christine's gaze darted around wildly. There was no one nearby, no one to appeal to for help. She made a snap decision—she wouldn't go one step farther with this thug. She opened her mouth and screamed with every cubic inch of breath in her lungs.

"Shut up, would you?" He cuffed her head, hitting her sore jaw. "Damn, you're a mouthy bitch."

Just then a group of noisy Cub Scouts, squealing and shrieking the way children do, entered Amazonia. Their noisy entrance camouflaged Christine's screams of distress as the kidnapper dragged her along, but she just screamed that much louder.

"Ryan! Help! Fire!"

Ryan was there in an instant. He had to have been lurking nearby, she thought later, keeping a close watch on her. But right now, all she felt was pure relief. Ryan immediately figured the situation correctly. He gave the man a mighty shove. At the same time, Christine kicked him in the shin, then stepped on his foot. His grip on her arm loosened and she pulled away.

Ryan tried to grab him, but the man shook him loose and bolted through the entrance. Some Cub Scout stragglers, and their leader, stopped and stared.

"Something wrong?" the leader, a young, bookish-looking man in his thirties, asked.

"No, we're fine," Christine immediately answered. "Just a misunderstanding."

"If you say so. Come along, boys." He herded his charges into the building, giving the couple one last, suspicious look over his shoulder.

Ryan opened a door marked Entrance Only and ushered her outside, into the bright sunshine and cool, fresh air. No one seemed to care.

"Are you really okay?" Ryan asked, putting a protective arm around her. "Did he hurt you?"

She shook her head.

"What was that all about?"

"A, um, mugger, I guess. I don't know. He just grabbed me, and I panicked."

"You got a great set of lungs, I'll give you that. Let's go talk to the police. They have a station right here at the zoo—"

"No. I don't want to involve the police," she said, her voice firm. That was all she needed.

"But that guy's a menace. What if he hurts someone else?"

"He won't." Realizing her certainty sounded odd, she elaborated, creating the fantasy as she went. "He's a friend of my boyfriend's. I'm sure Robert sent him."

"That's ridiculous. How would he have found you?"

"He's probably been following me all along."

"From when you jumped out of your boyfriend's car last night?" Ryan's skepticism was apparent.

"He was with us in the car," she said brightly.

"And he jumped out after you, and…"

"Followed me. Or Robert followed me in the car. I don't know how he found me, but he did." There.

"And you still don't want to contact the police?"

"No. Robert has friends in high places. He would make things even harder for me, and no criminal charges would stick. Look, no police, okay?"

"Okay, okay. I just want to understand here." His voice softened. "You sure you're okay? I saw him hit you." He ran one finger lightly along the curve of her jaw.

It would have been so easy to lean into him, to offer herself up for another kiss. But that would be insane. She was engaged. Not that she intended to remain that way for long, but a woman with class would not line up a replacement for a fiancé she had yet to dump.

She shied away from Ryan's touch. "So, I'll have a new bruise on top of the old one. Nothing's broken."

He pulled his hand back. "Okay, fine. Have you had enough of the zoo?"

"I guess so." The zoo was proving hazardous to her health.

"Let's head for the exit, then." He paused to study a map. "We can stop and see the seals on the way out. If any animal can cheer you up, it's a seal."

Christine smiled, despite her misfortune. Ryan was right. Seals were funny.

On the way to the seals and sea lions exhibit, she burst into tears.

Chapter 5

Ryan felt something akin to panic as he witnessed Chrissy's breakdown. He was worthless when it came to crying females. He still remembered all those nights he'd listened to his sister, Josette, pregnant with a rapist's baby, crying herself to sleep at night. He could hear her through the cheap walls of the apartment they lived in with their parents.

He'd been eighteen, on the verge of manhood and independence and freedom, while she'd been trapped in a situation she'd asked for—or so she was told over and over. He'd wanted to go to her, comfort her, tell her everything would be okay. But he hadn't been able to make himself do it. He'd been terrified that he would fail, that he would make her feel worse…or that he was wrong, and nothing would ever be okay for her again.

So he'd cowered in his own room, put the pillow over his head, and done nothing.

He would do better with Chrissy.

"Hey, take it easy," he said to her, leading her to a park bench. Even though he was quaking inside, he was deter-

mined to give her some comfort. He removed her sunglasses, pulled her against him and let her cry on his shoulder. "Are you hurt? Should I get you to a doctor?"

"N-no," she sobbed. "I'm o-okay."

"You don't sound okay."

The crying storm didn't last long. After a minute or two,
her sobs slowed down. She sniffed away the last of the
tears, wiped her eyes with the backs of her hands and hic-
cuped. "I'm fine. Just shaken up. It was a delayed reaction."

"I think we should go to the police," he suggested again.
He didn't *really* want to involve the authorities, because
that would mean giving up his exclusive. But Chrissy's
reticence intrigued him. He hoped that if he pressed her,
she would cave in and tell him the truth.

She sighed. "Maybe you're right. I've been playing a
very dangerous game, and I almost lost."

"What do you mean?" Ryan asked innocently.

"I haven't exactly been straight with you. In fact, I've
pretty much been lying through my teeth. I hope you won't
be too mad."

"Hmm…that depends."

"On what?"

"On why you lied, and what the real truth is."

She thought for a moment, chewing on her bottom lip.
"I lied because I wasn't sure I could trust you. I was scared
and confused. But now that I've gotten to know you, I can
level with you." She sat up straighter, and there was a
determined gleam in her eye. "I wasn't drunk last night. I
was drugged up."

"Oh?" He tried to sound as if this were no big deal to
him, that he encountered illegal drugs every day. "What
was it, heroin?" He'd heard heroin was making a comeback. "Coke? LSD?"

"Good heavens, no! Not that kind of drug. I don't even
know what it was. It came out of a syringe, and it was
given to me against my will."

"Uh-huh. Go on."

"My name's not Chrissy Green, it's...it's Christine Greenlow. My father is Stan Greenlow, a senator from Pennsylvania." She stared at him, waiting for a reaction.

Ryan pretended ignorance. "Name sounds familiar, but I don't read the papers that much."

"Oh. Well, anyway, I was kidnapped from my father's home three days ago by some environmental terrorists. They call themselves the National Allegiance to Something-Something-Something—it spells out NATURE. They're mad at my father about some stupid legislation, and they wanted a million dollars from him to help clean up this wildlife habitat. They kept me for about forty-eight hours, I guess, although my sense of time is a little messed up. Then I escaped, but they drugged me just before, so that's why I was wandering around in a daze when you found me."

Mentally Ryan rolled his eyes. He'd been prepared for another made-up story from her, but was she ever bad at creating fiction. Environmental terrorists? She'd probably heard about her supposed kidnapping, as told by Stan Greenlow, and now she was devising this hokey story so her father wouldn't be proved a liar.

Ryan didn't buy it for a minute. But he had to be very careful. He needed to dig down to the truth, but he couldn't risk alienating Chrissy. He wanted this story, bad.

"That must have been terrible!" he said, giving her shoulders a squeeze. "How did you get away?"

"First I kicked this guy in the... Well, you know. Then, when they drugged me, I pretended like I was unconscious so they wouldn't bother tying me up, and when they left the room I jumped out a window. From the second story. I landed in a bush—see the scratches on my legs?"

He gave her long, elegant legs a brief perusal, preferring not to dwell on them. He'd seen enough of them last night to provide him with a month's worth of fantasies. Their shape, their texture, were branded into his memory.

"And then what happened?"

She shrugged. "I don't remember much after that although some of it is coming back. I have a vague recollection of talking to a scruffy-looking man on the street, and then trying to get away from those boys who thought I was a prostitute or something—''

''Those 'boys' were members of the Pit Bulls,'' he reminded her.

She shrugged again, seemingly unaware of the gang's deadly reputation. ''Anyway, you know the rest.''

''That's an extraordinary story, Chrissy. I mean, Christine.''

She smiled, her eyes still a little misty. ''You can keep calling me Chrissy if you want. I kind of like it.''

Good, he thought. He had a real hard time thinking of her as anything else. ''I just have one question.''

''Yes?''

''Why haven't you called the police?''

''Well, I… Um, I don't really know, exactly,'' she said, clearly hedging. ''Something happened to me during the time I was held captive. Maybe it's the drugs, but I'm just not myself. I haven't been thinking too straight.''

That was an inadequate explanation if he'd ever heard one.

''I was going to call them,'' she continued, perhaps sensing his skepticism. ''But I started thinking about all the questions, and the reporters— I really can't stand reporters. They're so nosy, and they think they own you just because you happen to have money and your father's a public figure. One time a reporter asked me what size bra I wore!''

''Pretty tacky,'' Ryan said, inwardly smarting from her criticism. As a reporter, he'd seldom had anything to do with celebrities or politicians. But he couldn't deny that he'd at times been intrusive, annoying and even nosy, asking the most uncomfortable questions.

Even now he was wondering…what size bra *did* she wear? He'd guess she was a B cup. But he wouldn't ask her. A bazillion *Primus* magazine readers didn't need to know that. He had a few scruples.

''Anyway, you were so nice, letting me borrow your

clothes, feeding me breakfast. If I'd gone to the police, I would have had to explain that I spent the night at your house, and it would have sounded so tacky, and I just didn't want to face reality yet. You'd have been on the hot seat, too, you know.''

"So you were protecting me?"

"In a way."

"Hmm." There was a long silence, which grew to uncomfortable proportions. He broke it. "You know what I think, Chrissy?"

"What?"

"I think I like the abusive-boyfriend story better."

Every muscle in her body—at least all the ones pressed against him—stiffened. "Excuse me?" She sounded outraged.

"Don't get all hot and bothered," he said soothingly. "I understand, really I do, and I don't blame you a bit. I can picture it now…. You got tired of the Washington society scene, the responsibility of always being respectable, the senator's perfect hostess. You went a little bit wild, hanging out with a fast crowd. Some drinking, a little coke. But the whole thing spun out of control. You got stuck in the fast lane, didn't know how to get out.

"Maybe there was a boyfriend, someone totally inappropriate for you, putting the pressure on you. You started forgetting your obligations, staying out later and later. Then you didn't come home at all."

Ryan was just getting warmed up. It was the kind of story he loved to write, filled with human emotion, relationships, mistakes, regrets.

"Your father had to explain your absence somehow," Ryan continued, "and he couldn't very well tell the truth. So he fabricated the kidnapping. The story addressed all his problems, and it brought him some publicity and public sympathy.

"You got wind of the story—you might have read my newspaper this morning—and now you're backing up Dad's claims. Is that pretty close to the truth?"

He'd imagined Chrissy wilting as she was hit with the unvarnished facts, amazed at his deductive abilities, maybe even turning to him for help in changing her life around. Instead, she pulled away from him and turned the full force of an angry green gaze on him.

"That's what you think, huh?"

"It's not so far from the first story you told me, Abusive boyfriend, booze—"

"I made that part up! What I just told you is the truth, every word."

"I'm not blaming you. I'd like to help you. I'll take you home to your father. You can make up something to satisfy the police, say it was a misunderstanding. That's more or less the truth, anyway."

"That's not the truth! There was no party, no abusive boyfriend, no drinking. It was a drug the kidnappers gave me with a needle. Look, I'll bet you can still see the mark on my arm." She frantically rolled her sleeve up, then turned her arm this way and that, peering at her own creamy flesh.

Ryan found himself peering, too. She was incredibly flawless, even in bright April sunlight.

"There. Right there," she said triumphantly.

Ryan looked. She was pointing to a tiny red mark that could have been anything, even a self-inflicted pinch or scratch. "Uh-huh."

"They posed as UPS men, and they grabbed me off the front porch of my father's house."

"Uh-huh."

"Damn it! I knew there was a reason I didn't tell you all this in the first place. You wouldn't have believed it then, either."

"You have to admit, Chrissy, it's a crazy story. Can you show me even a shred of proof? Can you take me to where you were held? If you were really kidnapped, why didn't anyone take credit or contact your father?"

"They did! They demanded a million dollars. Only for some reason that part didn't get in the paper."

"Uh-huh."

"Oh, just forget it." Abruptly she stood and began walking away.

"Wait, Chrissy! There's no reason to get angry."

"I happen to think there is."

"Where are you going?"

"I don't know."

"I'll go with you, make sure you get there safely."

"No, thanks." She shook off his hand when he tried to physically stop her. A young couple with a baby cast curious glances his way, both of them frowning with disapproval. He backed off. Short of throwing her over his shoulder fireman-style, as he'd done last night, he couldn't stop her.

Fran reappeared at his side. "What did you say to tick her off?"

"Nothing! All I did was express a bit of skepticism when she told me this cock-and-bull story about environmental-terrorist kidnappers. I was very tactful..."

"You?"

"...but she was mad that I didn't hang on her every word."

Fran appeared thoughtful. "Wait a minute. Did you say environmental terrorists? As in a group that calls themselves NATURE?"

"Um, she mentioned something about that."

"These guys are all over the place! They tried to bomb the EPA, sabotage oil-company freighters, all kinds of stuff. Kidnapping a senator's daughter would be right up their alley."

"Fran, you don't actually believe she was kidnapped, do you?" Ryan asked, feeling the first prickles of unease. Chrissy couldn't be telling the truth. That guy who tried to grab her was either her pusher or connected with the Pit Bulls.

"It's not likely," Fran admitted. "Still, shouldn't we follow her?"

"Oh, I plan to," he said. He'd never taken his eyes off

of her. But he wanted to make sure she didn't spot him. "C'mon, let's go. It'll be interesting to see just where Miss Chris-Chrissy goes."

He felt only a twinge of remorse at having thrown away the fragile trust that had started to build between them, the camaradrie…the kiss! All of it was based on lies anyway, both his and hers.

Chrissy's anger billowed around her like a fog, dense, palpable. But it dissipated quickly, leaving her spent, disappointed and afraid. Where could she go from here?

She'd better just call the police, she decided. That horrible man might still be lurking around—the terrorist guy, not Ryan. Ryan wasn't horrible, just infuriating. He'd had no trouble believing her when she told one whopping lie after another. So why couldn't he have believed her when she trusted him with the truth?

There were pay phones near the zoo's exit. She paused in front of one, gathered her courage, lifted the receiver and dialed 911.

"This is the 911 operator. What is your emergency?"

"This is Chrissy—um, Christine Greenlow. I was kidnaped but now I'm free and I need to talk to the police, because someone's still after me. I'm at the zoo."

"The…zoo?"

"Yes. I know it sounds crazy, but someone tried to grab me in the women's rest room."

"Are you in immediate danger, ma'am?"

"I don't know," Christine said impatiently. Why had she ended up with the one person in the city who had never heard of her and knew nothing about her disappearance? "Could you just send someone to pick me up?"

"I can send someone out to make a report."

That would have to do. Once she got hold of a cop, she could tell her whole story and hope she did a better job convincing him than she'd done with Ryan. Surely they would take her to a police station and put her in touch with whatever detective was assigned to her case.

Christine waited by the main zoo entrance, keeping in full view of the ticket sellers and the swells of people, in case her terrorist was lurking about, waiting for her to drop her guard. She also kept an eye out for Ryan, halfway hoping he'd come around again. She'd been pretty hard on him, and in hindsight she couldn't blame him completely for doubting her. After all, she'd lied to begin with, so why should he instantly believe her, especially when the truth was so peculiar?

Even the police dispatcher had been confused and dubious about her story.

But Ryan didn't show. She felt a strange heaviness— regret, perhaps—as she climbed into the patrol car that showed up forty-five minutes later.

"Oh, yeah, your picture was on the front page of the paper this morning," one of the officers said, squinting at her when she took off her hat and sunglasses. She would have to return her borrowed "disguise" to Ryan, she realized happily. By then, her story would have been verified by all the papers, and she could apologize for losing her temper with him

And he could apologize for not believing her.

"And how did you end up at the zoo?" asked the other officer, who was driving.

"I escaped from the kidnappers yesterday, but I'd been drugged and I was pretty woozy. A Good Samaritan took me in for the night—"

"But you didn't call us then?" His voice clearly reflected skepticism.

Oh, dear. What if no one believed her? "I was out of my mind, and my Samaritan had no idea who I was. He thought I was just drunk."

"Okay," the officer said, "so he took you home with him, you slept off whatever drug you'd been given. That part I understand. Then you got up this morning, and...you went to the zoo?"

"I was still a little confused," Christine said. "Look, would you mind awfully much if I waited and told this whole story to Detective— What's his name? The one in charge of my case?''

"*Her* name. Brich. Lieutenant Wilma Brich," the other officer supplied. "I don't know, it was just getting interesting."

The first officer laughed. The other one joined in.

"I'm glad you both think this is so funny," she said huffily. She wasn't accustomed to being laughed at, at least not to her face. Stan Greenlow was an influential man in the Senate, and it wasn't wise to offend him, if you wanted to benefit from political favors in the future. He had a memory like an elephant. She thought about informing these two that with one phone call her father could have their jobs. He could, too. But he didn't normally abuse his considerable clout, and probably wouldn't in this case, even if she asked him to.

She decided to ignore the clowns.

The two officers sobered, even without the threat. "Sorry, Miss Greenlow," the driver said. "It's just that we don't rescue many kidnap victims at the z-zoo."

In the rearview mirror, she could see that he was struggling to keep from bursting into laughter again. With a sigh, she leaned back in her seat and tried to mentally prepare herself for the grilling to come.

Half an hour later, when she finally met Lieutenant Brich, Christine's situation didn't improve. The detective assigned to her disappearance was a big, blustery woman with ruler-straight red hair cut in an unflattering pageboy. Her bearing screamed, "Military." She disliked Christine from the start, solely on the basis of the fact that Christine had been born with money and privilege—at least, that was what Christine was able to infer from the frequent snide comments Brich made about Stan Greenlow's "mansion" and the two-carat engagement "rock" stolen by the terrorists.

"You'll forgive me if I'm having a problem with this," Lieutenant Brich said, after over an hour of questioning, during which a skeptical FBI agent was called in to participate. "But your story doesn't exactly jibe with what your father told us. He said no one ever contacted him with a ransom demand—"

"But they did! I heard them make the phone call myself. Maybe Dad was afraid to tell the police, afraid these loonies would hurt me if the cops got involved."

"He was downright uncooperative from the beginning," Brich said harshly. "It was the maid who finally called us, you know—against his wishes."

Good old Connie. Christine had guessed right about that part. "I'm sure he had his reasons."

"You called him this morning from a coffee bar in Georgetown. Yet it was several more hours before you called the police—"

"Look, it doesn't really matter if you believe me. I've told you everything I know. I just want to leave now." She had no idea where she would go. She could stop by her father's house and pick up a few things, but she didn't want to face Stan just yet. He hadn't even called the police? Hadn't he been worried at all? Or had he grown to hate her and her threats and ultimatums?

She toyed with the idea of calling Ryan, if his number was listed. He might still be angry with her, but he'd offered to take her to her sister's home. He seemed like an honorable man. Maybe he would honor that promise.

"There is a small problem," Lieutenant Wilma Brich said, an unpleasant smile threatening the corners of her full mouth. "The police don't take it too kindly when people waste their time."

Oh, dear. "Are you saying you want to charge me with a...a *crime* of some sort?"

"How about interfering with a police investigation?" The smile took on malicious proportions.

"But that's ridiculous! Everything I've told you is the truth."

"Yet you haven't provided us with even a teensy-weensy bit of evidence."

"What about the bruise on my face? And the scratches?"

"That could have happened any number of ways." Brich cleared her throat. "To me, it sounds like you and your pop have pulled the granddaddy of all publicity stunts."

"No." Christine was out of her chair. "He might be a little flamboyant, at times, but he would never make up something like this. Neither would I."

"Then give me some proof. For instance, this supposed 'Good Samaritan' who rescued you last night when you were on drugs, wearing ripped clothes and all—what happened to him?"

She hadn't wanted to involve Ryan any further, but if the police were going to toss her in jail, she supposed, she had no choice. "His name is Ryan Mulvaney," Christine said. "I don't know his phone number, but I think I remember where he—"

"Mulvaney? The reporter?"

Christine's blood went ice-cold. *Reporter?* Good Lord, what had she done? What all had she told him? "He said he was a mechanic," she said, almost desperate now to believe what she'd suspected all along was a lie.

"Tall guy? Late twenties? Dark hair, good-looking enough to make a woman do things she never dreamed of?"

"That's him," Christine said, sagging in defeat. If he wrote about her, about everything she'd said and done over the past twenty-four hours, she wouldn't have to worry about how to cut the strangling ties between herself and her father. He would disown her in a heartbeat.

The FBI agent, who'd remained detached throughout, smiled with undisguised amusement.

"Honey, I think you've been hoodwinked," Brich said. "I know how to get in touch with him. Shall I call, see if he'll verify that part of your story?"

Why bother? she thought. He might verify some of the facts, but the ones she really needed verified—the fact that she'd actually been kidnapped, for instance—he didn't believe, either.

"No," she said. Then she had another idea. "What if I

could take you to where the terrorists held me captive? If I could show you the pipes where they had me tied up, and the dirty mattress, and the window and the bush—''

Lieutenant Brich put an impatient hand to her forehead. "Why didn't you say so in the first place? You can actually take me there?"

"Well, if you could help me find the general area, I could probably find the place. It was a really bad neighborhood."

"We got lots of those." Brich was once again skeptical. "There's a gang that hangs out there. The Pit Bulls?"

"Ah." The sergeant nodded as recognition dawned. "I can take us to their territory. But I'm warning you, I don't have a lot of time to waste with some wild-goose chase. I want some evidence, or I'm tossing your rich little butt out on the street, and I *don't* want to hear from you again."

"I'll find evidence," Christine said, determined to redeem herself. It was a terrible feeling, being falsely accused of making up a wild story as a publicity stunt or as a means of covering up an even uglier truth. No one had ever doubted her word before today. "Can we go now?"

Lieutenant Brich's car was a major pigsty, with fast-food wrappers, crumpled, sweaty clothing and odd smells filling up every corner. The FBI agent took one look at it and decided he had pressing business elsewhere.

The lieutenant cleared a space in the front seat, and Christine gingerly sat down. What had she gotten herself into now?

Whatever the car lacked in aesthetic virtues, it made up for in performance. The horses under the hood sped them across town in record time. Soon they found themselves in a hideously depressed area that seemed vaguely familiar to Christine.

"This is it," Brich said. "Where to now?"

"There was some kind of barbecue restaurant," Christine remembered aloud. "Neon lights. Crowded parking, a lot of abandoned cars in weedy vacant lots." She was surprised at how much was coming back to her, now that the neighborhood was stimulating her drug-impaired memory.

"That sounds like Peak Street to me. I used to walk a beat there. Rudy's Barbecue?"

"That might be it." The name Rudy rang a bell.

Five minutes later, they parked in front of the place called Rudy's. But there Christine's sense of déjà vu ended. "No, I'm afraid this isn't right," Christine said glumly.

They drove around for a few more minutes, past one boarded-up building after another. Christine couldn't make heads or tails of anything she saw.

"Any bells ringing for you?" Brich asked, clearly put out that their field trip was for nothing.

"I'm sorry, Lieutenant Bitch—" The Freudian slip was out before Christine could stop it. "I mean, Lieutenant Beach—" No, that wasn't right, either.

The car screeched to a halt. "You're real lucky I don't haul your butt to jail and book you," the detective said harshly. "If you're out of my car in ten seconds, I'll think about forgetting this whole deal."

"But what will you tell—"

"Ten, nine, eight—"

"I'm sorry," Christine murmured before climbing out of the car, which sped away almost before she could get the door closed.

Great. She was in this horrible neighborhood again, helpless as a newborn kitten. She hurried along the street, thinking furiously. She would have to call her father now, she supposed, and pray she didn't get assaulted before the limo arrived to pick her up.

If her father would even send someone. Maybe he'd prefer for her to become a crime statistic.

Swallowing back that thought, she ducked into the first open business she came to, a liquor store. The bored clerk, a starkly gaunt woman of indeterminate age, stared at her when she asked to use the phone.

"Hey, you're the one from the paper. That political guy's daughter."

What a time to be recognized. Why didn't these things ever work in her favor? "Yes, I'm Christine Greenlow, and

I really need to use the phone. I'm lost, I'm stranded…''
And she was close to tears again.

"Here, you can use this one," the clerk said, with more
sympathy than anyone had shown Christine all day—not
counting Ryan's false show of concern. The clerk pulled a
battered desk phone from beneath the counter.

With a nod of gratitude, Christine started to dial her father's private line, then stopped. Why didn't she call Robert? He was still technically her fiancé, and she could hang
out with him until she decided what to do. Maybe he would
even arrange for her transportation to Raleigh to see her
sister.

She quickly punched out Robert's number.

He answered on the sixth ring. "Hello?"

"Robert? You're out of breath."

"I was out by the pool, and the cordless picked a hell
of a time to run out of batteries— Christine?''

"Yes, it's me."

If she'd expected to hear relief and concern in his voice,
she was sadly disappointed. "Christine, where the hell are
you? You know you've worried your father and me half to
death? We've got the cops and reporters breathing down
our necks—''

"I'm in a liquor store on Peak Street," she broke in.
"It's called Discount Liquors. Could you come get me,
please? Then I'll explain everything."

"Have you called your father?"

"I called him earlier." This wasn't going at all the way
she'd planned it. "Dad didn't sound all that pleased to hear
from me."

"That's ridiculous, Christine. He must have been ecstatic
to know you're safe."

"Yeah, about as ecstatic as you."

"What's that supposed to mean?"

"Nothing. For your information, I'm not in a particularly
safe position. If you'll just come get me, I'll try to explain
everything." She owed him that, she supposed.

"Where are you again?"

"Peak and…" She turned to the clerk. "What's a nearby cross street?"

"Twenty-third," said the clerk, who was hanging on Christine's every word. She was probably the type who liked soap operas and tabloids, Christine thought. And who knew? Tomorrow the woman might be able to read about Christine in some tabloid.

"Peak and Twenty-third," Christine told Robert. "How soon can you get here?"

"Um, that's a pretty grim neighborhood, sweetheart."

"You don't have to tell me."

"I'm not sure I… Can't you get a cab or something?"

"There aren't any cabs down here. Robert, for God's sake, come get me?"

"Christine, I drive a Jaguar." He spoke slowly, as though trying to make a point with a dull child. "The hub-caps alone could get me killed. Be a good girl and call a cab."

Christine could *not* believe her ears. The man who professed to be the love of her life was leaving her stranded in this awful neighborhood? "Robert?"

"Yes, dear."

"I'm really sorry I bothered you. Oh, and by the way, the wedding's off!" She slammed down the phone hard enough to make the clerk jump. Now what? She had friends she could call. But then she would have to do more explaining, and she didn't think she was ready. Maybe she should just call a cab and go home. Once she got access to her things—cash, credit cards, her checkbook and a change of clothes—she wouldn't be helpless anymore. No law said she had to stay under her father's roof.

"Got a phone book?" she asked the clerk, who had already hidden the phone away.

"No, sorry. And if my boss catches me letting customers use the phone, I'll be in trouble. There's a pay phone down on the corner."

"Okay, thanks." She didn't even have a quarter on her. But she supposed the operator would let her charge a call to her home number. Connie would answer Christine's private line, and she would okay the charge.

Christine was walking down the street toward the pay phone on the corner, mulling over her options, when she nearly ran right into a man standing in her way.

"Oops, I'm sor—" The apology died in her throat. It was him. Denny the terrorist. How did he keep finding her?

"We meet again," he said, smiling, exposing yellow teeth. "Are you coming easy this time, or do we have to do it the hard way?"

Chapter 6

Ryan squinted through the viewfinder of Fran's camera, which was equipped with a telephoto lens. It worked better than his binoculars. He and Fran were parked around the corner from Discount Liquors, Chrissy's last stop.

"She just left the liquor store," he announced.

Fran perked up. "She is one busy lady. Where'd she get the money to buy the booze?"

"She didn't buy anything. She's empty-handed. And... Uh-oh." Ryan's whole body tensed. "We've got trouble."

Fran peered out the window. "What?"

"Someone's hassling her. Oh, hell, it's that same jerk from the zoo."

"The Pit Bull? Quick, Ryan, we can't let him hurt her."

Ryan already had the Vette's engine started. He roared up the street, screeched to a halt in a no parking zone and jumped out. He didn't have a plan in mind. He just knew he couldn't let that jerk get hold of Chrissy. "Call the police on my mobile phone," he told Fran before slamming the door.

The man in the leather jacket, intent on his prey, didn't

notice Ryan's approach at first. Chrissy, apparently frozen with fear, didn't look at him, either. Then, before he could do anything, she moved. With a maneuver that would have made Chuck Norris proud, she kicked the guy in the knee-cap, then turned and fled.

Right into Ryan.

In a blind panic, she tried to get around him. He grabbed her arm. She screamed. He held on more tightly.

"Easy, Chrissy, it's me." He held her fast until she stopped struggling. Even under these dire circumstances, he was instantly aware of her as a woman—the feel of her feminine muscles beneath her sleeves, the smell of her fear, which was strangely erotic.

She was afraid, yes, but not helpless. After the blow she'd dealt her enemy—he was temporarily incapacitated, clutching his knee—Ryan's respect for her had eased up a notch.

"Ryan?" she gasped, peering up at him with those huge emerald eyes.

"To the rescue again. You okay?"

"No! That man—" She turned to point at the culprit. He had straightened up, and was staring at her with such animosity that it took Ryan's breath away.

"Give her back to me," the man said to Ryan. "She's ours. We found her, we did all the work catching her in the first place."

Ryan didn't remember seeing this particular man among the group of Pit Bulls he'd rescued Chrissy from yesterday, but the guy must have been there. A while ago, Ryan had called a friend of his who worked on the youth gang detail for the police department. He'd asked the friend to check and see what the word was on the street—whether the Pit Bulls had a vendetta against him for stealing Chrissy from them. He hadn't gotten an answer yet, but he already strongly suspected what he would find out.

The vendetta was staring him in the face.

"You think she's yours, huh?" Ryan said, using his rusty bravado from the days when he'd been a tough customer on the street himself. "I took her away, fair and square. And she wants to be with me, right, babe?"

"Uh, yeah," Christine murmured, clinging to Ryan, her gaze glued to the man.

"Maybe this will change your mind," the man said, pulling an object from his jacket pocket. A blue steel revolver. The gun didn't look like some cheap Saturday night special, either. It was amazing what gangs were carrying these days. The only thing that puzzled Ryan was why this young man was working alone. Where was his backup? Gang members always traveled in packs.

Instinctively Ryan pushed Chrissy behind him. "She's not worth that, man."

"I think she is." The man stepped closer, an inch at a time. Clearly, he intended to simply wrest Chrissy away from Ryan, using the gun as insurance.

Ryan caught a movement from the corner of his eyes. Fran! If ever there was a time when her talent for stealthy movements would come in handy, this was it. No one else was on the street to witness the assault. Even if there was, Ryan wasn't sure anyone would care. Fran was his best hope.

She sneaked up behind the man, quiet as any cat, and bided her time. Ryan tried not to give her away by looking at her.

The man was close enough to touch now. He reached out with his left hand, while the right hand held the gun just out of Ryan's reach, pointed toward the empty street. "Come on, now, girlie. Don't make me hurt your boyfriend here."

"I'll go with him, Ryan," she said in a quavering voice. "There's no use in your getting yourself killed."

No way was he letting her go. He'd seen his sister destroyed by members of this same gang. That fate would not befall Chrissy. He held her tightly with one hand.

Fran chose that moment to strike. She kicked against the back of the thug's knee, the same one Chrissy had injured, throwing him off balance. Before he could recover, Ryan lunged for his gun. The thing discharged, sending a bullet into the air. Chrissy jumped into the fray, pummeling the man's head with her fists.

At last he relinquished the gun. Without his weapon, he was a lot less brave. He turned tail and ran.

Chrissy slumped in relief against Ryan. "Thank you. Thank you so much. And you." She addressed Fran. "Whoever you are, I don't know how to begin to thank you."

"I'm Fran," the photographer said cheerfully. "And if you really want to thank us, why don't you hop in the car with us, and we'll take you someplace nice for dinner. We have a proposition for you."

She looked up at Ryan suspiciously as the first waves of relief subsided. "She's with you?"

"Uh-huh."

"And I don't suppose your showing up here was coincidence?" She sounded a lot less grateful all of a sudden. She looked back at Fran. "I remember you. You got on the train ahead of us back in Foggy Bottom."

"She's been following us all day," Ryan explained. "She and her, um, camera." He winced inwardly as he waited for Chrissy's reaction. He and Fran had already agreed to level with Chrissy. They could get a hell of a lot better story with her cooperation. Right now, it appeared she was completely alienated. They were her only friends. Even the police had abandoned her. But she wasn't going to like the fact that she'd been hoodwinked.

"Come on," he coaxed, when he couldn't get a reaction out of her. "The car's right here."

"All right, I'll go with you," Chrissy said, though he could tell she would have preferred it if some other choice had been offered. "Anything to get out of this neighborhood. But then you have some explaining to do, ace."

They all piled into Ryan's Vette. Ryan got in last, and he noticed his hubcaps were missing. Jeez, he'd taken his eyes off the car for, what, sixty seconds? Those were some brazen thieves. Then again, the hubcaps were pretty cool.

Custom design. Damn, this story better be worth it. He stuck the gun in his glove compartment.

Fran squeezed into the tiny back seat, giving Chrissy and her long legs the front passenger seat. Chrissy locked her door, glancing around nervously, jumping at every shadow, every pedestrian, until the car made it to the freeway.

No one had said anything. Now Chrissy broke the silence. "So, Ryan, you're a reporter."

"Yup. I guess it wasn't too hard to figure that out, since I'm toting around a photographer."

"Oh, I knew before I met your friend here."

"Really?" He was reasonably certain he hadn't given himself away. He hadn't flashed any notepads or tape recorders, and he'd kept his questions casual and friendly.

"The detective who was handling my case knew you, or of you, anyway. Lieutenant Wilma Brich."

Ryan gave a low whistle. "Yeah, I know her, and I wish I didn't, the old battle-ax. She was in charge of trying to solve your supposed kidnapping?"

"It wasn't a *supposed* kidnapping, and if you don't believe me, you can let me off at the first corner."

"Okay, okay. It's possible you were kidnapped." Barely. "The point is, did *she* believe you?"

Chrissy sighed. "Not a word. The more I tried to explain, the worse it got. I thought I could lead her to the place I was held captive, but I couldn't remember well enough. Then I got so flustered I, um, sort of mispronounced her name."

"You didn't. You did?" Ryan tried not to laugh, because he knew it wouldn't win any points with Chrissy.

"I called her 'Lieutenant Bitch.' She couldn't stop the car and throw me out fast enough."

Ryan did laugh then. He'd been watching, but he'd assumed it was Chrissy who'd insisted on being let out in the middle of Peak Street. Now he could just picture Brich getting her girdle in a twist over a wild-goose chase and her passenger's lapse in phonetic ability.

He would love to hear Brich's take on the story, if she didn't stonewall him, the way she usually did. She didn't much care for reporters.

Neither did Chrissy, he reminded himself. And he'd better apply himself now to changing her opinion.

"So you two have been following me since the zoo?" Chrissy asked.

"Uh-huh. We took a cab and followed you to the police station. Fran stayed there and kept an eye on things while I went back to get my car."

He paused for impact. "We have a very interesting story shaping up. With pictures."

Chrissy turned visibly paler as she took in the implications; then she turned on Ryan like a she-wolf. "I'll just bet, full of lies and unfounded suspicions. Is that how you earn your living? Printing half-truths and downright lies about innocent people?"

She sounded like she was ready to cry again. Ryan wasn't particularly enjoying himself. But he couldn't quit now, just because he was getting soft in his old age.

"I don't work for a tabloid. My story will contain just the facts."

"What facts? If you print one word of your theories about drugs and drunken orgies and an abusive boyfriend, my father will sue you so fast your head will spin."

"The abusive boyfriend was your story, not mine," he reminded her softly.

"And I recanted it."

"As for the rest of it, no, I don't plan to mention my suspicions, only things I can prove. You were wandering around Peak Street in a dirty, torn red dress, unable to walk straight, slurring your words. Do you deny that part?"

She dropped her chin. "No."

"You spent the night in a strange man's apartment. You went shopping at Target the next day, went out to breakfast, went to the zoo. You never made any attempt to contact the police until after three o'clock this afternoon. Have I got anything wrong so far?"

"No, but you're leaving out some crucial facts—like the terrorist guy who tried to rekidnap me in the ladies' room, then again on the street."

"He's with the Pit Bulls—the gang that was messing with you last night—and they want you back," Ryan said, in what seemed a perfectly reasonable explanation for what he'd seen.

"I don't know anything about the Pit Bulls," Chrissy insisted. "He was one of the ones who held me in that nasty apartment. He was threatening rape, threatening to cut off various body parts and send them to Dad. Maybe he's affiliated with this gang of yours, but he's also one of these radical environmentalists."

Ryan paused to think. Chrissy certainly seemed passionate about this environmental-terrorist fairytale. She hadn't wavered from it since she first told it to him. When he recounted it to Fran earlier, she'd thought it sounded more plausible than he did. And there was some guy trying to grab her, who *might* be associated with the Pit Bulls but wasn't wearing the official jacket.

Could it be Chrissy was telling him some version of the truth? He wanted to believe she was. He hated thinking of her as some fast-lane junkie. That image hadn't jibed with the Chrissy he'd gotten to know today, the one who laughed at the monkeys' antics and sniffled over a baboon baby.

"Okay," he said, "I'm willing to give you the benefit of the doubt. So convince me. I can go with the story I have, or you can cooperate with me, answer my questions, and let your side of the story be heard."

Her sigh was world-weary, too much so for a young, beautiful woman with money and privilege. "You don't give me much choice. I guess I have to cooperate. But you have to promise you'll treat me fairly. If you mention the part about me spending the night in a strange man's apartment, for instance, will you mention that I was unconscious? That I slept alone?"

Ryan heard a snicker from the back seat.

He cleared his throat. "I'll be fair. I'm always fair."

"He is," Fran interjected, sounding perfectly serious for once. "He doesn't take cheap shots. It's one of the reasons I like working with him." Then she laughed, ruining the effect of her testimonial, and tugged on a lock of his hair. "Aside from the fact that he has great buns."

Ryan cringed. Fran always did this. She just had to make sure *everyone* knew the two of them had once had a thing going. She did it just to embarrass him, or maybe as retribution because he was the one who'd called things off. Or maybe to convince him it wasn't a big thing to her anymore. She'd already ribbed him good and hard for "having the hots" for a society babe.

Regardless, Ryan saw that Fran's comment had had its desired effect on Chrissy. She was studying him with renewed curiosity, probably wondering just exactly what his relationship with Fran was.

It didn't matter, he told himself. What mattered was gaining Chrissy's cooperation. It would be nice if she gave him her trust, too. But he would have to work hard to earn that back.

"Um, Ryan, I don't want to alarm you," Fran said, "but a red Firebird has been on our tail for a while now. He could be our friend."

Chrissy whipped her head around, clearly alarmed. "Shoot, doesn't that guy ever give up?"

"Jeez, Ryan, she doesn't even cuss," Fran commented. "If ever a bad word was called for, this is the time."

Ryan glanced in the rearview mirror. "Ha. A Firebird. Does he really think he can keep up with me?" He punched down the gas pedal, and his Vette took off like a comet. All that tinkering he did under the hood paid off sometimes.

Chrissy gave a little squeak of surprise. "Are you sure this is wise? What if you get a ticket?"

"It wouldn't be the first time," he said as he pulled between a couple of semis, then cut in front of one. Immediately he took the first exit. "Actually, I'd welcome a cop's intervention." He glanced in the mirror again, then turned his head to his left to look up on the highway. "It worked! The jerk didn't make the exit." He made a quick right at the light. "Anybody know where we are?"

"I do," Fran said, her voice exhibiting none of its usual bravado. "There's a coffeehouse about five blocks straight ahead."

Ryan glanced at her in the mirror. Her face was pale as milk, each of the freckles sprinkled across her nose standing out in stark relief. "Did my driving scare you, Franny?"

She snorted. "Of course not."

"How 'bout you, Chrissy?"

She didn't answer. She was bent over, her head on her knees, her hands clasped behind her neck in the classic airplane-crash position.

He nudged her. "Hey, sweetie, it's over. We didn't die."

She raised up slowly and looked behind her. "Is he gone?"

"For the moment," Ryan replied. He didn't mention the fact that he'd spotted a sticker on the guy's rear bumper that gave him pause: Save the Wetlands. An odd sentiment for a Pit Bull.

Chrissy gave him a shaky smile. "That was very interesting driving, Mr. Mulvaney. You scared the heck out of me, but you did the job."

Ryan wasn't sure what to make of her praise. She'd been blazing-mad at him just a couple of minutes ago. "I used to race stock cars," he said. "Till I realized I was mortal." He spotted the coffeehouse, Java Joe's, and pulled into the parking lot. He found a space in back, where his car couldn't be easily spotted from the street.

Chrissy reapplied her disguise of hat and sunglasses, then followed him inside without further comment. Fran trailed along behind, doing something with her camera.

It was early evening, and the coffeehouse was almost deserted, so Ryan had his choice of tables. He requested a booth in the back, then sat where he could watch the door. He ordered black coffee, and Fran followed suit.

"I'll have a mochaccino, please," Chrissy said. The other two stared at her. "Well, have you ever tried one? They're good. What's the point of coming to a place like this and ordering plain coffee? And can I order some food? I'm hungry."

"That figures," Ryan muttered, but he shoved a menu at her. He wanted her cooperation. The story would be ten times better if he could question her directly. "Order whatever you want." He could afford to be generous with Fran's money.

"A hamburger," she said promptly to the waitress. "With cheese. And french fries."

"Yeah, sounds good. I'll have one, too," Ryan said. Except for popcorn, he hadn't eaten since breakfast, either. Fran gave him a dirty look, which he supposed he deserved. But he'd pay her back, every nickel, with interest.

"I'm gonna catch a cab home and develop some film," Fran announced suddenly, scooting out of the booth. "I think you'll both be interested in the shots I took today. Ryan, I'll catch up with you at your place later." She melted away, gone almost before Ryan could blink.

Chrissy, clearly unnerved by the mention of photographs, stared at the empty space where Fran had been. "She doesn't care for me much."

"She's got nothing personal against you," Ryan said, almost believing himself. "She's just temperamental. If anything, she's mad at me."

"Because I spent the night with you?" Chrissy asked, raising one inquiring eyebrow.

The waitress showed up with their coffees. Chrissy managed a smile of anticipation just before she scooped up some whipped cream on the end of her tongue.

Ryan tried not to groan aloud at the sultry image she presented. He stared at the sugar shaker until he could talk normally. "Fran's mad at me because I borrowed money from her, and because I wouldn't pay her up front for working this story with me. She most assuredly doesn't care who spends the night in my apartment."

"You mean you and Fran aren't, um—"

"No. We used to be, but it ended almost a year ago. We're just friends now." And why did it matter that he make this so clear? he wondered.

"Why would you need to borrow money from her?" Chrissy asked.

"'Cause I didn't have any cash on me. When I told you I was unemployed, I wasn't exactly lying. I'm a freelancer. My income is somewhat…oh, erratic. I guess that's something you've never experienced."

"Ha! Ever since those guys kidnapped me, I haven't had a cent on me. I have to admit, it's a weird feeling to be without money and credit cards, no car at my disposal."

Ryan reached into his shirt pocket and pulled out a tiny notebook and pencil.

"Huh-uh, wait a minute," she objected. "I didn't consent to any interview."

With a shrug, Ryan closed the notebook and pushed it aside. "I have an audiographic memory anyway. I won't misquote you."

He could almost see the steam rising off her. "Then from now on, everything I say is off the record. If you're a decent reporter of any kind, you'll respect that."

She had him there. "Yeah. Okay. We're now officially off the record. But we either go back on real soon, or this gravy train comes to a screeching halt. No more free meals, rides, or roofs over your head. No more rescues."

She gave him a nervous smile. "Just give me a little time, okay? Whatever I tell you, it'll haunt me for the rest of my life."

At least she'd gotten that right, Ryan thought.

Part of Christine wanted to simply walk away from Ryan and his sleazy story. But another part of her realized that he was the only hope she had of convincing the world at large that she hadn't made up the kidnapping as a publicity gimmick, or to cover up some less savory story.

If she walked away, Ryan would print what he knew,

and she and her father would look very bad. Her father's entire political career depended on the decisions she made in the next few minutes, and on whatever she told Ryan during the next few hours. She was angry with her dad, but she didn't want to permanently alienate him. She needed a little space to figure out her life, a little distance from his overwhelming influence. But "a little space" didn't mean a lifetime of estrangement.

Their hamburgers arrived, and Christine ate hers with gusto. She couldn't remember having consumed anything so wonderful since her college days. Her father had a chef who prepared all their meals at home, with special attention to lowering fat, salt and sugar content. The meals were usually okay, but predictably heavy on steamed vegetables, broiled fish and dry brown rice.

Then there were the rubber-chicken fund-raising dinners, and the meals at four-star restaurants, spent schmoozing and pressing flesh. She nearly always ordered a salad from the menu. Every once in a while, Christine craved something really decadent, with nutritional values that would give her father's chef coronary thrombosis just from thinking about them.

"Are you going to eat those pickles?" she asked Ryan.

He shook his head and nudged his plate toward her. "Be my guest. You can have some of my fries, too, if you want. I'm full."

"Thanks." As she popped the last fry into her mouth, she noticed that he was staring at her, his face brimming with amusement. "What?"

"Sorry," he said, "but I never saw a beautiful woman eat so enthusiastically. You don't have what I'd call a delicate appetite."

Oh, was that all? And did he really think she was beautiful? some girlish part of her heart asked. She licked some ketchup off her thumb. "Nope, no one ever accused me of being a picky eater. I'm over five-eight, you know, and I'm pure muscle." She plucked the pickle slices from his plate. "I burn a lot of calories just by breathing."

"Can I put that in my story?"

She frowned. "Why would you want to? Who cares about what I eat?"

"Chrissy, honey, I don't know how to break it to you, but you're a bona fide media event right now. The TV and radio stations have just enough details about your sup—" he caught himself "—about your kidnapping to present a very intriguing picture. Everybody wants to know, were you really kidnapped? If so, are you okay? Have you been freed? If not, what really happened? Was it a publicity stunt? Why didn't your father want to cooperate with the authorities? Who made that phone call from Costello's this morning?"

Christine gasped. "You mean the media is already speculating? They know about the phone call?"

"Reporters are curious and tenacious. This is one bone they're not going to let go of. The less you and your father cooperate, the more condemning the public will be."

Darn, he was right. She downed the last of her mochaccino, wiped her mouth with her napkin and came to a decision. "Okay, Ryan, here's the deal."

He leaned forward expectantly. "Yes?"

"I'll cooperate with you. I'll give you an exclusive. I'll answer all of your questions, within reason, to the best of my ability, and I'll even tell you something I've been holding back. But I want you to do something for me."

"Anything."

"Let me stay with you tonight. I don't have any other place to go. And tomorrow, I want you to take me to my friend's house, like you originally promised. I don't want to be around when the story hits the papers."

He nodded. "I understand. I'll be happy to take you anywhere you want to go, once the story's done. But…why don't you just go home? It doesn't make sense for you to stay away."

"It will, when I tell you the whole story." She'd committed herself now. She was going to admit, publicly, that her father hadn't tried to get her back, even when it was completely within his power.

She hadn't decided whether she would tell Ryan about her father's drug problem. Probably not. A candidate for office could cheat on his wife or be convicted of shady business dealings and survive politically, but for some reason, if there was any hint of drug dependency—even on prescription drugs—the public was not so forgiving.

"One other thing, though," Ryan said. "The story won't be hitting the papers, at least not at first. I'm not working for the *Guardian* on this thing."

Christine tensed. "Then who…?" Please God, not some sleazy tabloid.

"*Primus* magazine. Still on spec, mind you, but they've said if I can deliver what I've promised, they'll buy it."

Primus! Everybody read the weekly newsmagazine, even her grandmother. "And what exactly did you promise?"

Ryan looked everywhere but at her. He didn't want to lie to her, not anymore. "I'd rather not say."

Chapter 7

Christine Greenlow on a plate. That was what Ryan had rashly promised the editors at *Primus.* Now, as he pushed a cold french fry around in a pool of ketchup, he was feeling somewhat differently. For one thing, he'd assured Chrissy that he would be fair. Not that he wasn't always, but her definition of fair and his were probably quite different.

Ryan prided himself on his ethics. He might employ a little subterfuge now and then to get a story, but he wouldn't out-and-out lie to a source once the cards were on the table. He could only hope that the unenhanced truth—when he found out what it was—was racy enough to please his hungry editors.

The check came, and Ryan paid it. ''Ready?''

''Sure.''

''Anywhere you want to stop before we head back to my place?''

''I'd like to go home and get some of my things,'' she said, with a certain longing in her voice. ''But...I guess I can't.''

"Why not?" Ryan was thinking how enlightening it would be to actually speak with Senator Greenlow, to see the big blowhard and Chrissy together.

"Because I'm afraid my father will talk me into staying."

"Only if you let him."

She pressed her lips together. "He can be very persuasive. He didn't get where he is by caving in to other people. He usually gets his way."

"Yeah, but, Chrissy, I don't sense that you're some kind of marshmallow. You've got a pretty strong will yourself. You kicked a kidnapper in the crotch and jumped out a second-story window, after all." As he said it, he realized that, for a few seconds there, he'd been talking as though Chrissy's crazy story were true. He'd actually believed her for a short time.

He kept thinking about that Save the Wetlands bumper sticker.

She seemed to be thinking, too, real hard. He couldn't see her eyes behind the sunglasses, but her brow had delicate furrows in it. "I'm learning to fight for what I want," she finally said. "Listen, would you mind if I made a couple of phone calls?"

"Not at all. Need some quarters?"

"Yes. I'll pay you back for all this as soon as I get situated someplace."

"Don't worry about it." He started to hand her fifty cents from his pocket, then held it back at the last moment. "Who ya calling?"

Her face stiffened. "For a minute there, I thought you were being a normal, nice person…as opposed to a reporter. I'm calling my friend, to let her know I'm coming, and my father. I want to let him know that I won't be home tonight, and not to worry. You don't suppose the police are still tracing calls, do you?"

Ryan shrugged. "You never know, with the police." He gave her the quarter. "Make it short, and we'll get out of here before anyone has a chance to find us.'' He scooted out of the booth.

Ryan eavesdropped unabashedly while Chrissy made her phone calls. The one to her sister was brief, but comfortable and cordial. The one to her father was less than successful—she spoke to a chain of servants, but never got the man himself on the line.

When she talked to someone named Connie—the maid who'd become worried when Chrissy went missing and called the police, Ryan gathered from the conversation—Chrissy's whole face lit up with warmth and obvious affection.

''I'm fine, I promise,'' she told the woman. ''I'm staying with a friend tonight. I just can't face Dad right now.... Why not? Well, I'm a little angry with him over the way he handled things the last couple of days.'' She cast a sideways look at Ryan.

He studied his fingernails, pretending to be uninterested, but he figured he wasn't fooling her. Although she'd promised to cooperate, she would be very carefully choosing any words she spoke within earshot of him.

''It's complicated, Connie. I'll explain it all to you sometime, I promise.... No, don't wake him. You wouldn't be able to, anyway. Just tell him I'm fine, and...that...I love him.'' She hung up. She was still wearing the sunglasses, even though it was dark outside, so Ryan couldn't see her eyes, but he suspected she was crying.

Christine was mostly silent on the ride back to Ryan's apartment, mulling over what she could safely tell him, what would work best to convince him she was telling the truth.

Maybe when she explained that her father hadn't tried to ransom her, and how shocking and upsetting that was for her, he would understand why she had delayed calling the police.

And speaking of police...there was a squad car, lights flashing, sitting out in front of Ryan's building.

"Now what?" he wondered aloud as he pulled into the alley. "I hope to hell this doesn't concern us."

She liked the way he said "us." As if they were a team. She needed someone on her side right now, even if the camaraderie was only illusory.

Then she shook her head. She couldn't afford illusions. He was using her for his own material gain. All his kindnesses had been calculated to gain her cooperation.

She had to remember that.

"Do you want to wait in the car while I check this out?" he asked her.

"No," she answered quickly, feeling a swell of panic. "That guy could be waiting to get me alone again."

"Mmm…good point. You know, my landlady will throw a fit if she sees you."

"You don't think she bought the 'Cousin Chrissy from Jersey' story?"

"Not for a minute. She was on the phone this morning the minute we left, calling my mother to find out if I really did have a cousin Chrissy. I doubt my mother covered for me."

"Oh. Well, I'll be very quiet."

"No more choruses of 'Everything's Coming Up Roses'?"

"What?" What was he talking about now?

"That's what you were singing last night, while you were slung over my shoulder. At the top of your lungs."

No way. She shook her head vehemently, unable to even imagine herself engaged in such a behavior. "I don't even know that song."

He nodded. "Oh, yes, you do. It's lodged in your subconscious somewhere. Come on." He handed her the bag from Target, which contained her new underwear and toothbrush, and got out of the car.

As it turned out, there was no opportunity for anyone to sneak. A uniformed officer was poking around the back of Ryan's building with a flashlight. He stopped them as they started up the back stairs.

"Excuse me. You live here?"

"Yes, sir," Ryan said as Christine cowered behind him, hoping that for once she wouldn't be recognized. "I'm on the third floor."

Just seeing the uniform gave her a knee-jerk reaction of pure tension. She used to consider the police her friends, her allies, but after her experience with Lieutenant Brich, she despised all of them.

"Well, your landlady caught someone trying to break into your apartment a few minutes ago. He was going at your back door with a crowbar. Got it open, but she came after him with a baseball bat and scared him off before he could take anything."

Bless Ryan's nosy landlady! Christine had no doubts as to who the would-be burglar was. He was probably not far away, watching, waiting for the police to leave so that he could make another move. He'd probably armed himself again, too.

He wouldn't kill her, as long as there was a chance she was more valuable alive than dead. But Ryan didn't have the luxury of a millionaire father. She would never forgive herself if she caused him harm, even if he was a leech reporter.

Another officer came down the stairs. "I secured the door temporarily," he said, looking at Ryan. "Are you the one who lives here?"

"Yes, sir," Ryan said.

"You'll have to use the front entrance. And you might think about getting a stronger door. Those French doors are a piece of cake for a burglar."

"Thanks, I will."

"Any sign of the guy?" he asked his partner.

"Nah, he's long gone."

Ryan answered a few more questions for the police report. Then he and Christine walked around to the front and let themselves into the foyer.

Mrs. Reiser's door immediately opened. "Oh, Ryan, I'm

so glad you're back. Something terrible happened.'' She was still clutching her baseball bat.

''I know all about it,'' Ryan said soothingly. ''I met the police out back. It's okay now, the burglar's gone, and thanks to your quick actions, he didn't get anything. He'd be a fool to come back to *this* building with you on the alert.''

Mrs. Reiser preened herself over Ryan's praise. It figured, Christine thought. What female of any age could be immune to Ryan's charm when he turned it on? She herself had certainly fallen victim to it.

''I try to keep an eye on things,'' Mrs. Reiser said. Then she peered around Ryan to where Christine was trying to be inconspicuous. ''Your cousin is still here, I see,'' she said, more ''alert'' than Christine cared for her to be at the moment.

''Yeah,'' Ryan said with an easy smile. ''She was supposed to meet up with my other cousin Merle earlier today, but things got mixed up and it turns out Merle is in Albuquerque till tomorrow. So I'm getting ready to drive Chrissy to my grandmother's house.''

Christine hoped she wouldn't have to say anything. Her fake Jersey accent could only stretch so far.

''That's very nice of you, Ryan,'' Mrs. Reiser said. ''I tried to call your mother today, but she wasn't at home.''

Thank goodness, Christine thought. Then, in a moment of insanity, she decided to speak. ''I'll be seein' Auntie tomorra, prob'ly. I'll be sure and give her your regards.''

Ryan looked at her with undisguised horror. Was her accent that bad?

''Thank you, that's very kind,'' Mrs. Reiser said. ''Tell her I'm getting my hair done at Tony's on Thursday, if she wants to meet me there. Eleven o'clock. We can have lunch afterwards.''

''Sure,'' Christine said. The word came out sounding like ''Shoo-ah.''

After that, Ryan quickly bade his landlady good-night and dragged Christine up the stairs. He didn't speak again until they were safely inside his apartment. "You a frustrated wanna-be actress, or what?"

Christine giggled nervously. "I felt stupid, just standing there like a mute. I thought I'd support your story."

He gave her an appraising look. "You lie without batting an eyelash, don't you?"

"So do you," she countered, feeling thoroughly insulted. "We all do what we have to do. Oh, please tell me you're not going to include my Cousin Chrissy act in your story."

"I don't know what I'll include, yet," he said mildly, and then he laughed. "Not for *shoo-ah*." He mimicked her perfectly.

Her stomach swooped. By the time Ryan got done with her and all of America had read his story, she was either going to be a heroine, an evil villainess, or a laughingstock.

Right now, she was voting for laughingstock.

Ryan turned serious. "We can't stay here tonight. It's not safe."

"I was hoping you felt that way," she said. "Where can we go?"

"We could get on the highway and drive to your friend's house. But I don't like to be on the road at night with some maniac after us."

"Me neither."

"A hotel, then. Don't look at me that way. We'll have separate rooms."

Did she dare tell him that separate rooms was what she feared most? She didn't think she could bear sleeping alone tonight, knowing that crazy Denny would break through any window or door to get to her. She'd gotten the feeling that this whole kidnapping thing had become very personal for him. He was working alone, perhaps believing that if he returned her to the terrorist group, he would be rewarded.

And avenged. She shuddered to think what he might do to her, if he did catch her, before he turned her over to the group at large. Yesterday—was it only yesterday?—he'd had rape and mutilation on his mind.

"I'm going to gather up a few things," Ryan said. "And I want to make a quick phone call. Then we can go."

The sooner the better, Christine thought. She couldn't even make herself sit down; she was too nervous. She paced the small living room and chewed off a broken cuticle. When she realized what she was doing, she shoved her hands in her pockets.

Ryan was ready a few minutes later. He had his cellular phone, a laptop computer, reference books, telephone books, his Rolodex, a miniature TV and a road map—everything the modern reporter on the move needed. He stuffed it all into a Gore-Tex duffel bag.

The tools of his trade left Christine feeling cold. She wished, as she'd never wished for anything, that Ryan wasn't a reporter, that he really was an unemployed mechanic whose only motive was the desire to help out a fellow human being in need.

And sex. She wouldn't mind if that was one of his motives. Not that she'd fall into bed with him. But the fact remained, she didn't go more than a few minutes without reliving that kiss and wondering if it had meant anything, anything at all.

In minutes, they were back in Ryan's car, on the road. Ryan weaved in and out of side streets, while Christine kept watch out the rear window, watching for a red Firebird or any other suspicious cars. But no one followed. Maybe her terrorist friend had retreated to regroup.

"Where are we going?" Christine asked.

"How about the Sheraton?"

"Mmm…nice digs." She was surprised. A cheap motel would have been fine with her, but a first-class hotel sounded better—and safer.

"I can use my frequent-flier miles there." Ryan explained, blowing away any illusions she might have had that he'd chosen a nice hotel to soothe her sensibilities. Dollars and cents. That was what it all came down to.

It took only a few minutes to reach the Sheraton. Christine studied her surroundings as if she were studying for a test, in case she needed to find her way around in a hurry. Actually, she'd never seen a hotel garage before, and it wasn't very glamorous. She'd always had a chauffeur to deal with annoying things like parking.

"I don't let valets touch my car," Ryan explained, even though she hadn't said a thing. He was getting very good at reading her thoughts, which was a scary realization.

With her hokey disguise in place, knowing she looked scruffy and unkempt in Ryan's borrowed clothes, Christine felt ridiculous. But no one seemed to notice her. In fact, she'd been more anonymous today than she could ever remember being in her life. She was accustomed to attention. It was nice, but a little weird, not to have it.

"I'll need two rooms, please," Ryan said, placing his credit card and frequent-flier card before the registration clerk.

"Um, Ryan, wait. Just get one room, okay? You don't want to waste your miles."

He gave her a look that made her feel like a steamed lobster. Surely he didn't think she was suggesting anything improper. Well, if that was what her suggestion had implied, she'd set him straight as soon as they were alone.

"One room," he amended to the clerk. "Two beds."

The paperwork seemed to take forever. That was something else Christine wasn't used to. Normally when she checked into a hotel, traveling with or without her father, she got VIP treatment—instant recognition, and no fussing with credit cards. Just an attentive bellman to whisk her things up to some elegant suite.

Ryan carried his own bag. She carried her paper sack from Target, which contained all her worldly possessions, at least for the moment. They took the elevator to the fourth floor and walked down a long hallway, and Ryan opened the door to their room with an electronic key.

It was not a large room, but it was nicely furnished, and it did indeed have two double beds. Christine sat down on one of them. She was suddenly exhausted.

Ryan crossed to the other bed and dropped his duffel on it. "This'll do."

"Comfortable," she agreed.

He immediately began pulling out the things he would need to work on his story. Christine watched, feeling detached from the whole thing. She'd boarded a runaway train and she couldn't get off, but she almost didn't care anymore. At least she was safe.

"About sharing a room," she said. "I hope I didn't give you the wrong idea."

"I asked for two beds, didn't I?" he said gruffly, not even looking at her.

"It's just that I'm afraid to stay alone. That Denny guy could break into my room and spirit me away without anyone the wiser. But if you're here, sleeping in the next bed, that can't happen."

"I understand."

"I'll try to stay out of your way."

"I'm sure it won't be a problem." He began tapping on the keys of his laptop, evidently immersed in his own thoughts.

Christine couldn't escape the feeling that he was angry with her about something. True, if not for her, no one would have broken into his apartment. He wouldn't have lost his hubcaps, and he could be relaxing at home now, microwaving a pizza for dinner, or inviting over his girlfriend, instead of being on the run, the target of a terrorist.

Did he have a girlfriend? she wondered. He'd made it clear that Fran was an ex, but Christine would be surprised if he hadn't found a replacement.

"Do you have a girlfriend?" she asked.

He looked at her then, appearing amused at the question. Then he shook his head. "No."

"I didn't want her to be mad at you because of me."

"I wouldn't date a girl who got mad at me for spending time with the subject of a story I'm writing." He returned to his typing.

"But you kissed me. A girlfriend would have a right to

be miffed over that.'' Immediately she wished she'd kept her mouth shut. He probably hadn't given the kiss a second thought, and here she was, dwelling on it, making it obvious that she'd placed some importance on it.

He looked up again. ''That kiss didn't mean anything.''

''I know. But a girlfriend wouldn't care. She'd still be mad.''

''There is no girlfriend, so this is a really pointless discussion, don't you think?''

''I suppose.'' She paused, looking around the room, wishing she'd thought to grab one of Ryan's books to read. ''I think I'll take a bath, okay?''

''Sure.''

She was feeling really grungy. Gosh, how long had it been since she bathed? Since before the kidnapping... No, that couldn't be right. That was three days ago, and she wasn't that grungy.

She paused at the bathroom door. ''Did I take a bath last night at your place?''

''Uh-huh.''

''But I thought I was unconscious.''

''Most of the time you were. You fell asleep in the tub and almost flooded the bathroom.''

''Yikes. You caught it in time?''

''Uh-huh.''

''Then how did I get...from the tub...'' She could feel her face turning three shades of red. When she looked at Ryan again, he was grinning wickedly at her.

''Now that,'' he said, ''is a subject best left undisturbed, if you know what I mean. Suffice it to say that my mythical girlfriend would have every right to be miffed. And you have a cute little mole on your left upper thigh.''

She couldn't begin to come back with a smart reply to that revelation. Ryan had seen her naked! He'd pulled her unconscious body out of a bathtub, dried her off, tucked her into bed...and he'd looked.

He could have done a lot more, she reminded herself as she entered the bathroom and slammed the door.

Ryan fell back against the pillows with a groan. He hadn't counted on this. The longer he spent with Chrissy, the harder it was for him to keep his hands off her. Now he had the fantasy image of Chrissy in a bubble bath to deal with, and he didn't even have to rely on his imagination. He *knew* what she looked like without her clothes. His traitorous brain called the image up every ten seconds or so, with or without his consent.

He'd been lying when he said the kiss meant nothing. He wasn't even sure why he'd said that, unless it had been a desperate attempt to keep things on an impersonal level.

He wasn't the kind of guy who played hard to get. When he saw something he liked, he normally went for it. He was no Casanova; sometimes he made a conquest, sometimes he got shot down. He certainly never sweated it.

But Chrissy Greenlow had him tied up in knots. Now he was sharing a room with her! If she even hinted that she might feel an inkling of desire for him…

Ah, hell, who was he kidding? She was engaged. Even if she wasn't, she wouldn't go for him. He represented everything she hated.

Still, why hadn't she turned to her fiancé for help? Ryan understood that there was something weird going on between her and her father, but what about this…what was his name? Richard, Robert, something like that?

Ryan needed to make some phone calls while Chrissy was in the bath. Forcing his mind to the job at hand, he called Fran first. She wasn't at home, so he tried the darkroom at the *Guardian,* where she sometimes did her developing and printing, because she could scam free chemicals and paper.

He hit pay dirt. "Hey, wait till you see some of these shots," she said excitedly, not even giving him a chance to speak. "The one of you and her in a lip lock is pure gold. Sex and steam and exotic birds—"

"I don't want you to use that one, Franny," he said abruptly.

"Why not? Your face isn't recognizable."

"I've decided I'm going to have to be up front about my role in all this. *I* took her to the zoo. *I* kissed her. If I don't admit that, it's like— Oh, I don't know. Entrapment."

"Oh, Ryan, don't get all sensitive on me at this late date. I know I ribbed you earlier about having a case for the society babe, but you don't really, do you? I mean, you don't have a soft spot for the princess, do you?"

Ryan didn't answer right away. When he finally responded, his answer surprised even him. "I like her, Franny. I'll do the story—it's not the kind of thing you stumble across every day—but I don't want to run over her with a bulldozer. Besides, I'm beginning to think there's something more to it than we originally thought. This society-girl-in-the-fast-lane idea isn't working. She's not like that."

"Hmm. What angle are you aiming for, then?"

"I don't really know, yet. But I'll tell you one thing. This scumbag who's trying to grab her is one persistent S.O.B. He's not acting like any gangbanger I've run across. And he had a Save the Wetlands bumper sticker on his car."

He paused to let that sink in.

"You think those NATURE guys might really be involved?" Fran asked in a hushed voice. "That they really held her hostage, like she said?"

"I'm beginning to think it's a real possibility. I'll know more in a little while. As soon as she finishes her bath, I'm going to get into the interview, full swing."

"If anyone can find cracks in her story, you can," Fran said. "Want me to drop by with some of these photos?"

"Sure." He told her where to find him, and why he and Chrissy weren't at his apartment.

"A break-in? Jeez, that's scary," she said. "I'll be by the hotel in an hour or so, then."

"Make sure you're not followed." With that warning, he disconnected and dialed another number. He'd tried earlier, at his place, but hadn't managed to connect with his policeman friend on the youth violence detail. This time, his friend Jerry answered his cell phone on the first ring.

"Hey, Mulvaney. Yeah, I did some checking up for you—talked to my little Pit Bull snitch. He'd heard about the blonde in the red dress, flying higher than a kite, all right. But there was no mention of you specifically, just that the girl went off with her boyfriend."

"And…"

"And, that's it. This was pretty much a nonevent in their books. They never realized it was you that took the woman away from them. These were younger guys, you know. They don't remember the business with the stories you wrote, the harassment, nothing. Your name doesn't even ring a bell with them."

"Really?" Then Ryan had an inflated view of his own importance, he supposed. Could the gang really forget him so easily? His involvement with the Pit Bulls had changed his whole life. "Then there's no vendetta? No wild-eyed older member out to teach me a lesson?"

"Nada, dude. If someone's out to get you, he's not with the Pit Bulls. You sure you're not being paranoid?"

"Oh, this guy's real, all right. I took his gun away from him. It's still in my glove compartment, as a matter of fact."

"Well, hell, bring it over here. We'll check it out, tell you who it belongs to, if it's legal—which it probably isn't."

"Yeah, maybe I'll do that," Ryan said. But he really didn't need to. He knew who the guy was, now. His name was Denny, and he was an environmental terrorist.

Chapter 8

Christine had a record-breaking soak in the tub. She was sore all over—from being manhandled, from jumping out a window, from being bitten by a parrot. She could easily have nodded off in the warm, sudsy water, and almost did a couple of times. But the thought of Ryan finding her as he had last night frightened her into wakefulness.

She didn't remember last night's bath, but there was no doubt she'd awakened this morning clean and naked.

It wasn't so bad that Ryan had seen her in the buff, she supposed. The bad part was that she didn't remember it. He could have climbed into the tub and bathed with her, and she wouldn't have remembered it! Her deviant mind wondered what *he* would look like naked.

All right, so she was indecently attracted to the guy. It was only natural. He was gorgeous, they were in close proximity, and she'd been a long time without really good... No, that wasn't it. It wasn't just that she wanted sex. It was him. She felt a special attraction for Ryan Mulvaney that was a new experience for her.

How did he feel about her? she wondered. Contempt?

Desire? Indifference? The thought of his indifference was the hardest for her to handle.

Oh, what was she thinking? She was at a turning point in her life, facing estrangement from her father and possible poverty, not to mention national notoriety—the kind nobody wanted. She was too mixed-up to think about getting involved with another man, even in a purely frivolous way.

When she finished her bath, she toweled off, then donned the complimentary hotel robe hanging on the back of the door. She had her clean underwear and T-shirts but a good airing-out would have to suffice for the shorts. Maybe the hotel would launder them—but no, that was what rich people did. They sent all their clothes out to be daintified.

Next she donned a new pair of panties, after debating mightily over her choice of colors—purple, pink or blue. She would sleep in the robe, she decided. She brushed her teeth and finally felt ready to face Ryan again.

He was deep into his computer screen when she exited the bathroom, and seemed hardly to notice her. Fine. She would watch TV until he was ready to interview her. Television was another luxury she seldom had time for, unless it was C-Span.

She found the remote and turned on the TV, volume down low. She didn't really care what she watched, just anything to occupy her mind and keep her more dismal thoughts at bay. So she channel-surfed.

"Do you think you could light on something and stay there?" Ryan asked, sounding peeved. He didn't even bother to look up when he spoke to her.

"Sorry," she said, not sorry at all. She was providing him with a hot story; the least he could do was pay attention to her.

All right, so maybe she was the one who was being peevish. She was used to people noticing her. She was spoiled. Very soon, she would be just another working woman worrying about the price of panty hose and dining on fast food or Chinese takeout because she was too tired to cook.

Heck, she wasn't sure she could remember how to cook.

She'd attended a French cooking school for a few weeks the summer she graduated from high school, but not much of it had stayed with her.

"Ryan, what kind of job do you think I could get?" she asked.

"Um, I don't know." He finished typing a sentence. Christine thought that was all she would get from him, but suddenly he looked up. "What do you know how to do?"

"I don't have a college degree."

"Neither do I. It doesn't matter that much, unless you want to be a doctor or a C.P.A. or something."

"Neither of those careers appeals to me." So maybe her lack of a university education was okay.

Ryan pushed his computer aside, stacked his two pillows behind him and leaned up against the headboard. "Okay, so what skills do you have?"

"Well…I can host a mean dinner party."

"Hmm. I suppose you could get a job as a professional party planner. Your name's well-known enough. I'm sure all your friends would hire you."

Unless she became a pariah. After she dumped Robert and ruined her father's political career, it was possible that none of her friends would want to speak to her, let alone give her money.

"That's one possibility," she said, not wanting to dismiss Ryan's idea out of hand. It might work. "But what if I wanted to break away completely from the Washington society stuff? I might even move to another town. What could I do?"

"Can you type?"

"No."

"Wait tables?"

"I could learn that."

"Well, I'll tell you, most people with reasonable intelligence and no job skills take an entry-level job at a company where they might be able to advance if they prove themselves. You could answer phones, or work retail, or be a filing clerk."

She wrinkled her nose.

"On the other hand, most people with reasonable intelligence, no job skills but lots of connections start out considerably better. If you put out the word among your friends that you're looking for employment, you can probably land some cushy job, like being an assistant to an assistant to some bigwig."

Christine frowned. She didn't want to get a job using connections. She knew that others would think she was crazy, but she was tired of having things handed to her. She wanted to make her own way, achieve her own successes. She imagined that accomplishing things with hard work and nothing else gave one a terrific sense of self-worth.

"How did you become a writer?" she asked Ryan.

"Oh, I worked as a gofer at the *Guardian* for a couple of years. Then a proofreader, then a copy editor. I started doing my own writing on spec, which mostly got turned down. But then I sold a couple of pieces to magazines, and the *Guardian* took a little more notice. I started freelancing for them, then made it to staff."

"But you're not on staff now?"

"No." A shadow crossed his face. "I like working for myself, even if the income is chancy sometimes."

"I like to write," she said thoughtfully. "Not that I'm any good, but that's something I would enjoy learning more about. Do you think I could get a job as a… What did you call it? A gofer?"

"Most gofers are college kids. The pay is terrible."

"I can live with that. I have a small income that would supplement…" She stopped, noticing the moment Ryan went from "friend mode" to "reporter mode." He got this certain intent look on his face that Christine translated as meaning he was trying to remember the facts, the exact words, so that he could faithfully report them.

Why couldn't she remember that he was a reporter? He seemed so easy to talk to.

"Why are you thinking of getting a job?" he asked her.

"Because it's time. I'm not a little girl anymore. My father's had my undivided attention for ten years now. It's time for me to live my own life."

"Amen," he murmured. Then he studied her anew. "You might make a pretty good reporter at that," he said, twirling a pencil between his thumb and finger, as if it were a cigar. "You've certainly gotten me talking about things I usually keep to myself. You could even do TV. You're pretty enough."

"Hmm." She tried on a television voice. "'This is Christine Greenlow, reporting for CNN.' How was that?"

"Could use some work, but it's got potential."

Christine laughed at the idea of being a TV reporter. It wasn't what she wanted—not in the least. Hot lights and lots of makeup, rushing from disaster to disaster. Not for her.

All at once, her laughter died in her throat, as her gaze became riveted to the television screen. "Oh, my God. It's my father."

"So it is," Ryan said, not sounding very surprised. "Could you turn it up a notch?"

She was already reaching for the remote.

"We understand your daughter's whereabouts are unknown at this time," the woman reporter said. "Can you confirm or deny this?"

The two were standing in front of the Greenlows' Capitol Heights home. The ostentation of it suddenly repulsed Christine. Couldn't her father think of more worthwhile things to spend his money on than statues and fountains?

Lord, she was starting to think like a Democrat!

"I heard from my daughter this morning. She claimed at that time to be free of her kidnappers. But I have not been able to locate her or verify her whereabouts." There was a catch in his voice. Purely calculated, Christine was sure.

"Do you know the identity of the kidnappers?" the reporter asked, leaning in, practically ready to devour the senator, she was so hungry for a scoop.

"I'm not altogether certain there were actually any kidnappers," the senator said. "Christine has been under a great deal of stress lately—my fault, all my fault. When I campaign, she takes it very seriously, works herself to a frazzle—"

"So now I'm delusional!" Christine shrieked.

"Shh!" Ryan hissed. "I need to hear this." He was typing furiously while he watched and listened.

"Are you saying, Senator Greenlow, that you think the kidnapping was a hoax?"

"No, not at all. I don't believe my daughter was aware of the problems she left behind when she...when she disappeared. Christine would never deliberately manipulate me or the police or the press. I'm sure she's just tired and confused, and I hope that, wherever she is tonight, that she's safe, and that she knows I love her and that she can come home anytime, no questions asked."

"Oh—oh!" Christine cried, shaking her fist impotently at the TV screen. Her father wasn't there any longer. Some sportscaster had taken over the screen. "How could he say those things? He knows damn well the kidnapping was real. Why is he pretending like I made the whole thing up?"

She looked over at Ryan, who had stopped typing and was staring at her, his mouth gaping open.

For heaven's sake, was she making that big a spectacle of herself? Her robe was gaping, she realized. She tugged it closed self-consciously. "I don't suppose you'll ever believe me now," she said, her temper tantrum deserting her as quickly as it had come upon her.

Ryan found his voice. "On the contrary. I do believe you, Christine. I believe you were kidnapped and held captive by these NATURE creeps. I'll do my best to convince my readers, even without hard evidence, that you were a victim, not the perpetrator of a hoax."

Now it was her turn to gape. Hope welled in her heart for the first time in days. "Really? You believe me?" Then it occurred to her to ask, "Why?"

"I wish I could say it was blind faith, but I'd be lying."

He leaned back against the pillows and began untying his running shoes as he explained. "A number of small details had me doubting my own theory, pretty though it was."

"It was beastly and totally incorrect," she said petulantly, flopping on her own bed. She was careful this time to keep the robe properly wrapped.

"I made a few phone calls while you were in the tub. Turns out this terrorist group you mentioned really does exist, and this wouldn't be the first time they'd resorted to violence. Plus, this jerk who keeps trying to grab you couldn't possibly be with the Pit Bulls, like I thought, nor is he your pusher—"

"Pusher! You mean, as in drugs?"

"You haven't had any type of drug in the past twenty-four hours, unless you and Lieutenant Brich snorted a few lines."

"Very funny."

"And you're obviously not in withdrawal. So you're not an addict."

"Glad we have that little misconception cleared up," she said dryly.

"Ergo, your friend Denny, who, by the way, has Save the Whatever bumper stickers pasted to his car, could quite logically be an environmental terrorist."

"He could be," Christine said, a note of bitterness creeping into her voice. "But I'm sure your feverish little brain could come up with another alternative. That's still not proof."

"No, I don't have proof. But I believe you anyway. I guess there's a smidgen of blind faith involved."

"Why?" she asked.

He shrugged. "I'm tired of trying to convince myself you're a self-serving liar. You just…couldn't be."

Christine felt a rush of warmth so powerful it stole her breath away. He believed her! He would tell her side of the story. She would be vindicated. And her father…

Her father.

"Maybe," Ryan continued, "you've picked up on the

fact that, if you're telling the truth about the ransom phone calls, your father's behavior becomes increasingly odd. So you'd better start applying your energy to figuring out why *he's* lying. What does he have to protect by denying the kidnapping ever happened?''

Ryan watched the play of emotions on Chrissy's face—elation, gratitude, then puzzlement, and finally, a profound sadness. What, he wondered, did she have to feel so sad about?

That was his story. He would get to the bottom of Chrissy's melancholia if it was the last thing he did.

''My father has many things to protect, many secrets,'' Chrissy said. ''And you can stop licking your lips, I won't tell you what they are. But doesn't everyone have a skeleton or two rattling around in the closet?''

''Some skeletons rattle louder than others,'' he said offhandedly, as if her words weren't driving him crazy with curiosity. According to his research, although Stan Greenlow was often flamboyant, fond of grandstanding, always claiming to be the person who came up with a good idea, he wasn't known to be sleazy.

Reporters had tried before, and failed, to dig up dirt on the man. He had been an excellent student, had always attended church, hadn't ever smoked pot, had served his country admirably in the Air Force, then the reserves. He'd been a devoted husband when his wife was alive, and staunchly loyal to her after her death. As far as anyone could tell, Stan Greenlow hadn't even dated since becoming a widower.

He was known to run a hard-hitting campaign, and had made a serious run for the Republican presidential nomination in the last election, though he'd been squeezed out pretty early in the process. Rumor had it he was planning to try again, and darker horses had certainly won before.

So what did the man have to hide?

A thought occurred to him. ''Chrissy, where exactly did you want me to take you tomorrow?''

"To a...friend's house in Raleigh," she answered warily.

Did Ryan imagine that guilty flush gracing Chrissy's cheeks? Was it merely from her anger with her father, or the warmth of her bath?

He already knew she was a facile liar. And something about her reticence made him suspicious. And now she wouldn't look at him, pretending rapt interest in a baseball story on TV.

He was about to question her further when all at once she turned to stare at him. "No, that was a lie. Michelle is my half sister, my father's illegitimate child from a youthful indiscretion." The spontaneous confession came pouring out of her. "But Ryan, please, you can't put that in your story, really, you can't. It has absolutely nothing to do with what's happened the last few days. Please. Promise me you won't tell anyone."

Ryan was dumbfounded—first that she'd handed him the juiciest tidbit of his career, second that she expected him to sit on it. "This is the truth, now?" he asked, just to be sure. "You're not jerking my chain?"

"I wish you'd just forget about the whole thing," she said miserably. She stood and began pacing the small room. With each jerky step she took, the white terry robe flapped open, revealing her ridiculously long legs. "I wouldn't have told you, but you already knew Michelle existed because I told you about her before I knew you knew who I was. And I could have stuck with the lie that she was just a friend, but lying is what got me into so much trouble in the first place—the story about the abusive boyfriend and all."

She stopped pacing aimlessly and walked purposefully toward him, until she was standing right in front of him. "Ryan, I know you don't owe me this. But please don't tell anyone. It was a youthful indiscretion with unfortunate consequences, something that happens to all kinds of people all the time."

"People who are careless," Ryan said, though he

couldn't help thinking about Josette. His sister had made a mistake—a big one—in choosing the wrong friends, trusting the wrong people. She'd paid, first with the rape, then with the pregnancy, then with putting the child she'd grown to love, despite everything, up for adoption.

How would he feel now, if some reporter chose to splash that sordid story across the newspapers? Pretty hostile. With Stan Greenlow, the story was a common one. What made it interesting was the man it was attached to.

"Almost everybody is careless at one time or another," Chrissy continued. "Haven't you ever had unprotected sex?"

"Well, um…" How had they started talking about *his* sex life? "I never fathered any babies," he said defensively.

"Because you're lucky. Or there might even be babies you don't know about. In my dad's case, he and Michelle's mother weren't even dating. They'd gotten together at some frat party, and she'd been drinking. When she came to him a couple of months later, he was prepared to marry her. But it wasn't what either of them wanted. Both families had money. They got together, decided on a fair amount of child support, which my grandfather paid in a lump sum—eighteen years' worth, plus money for college."

"So he paid her off, made the girl and her baby disappear."

"That was the intention. But Dad has had contact with Michelle and her mother over the years. He couldn't bear the idea that his daughter would grow up not knowing anything about him. I've known about Michelle since I was old enough to understand, and we've spent a lot of time together. Sometimes she would come and stay with us for a few days—my 'cousin Michelle.' And we always did wish we could be real sisters, live in the same household."

Ryan said nothing. If this was all true, then Stan Greenlow had been a more responsible and caring unwed father than most. Chrissy was right—a lot of people were careless, especially when they were young. He hated to admit it, but he'd had unprotected sex at least twice that he could think of. But only a relative few paid the price. Like her father. Like Josette.

"You're not saying anything," Chrissy said, perching on the end of his bed.

"I'm thinking. And you're right, a hundred percent right. The fact that your father had an illegitimate daughter has nothing to do with his ability as a lawmaker, his effectiveness as a leader."

"But…"

"Damn it, Chrissy, I'm a reporter! I would be crazy to keep a secret like that. It's what we live for, what we dream of our whole careers—breaking that big story."

"What is so big about an illegitimate child? If you broke the story, it would be big news for a couple of days, then forgotten, right along with my father's whole career."

"But I can't—"

"You can, if you want to," she said softly. "I know a lot about you, just from spending one day with you. You're not a totally self-serving jerk, despite your profession. I know you'll do what's right."

She got up then, came to him, leaned down and kissed him on the forehead.

"Um, what's that for?"

"I'm laying a guilt trip on you. It's something else I'm good at."

"Yeah, well, maybe you should look for a job in the guilt-tripping field, because you're *damn* good at it."

She smiled. "I know. I'm going to bed now."

"Wait a minute. Don't you owe me an interview?"

"I never specified *when* the interview would take place, did I? Don't worry, I'll answer all your questions."

"When you're good and ready," Ryan mumbled.

She turned away and, without a backward glance, pulled back the covers on her bed and climbed underneath. Ryan could only stare at her back, totally befuddled, and watch her fall asleep. His forehead burned where her lips had touched it.

He ought to be thinking about his story. His deadline wasn't for a couple more days, so he could afford a few delays. But how could he possibly keep mum about Greenlow's bastard? If he didn't promise Chrissy he'd keep mum, how much cooperation could he realistically expect from her? And if he did promise... He didn't break promises.

All these thoughts were swirling around his brain like lazy bumblebees in the background. They should have been his primary concern right now. But all he could concentrate on was how much he wanted to turn off his computer and climb under the covers beside Chrissy.

Christine pretended sleep, the blankets pulled protectively up to her neck, her back turned toward Ryan, who continued to tap at his computer keys. What the heck was he writing, anyway? He hadn't even interviewed her properly. If he used all the bits and pieces he'd collected so far to write his story, there was no telling what the end product would be.

She ought to let him question her. But she was afraid. Look how much she'd already revealed to him! She still couldn't believe she'd spontaneously confessed the secret of "Cousin Michelle's" identity. But she couldn't bear for there to be any more lies between herself and Ryan. There had been too many already. She sensed a need for trust between them, if he was to write the most accurate story possible. And he would never trust her again if he caught her in another lie. But meanwhile, what other secrets would he pull from her? And how would he choose to reveal them to the public?

She didn't fool herself that he really would keep her secret about Michelle. No reporter could sit on that for long. She almost didn't blame him for blabbing it to the world, but she wished he could be the kind of man who, out of consideration for her, wouldn't betray her confidence.

A man like that... She could love a man like that.

She lay there for at least another hour, staring wide-eyed at the wall, before sleep overcame her.

The next thing she knew, she was in a life-and-death battle with the bedcovers. They were trying to strangle her. No, she was wrong, it was a man's strong arms pinning her down, shaking her.

"Let me go!" she bellowed. At once she was free of both the man and the covers. It took her a few moments to remember where she was, and with whom. "Ryan?" she asked in a trembling voice, though she already knew it was him. In the dark, she recognized his scent.

"Chrissy?" he asked back. "You okay? You were having a nightmare. I was trying to wake you up, but apparently I only scared you more. Sorry." He was sitting next to her on the mattress. She could sense, without seeing him, that he was naked, or very nearly so.

"A nightmare?" she repeated. "How Victorian of me. I haven't done that since the night terrors I had as a child."

"I had them, too," he said softly. "Monsters?"

"When I was a kid, I used to dream that my mother and father left me, and I would wake up screaming and screaming. I think it scared my parents more than it did me."

"And what were you dreaming about just now?" he inquired.

She sighed. "I don't remember, only that it was very scary. Was I screaming, or what?"

"Thrashing around, shouting. Something about... needles?"

All at once she remembered, and she shuddered so hard she shook the bed. "I know, now. I was dreaming about the terrorists. They drugged me through a needle. The last time, I tried to fight them, because I knew then what the drug did to me, but I couldn't—" The fear caught up with her again, tightening her throat, making her want to hide under the bed.

"It's okay, Chrissy. They won't get you again, not while I'm around."

Which would be exactly until sometime tomorrow, she

thought glumly. "I won't be safe until they're behind bars, every last one of them," she said.

"How many were there?"

"At least a dozen. Mostly men, a few women. The women had some power within the group—and some decency, too. They wouldn't let the men hurt me unnecessarily. But right before I jumped out the window, there were only two guys watching me, Denny, and another named Pete. They weren't decent at all." She shivered again.

An angry noise rumbled in Ryan's throat.

"Listen, you can turn on the light if you want, take notes. I won't be going back to sleep for a while."

"Mmm..." He didn't seem very interested in her suggestion.

"Or not," she added in a small voice. She was very aware of him next to her in the darkness, and she decided she didn't really want the light on. Warmth emanated from his body, and she was cold, despite the thick robe still wrapped around her.

"Do you want to tell me some more?" he asked. "I'll listen, if you want. Off the record. Sometimes talking things out makes them less scary. When I was little, my father used to make me describe the monsters. During the day, he'd ask me to draw pictures of them. The night terrors stopped pretty soon after that."

"Yeah, but your monsters weren't real. The terrorists are."

"You'd be surprised how vivid my imagination was. They were very real monsters to me."

Christine found that she did want to talk. She hadn't told Ryan anywhere near the complete story yet. But it seemed silly for the whole thing to be off the record. She'd only have to repeat herself tomorrow for his tape recorder.

"I was getting ready for a party," she said. "Um, before I go on, would you like to get more comfortable? You make me nervous just sitting there like that." So close, but not close enough. "I can hear you breathing, I know you're near, but I can't touch you."

"Do you want to touch me?" He sounded surprised. "You sure didn't a minute ago."

"I was in the throes of nightmare hysteria. Come on, get under the covers. It'll be like when my sister and I were little. We would snuggle under the covers and tell scary stories."

He stood up. "Uh, Chrissy, I hate to break this to you, but if I get under the covers with you, it most certainly won't be the same as two little girls."

Well, all right. She'd known that. Feigned innocence wasn't working, so she might as well fess up to the uncomfortable truth. She wanted Ryan Mulvaney to lie down with her. She needed to be held. That was the worst thing about being a hostage—the aloneness, her inability to articulate her fears to anyone who cared a whit.

She took a deep breath, then swung the covers back in a silent invitation.

Chapter 9

Ryan could hear his own heartbeat in the suddenly too-quiet room. Chrissy had just invited him into her bed, and he didn't know quite what to do.

He'd been propositioned by sources before. He often bought information from street-savvy prostitutes, and more than one of them had tried to turn a cut-and-dried business arrangement into a *working* arrangement. A couple of times, sources he was just about to nail had offered to trade him a high-priced call girl for his silence. And once, a high-ranking police administrator's wife had come on to him, a last-ditch effort to keep her husband's blatant corruption off the front page. He'd been smart enough to gracefully get out of all of those situations.

But this...this put him on a whole different level of temptation. His impromptu kiss with Chrissy, documented on Fran's film, was bad enough. But to compromise the whole story by sleeping with her was unthinkable.

Then why was he thinking about it? She might be manipulating him, trying to get him to have sex with her so that she could lay another big guilt trip on him. And she might just succeed. He was already having a hard time thinking about how he was going to nail Stan Greenlow to the wall; it would be a hell of a lot harder after sleeping with the man's daughter.

"Well?" she said. She was trying to sound cavalier, he could tell, but her voice quivered just enough that he knew his decision meant something to her.

He should have done the smart thing and taken a cold shower, but he couldn't make himself even stand up. Manipulation or not, he honestly believed Chrissy needed him, needed whatever comfort he could offer. If that made him a schmuck, so be it.

Anyway, no law said he had to do the deed with her. She claimed she was after a good snuggle, and he could provide her with that. He swung his legs up and under the covers in one smooth move, then eased down beside her. She felt warm, even through the thick terry cloth of that infernal robe. He remembered the way she'd glowed after her bath, both last night and tonight, her skin blushed to a delicate pink.

She took a quick, shallow breath as he smoothed the blankets up over them both. "You must think I'm extremely juvenile, or naive...or slutty," she said.

Ryan found it difficult to speak—all his senses were clogged up with impressions of Chrissy's long, lean body—but he managed. "I don't know what to think. You're either incredibly trusting, or you don't care much about your virtue."

"Is my virtue in danger?"

"I would hope so." His hands itched to stroke her, to at least acknowledge this newfound intimacy. "I'm not a eunuch, and I haven't exactly made it a secret that I find you attractive. At the same time, I know that the two of us...getting intimate is about the stupidest thing either one of us could do."

"I know," she said. "It's not really what I want, although..."

"Although what?"

"Nothing." She sighed.

"Then what *do* you want?"

"For you to hold me," she answered without hesitation. "I haven't had anyone do that in a long time—unless you count the kidnappers, and that was hardly comforting."

Suddenly, more than anything, Ryan wanted to erase Denny's obscene touch from Chrissy's memory. He felt a strong urge to break the nose of anyone who'd laid a hand on her. He slid one arm behind her neck. "Come here. I'll hold you." And that was all he would do, God help him. He'd been crazy to let her start this, but he was stuck with the situation now.

"Mmm, that's better. Certainly better than a sister could do." Her voice was laced with humor, nothing provocative, but she must not have known what that timbre did to him. He suspected she didn't have a true picture of just how enticing a creature she was.

"You're not a virgin, are you?" He needed to know.

She didn't seem offended. "No. I had a boyfriend in college. And then there's Robert, though I'm not sure I can count him."

"Why not?"

"Because he's...I don't know, almost asexual. I swear, the way he handles it, you'd think sex was some annoying but essential duty he had to perform. Maybe that's the way he sees it." She gave a little gasp. "Oh, God, Ryan, you wouldn't quote me on *that,* would you?"

"We're off the record, remember?" Ryan found that, at the moment, he didn't feel the slightest ambition to work these revelations of hers into the story. All he wanted was to keep holding her. The fact that she trusted him with such intimate details of her life, even when she knew what he was and what he was ultimately after, gave him a warm feeling like nothing he could remember.

"Oh, good." She relaxed another degree. "So, where do you want me to start?"

"Anywhere you like."

"I'd do better if you'd ask questions."

"Okay. Let's start with the kidnappers. Just who exactl
are these guys?"

"I've told you pretty much everything I know. They'r
part of this environmental group that's been the terror o
Capitol Hill the last two years. Now I guess they're takin
lobbying to an all new level."

"That's a good turn of phrase, Chrissy," he said. "Se
you could be a writer if you wanted."

"Oh…well…" she stammered.

"Sorry, I didn't mean to wander off the subject. S
you've never had trouble with this group before? I mean
you or your father personally?

Chrissy hesitated. "It seems I remember my father com
plaining about them a couple of times. But then, he com
plains about a lot of things, so it didn't really stand out i
my mind. The first I knew that Dad and I were targets wa
when they grabbed me."

"And how did they accomplish this feat?"

"They posed as deliverymen. The wedding is in abou
three weeks, you see, and I've been receiving a stead
stream of wedding gifts ever since the invitations went ou
I didn't think twice when the two men came to the doo
They wore uniforms and everything."

"Do you normally answer the door?"

"No. But I was close by, so I did this time. It amaze
me that they got so lucky. On a normal day, they wouldn'
have been permitted access to the house, much less to me
But I was there, in my party dress and my jewelry, Johnny
on-the-spot to rake in another wedding gift. Before I knev
it I was being wrapped in a blanket and stuffed into th
back of a truck."

"No one saw you?"

"Apparently not. Dad was probably in his office with hi
secretary. Connie would have been upstairs cleaning o
something. Our cook had the day off, I think. I don't knov
where the chauffeur was. That's all the employees w
have."

Ryan had visualized the Greenlow household as a b

more complicated. He would have to verify the situation through some other source, he supposed—

He stopped himself. He wasn't supposed to be thinking like a reporter right now. He was supposed to be Chrissy's surrogate big brother, slaying the dragons of the dark for her.

Only he was hard as a rock—a most unbrotherly attitude. She had only to move her leg a couple of inches to discover that for herself.

He tried to herd his thoughts onto more reasonable pathways. "When did they drug you the first time?"

"Oh, as soon as they grabbed me. I think they must have thought the drug would work faster, because I kept yelling and thrashing, and they seemed surprised that I hadn't passed out right away."

"How long before the drug took effect?"

"I think about ten minutes. First I got really happy and complacent, then I passed out."

Clioxydine. Ryan had done some research on the Internet on the various tranquilizers Chrissy might have been given. Clioxydine, a veterinary drug, seemed to fit the bill, given the symptoms she'd mentioned, and it was cheap and readily available. He'd heard that an oral variety had been the culprit in several recent date-rape cases.

He hesitated to ask his next question. But if the answer was yes, Chrissy needed to talk about it. "When you were under the influence of this drug, did these guys…you know, hurt you?"

There was a long pause. "I'm not really sure, but I think not. Wouldn't I know…I mean, wouldn't I be able to tell if I'd been raped?"

Involuntarily, Ryan shuddered, again remembering Josette. She'd been in the hospital for six days after she'd been raped. He'd interviewed other victims when he did a story about a serial rapist; his inclination was to believe that a woman couldn't be violated without knowing it. Anyway, he would tell Chrissy what she wanted to hear. "You'd know."

"Anyway, the drug lasted a few hours. When I woke up, I was in this terrible, nasty room, tied to a pipe, lying on a dirty mattress with no sheets. Through an open door there was another room, and the terrorists hung out in there, watching TV, smoking dope, drinking, and talking about how to deal with me."

"And how long were you there?"

"I'm not sure. I think two days, but my sense of time got all mixed-up."

"And for two days you just sat there? Did they feed you?"

"No. One of the women took me to the bathroom, and I drank water from the tap. And one of the guys gave me a sip of his beer. That's all I remember."

"What did they talk about?"

"About how to get my father to pay a million-dollar ransom."

"Did they give any indication as to why they'd chosen you as a target?"

Chrissy hesitated, and Ryan sensed the first evasion she'd shown all evening. "It was political. They didn't like the way Dad voted on some key environmental issues, and they said he took money from oil companies and other anti-environmental lobbyists."

"It seems a lot of congressmen would be targets, then, if that was all it took." Ryan had been researching Greenlow's politics, comparing his voting record to that of other senators. He definitely wasn't an environmentalist's dream, but he wasn't their nightmare. Others were worse.

"Maybe I wasn't the only target," she said, sounding the slightest bit defensive. "Maybe there were other attempted kidnappings, but I was the first successful one."

She was hiding something. Ryan's journalistic instincts were kicking in, despite his best efforts to keep them at bay, and he knew when a source was trying to explain away something that hadn't even come out yet. His impulse was to argue with Chrissy, to fluster her. But he couldn't. First off, they were off the record, so why bother? And sec-

and…he couldn't make himself be mean to her. Her father was involved in something sleazy, and she was the one who got caught in the middle.

Tomorrow would be soon enough to challenge her.

"Who knows what motivates animals like that?" he said, though he knew very well. Money. And for some reason, these environmental terrorists believed that they could get it out of Stan Greenlow.

"So did these guys contact your father?" Ryan asked.

Another hesitation. "They did." She yawned melodramatically. "I'm getting tired, now. Could we talk about this in the morning?"

Ryan knew that if he dropped the subject now, by morning she would have her story straight. Again, his journalistic impulse was to push. Whatever she admitted, he could work on getting it *on* the record tomorrow. Or confirming the facts through independent sources. But again, he couldn't make himself harass her.

"Sure, we can drop it till morning," he said. "I'm kind of tired, too." And horny. "Do you want me to stay here, or go back to my own bed?"

"Um…" Whatever her answer would have been, a knock on the door silenced her. Ryan pressed one finger to her lips, indicating that she should remain silent, then slipped out of the bed, his senses alert.

The knock came again. "C'mon, Ryan, open up."

Fran! He'd forgotten all about her. He flipped on the bedside lamp, then grabbed his jeans and pulled them on, zipping them up as he walked to the door. Not that Fran hadn't seen him in his underwear before, or that she would even blink, but he felt very uncomfortable with the idea of her seeing him so…casual with Chrissy in the room.

He peered through the peephole in the door, just to make sure Fran was alone, then let her in.

"Took long enough," Fran said, her eyebrows arched speculatively. "What's our little princess up to?"

"Don't call her that," he said, annoyed. At the moment, Chrissy was doing a beautiful job of feigning sleep. Ryan's

computer was still on, and his notes were laid out all ove
the bed, as if he'd been working. "She's been through hel
the last couple of days. And she's being a really good spor
about the inconveniences."

"Oh, some inconvenience. I wouldn't complain, either
if some guy put me up at the Sheraton so he could interviev
me. Has she made it worth your while?"

Ryan chose to accept a nonprurient slant to Fran's ques
tion. "I've got a hell of a story shaping up. Come out i
the hallway for a minute, and I'll tell you."

"You afraid the princess will miss some of her beaut
sleep? Jeez, if anyone doesn't need beauty sleep, it's her
She's so damn photogenic it's scary. Wait till you see thes
pictures." Fran handed Ryan a large brown envelope.

He laid it on the corner of the bed. "Come on." H
ushered her out into the hallway, leaving the door ope
only a crack. "This is turning into a better story than w
bargained for. I think Stan Greenlow's got a secret, a rea
dirty secret." He wasn't referring to the illegitimate daugh
ter, either. That was a secret Ryan had decided to keep
given that it wasn't relevant to his current story. "Chriss
has told me a lot of stuff, but she's holding something back
too. These NATURE guys and girls were trying to make
point by targeting Christine and her father. There's some
thing juicy beneath the surface here. I can feel it."

"So you really believe she was kidnapped?" Fran askec
clearly amazed.

"Unless she's an incredibly good liar. I can usually spc
liars."

"I don't know, Rye. Raging hormones can cause an
guy's judgment—including his lie-spotting abilities—to g
right out the window."

"My hormones are not raging," he lied succinctly.

"They are, too. What's she doing in your room, any
way?"

"It's our room. She didn't want to stay by herself, an
I don't blame her. She's really spooked. And in case yo

didn't notice, she's bundled up like an Eskimo and sleeping in her own bed.''

Fran narrowed her eyes. "She trusts you that much?"

"Yes, and I wouldn't even *think* of violating that trust."

Fran snorted. "Now I know you're lying. You might be able to curb your wayward impulses, but you'll never believe that you aren't at least *thinking* about... waywardness." She smiled coyly. "Hey, you want I should take a picture of her asleep?"

"No," he said hastily. Chrissy wasn't really asleep, and she would never allow Fran to point a camera at her now. "You can take more pictures tomorrow. She'll consent to it, I'm pretty sure. Let's not risk making her mad."

Fran rolled her eyes. "Okay. But I think you're going soft on me...parts of you, anyway. Your killer instinct has taken a hike." With that, Fran turned and sauntered down the hall toward the elevators.

Christine had made a dive for the envelope full of photos the moment she was alone in the room—she couldn't resist. Now she was flipping through one glossy eight-by-ten after another, horrified by what she saw. Here she was making a phone call at Costello's, and there she was stuffing her face with a cinnamon roll, appearing as if she didn't have a concern in the world.

Here she was fleeing down the street as the police arrived at Costello's; there she was riding the crowded subway. Smelling flowers at the zoo.

Lots of zoo pictures. She certainly looked as if she were having fun. My Lord, she thought, who would believe the woman in these photos had escaped from captivity just the previous evening? Who would believe she'd been threatened with rape and mutilation?

Christine flipped to the last picture and gasped. She and Ryan, wrapped up in a passionate kiss. His face didn't show. Hers did, quite clearly, despite the steam rising up around them.

The picture made her hot in more ways than one.

He was using her. The wholly natural attraction she felt
for Ryan would be her downfall. She could already imagine
the photo caption: And Where Is Fiancé Robert In This
Picture?

Not only would everyone think she was a liar, they
would think she was a slut, too. Well, hell, maybe she was.
Minutes ago, she'd been in bed with Ryan. And she was
still officially engaged, never mind that Robert, the slimy
invertebrate, cared more about his stupid car than about her.

Ryan came back into the room, alone. He froze when he
saw what she was doing.

She looked up at him and narrowed her eyes, then tossed
the offending photo across the bed toward him. "Want to
explain what you planned to do with this?"

Ryan picked up the photo, studied it. She wondered what
he thought of it, from an aesthetic standpoint. It was a beautiful photo, artistically composed, with just the right mixture of light, shadow and steam. All kinds of steam.

His face revealed nothing. "I wish you had let me explain about these before you looked at them. I told Fran
not to print this one, but I guess she couldn't resist."

"I'm listening now. But I don't think there's anything
you can do to make these photos less damning. It's taken
me all day to convince you I was kidnapped, if you're even
truly convinced. If people see these, they'll never believe
it."

"You underestimate my writing abilities," he said,
reaching for the rest of the photos. He scooped them off
her lap and spent a great deal of time studying each one.
"You said you would be able to explain why you didn't
call the police first thing this morning. You explain, I'll
write it in a way that makes my readers see it exactly as I
see it. The photos won't change that."

She didn't believe him, not for a second. They'd been
dealing in words all day. Words didn't carry nearly the
weight of those inflammatory images.

"I'll explain it, all right. Tomorrow." With that she
scooted back under the covers, flopped over on her side

facing the wall and pulled the blankets nearly over her head. She was too confused to deal with Ryan any more tonight. Tomorrow, when she was fresh, she would figure out how to tell him that her father hadn't wanted her back.

Ryan took the stack of photos to his bed, stripped off his jeans, then sat down to study the pictures at leisure. Fran was really good, he thought again. He could understand why she'd been excited about the kiss picture. It spoke. He was surprised the passion didn't burn right through the photographic paper.

But none of these photos was right for the story. Maybe he could use one or two of them, but he needed something else. Too bad no one had photographed Chrissy when he first found her, filthy, disheveled, beaten, half-starved, and being harassed by the Pit Bulls. That would have been a picture that told a story.

Now, here was one he really liked—Chrissy watching the mother baboon. The expression on her face was poignant, almost tragic—hardly carefree. He suspected that had been one of the few times today when Chrissy dropped her guard and let anyone see how she was really feeling.

What had made her so sad? he wondered. He glanced back at the bed, where she was again feigning sleep, or perhaps actually sleeping. It was getting late, and today had been exhausting.

He regretted Fran's timing, even though he knew, from a strictly intellectual point of view, that her awkward arrival was the best thing that could have happened to him. If Chrissy had said yes, she wanted him to stay in bed with her, he wouldn't have settled for a cuddle.

He was pretty sure she'd known that, too. For all her seeming innocence, she wasn't that naive.

What would she have answered? He probably would never know. She was good and mad about the photos, and he might never again achieve the degree of trust they'd shared earlier.

Still, the photos had had their desired effect. She knew

now, better than ever, how her behavior today had implicated her. He only hoped that now she would follow through with the whole truth. She still had a lot of explaining to do.

Ryan worked for another two hours on his story. During that time, Chrissy hardly made a sound, only a deep, sighing breath every so often. There were no more nightmares, for which he was thankful, though he wouldn't have minded another chance to comfort her. When he could no longer hold his eyes open, he knocked off for the night, but his sleep was restless. He kept imagining that Denny had found them and was trying to break into their room.

Dawn couldn't come soon enough. With early-morning light brightening the room, Ryan's heebie-jeebies melted away. Chrissy was still safe. Denny didn't have a clue as to their whereabouts.

Ryan got up, took a quick shower, shaved, elbowed his way into a long-sleeved T-shirt and jeans. Chrissy was still snoozing blissfully, or at least she seemed to be.

He called room service and ordered the works for breakfast, never mind that it cost the national debt. He needed sustenance if he was going to continue wrestling with this story, and he wanted to keep Chrissy fed and happy.

It occurred to him then that, since it was Monday, Chrissy could go to her bank and make a withdrawal. She wouldn't be dependent on him for anything after that. Anything except her safety. He was still betting that she wasn't ready to tackle life alone on the streets just yet.

She stirred. He tensed. "Chrissy?" he said softly.

She rolled over, opened her eyes, blinked a couple of times, as if trying to get oriented, then smiled. "I'm starving."

"That figures." The woman ate like a linebacker. "Breakfast is on the way."

"Oh, good." She sat up and swung her legs to the floor. The terry robe didn't come with them, and she hastily adjusted herself, hiding her thighs with the bedspread. Darn. "What did you order?" she asked.

"Legs, bacon, toast, orange juice and cof—"

"What? What did you say?"

Had she developed a hearing impairment from the drug? he wondered. "I said, eggs, bacon, toast, O.J. and coffee."

She smiled—a soft, secret smile, the meaning of which was a total mystery to Ryan. But at least her sour mood of last night had vanished. She licked her lips. "Mmm. I hope the bacon's crisp. Can we eat in the car?"

"Excuse me?" Maybe he was the one who needed his hearing checked.

"I was hoping we'd get an early start for Raleigh. You know, where my sister lives."

Raleigh. He'd forgotten all about his promise to take her to her sister. "Um, how early? There are a few things I'd like to take care of first."

She looked at the digital clock on the nightstand. "Earlier than this," she said with a frown. "Why did you let me sleep so late?"

"It's not even eight o'clock yet. I didn't figure we were on a tight schedule."

"I'm anxious to get going. I want out of Washington." She folded her arms. "You *are* still taking me to Raleigh, aren't you?"

"I was planning to. But I haven't exactly gotten that exclusive interview you promised," he reminded her.

"I thought we could take care of that on the way to Michelle's."

He shook his head. "I can't take notes or look things up while I'm driving."

"I could drive."

He laughed at that. "Do you even have a driver's license?"

"Not with me, but I have one," she said huffily. "About once a week, Dad's chauffeur lets me drive the limo around. I can drive as well as anyone you could name."

"Yeah, well, you aren't driving my Vette. No one does."

"Oh, all right. You can grill me during breakfast. I'm

sure you can eat and take notes at the same time. Then can we leave?''

He thought about it. He could get most of the information he needed in an hour or two. But he would have to do some digging here in town if Chrissy wasn't forthcoming about her father's dealings with NATURE—or even if she was. He would have to verify everything she said through second sources.

So, he supposed he could drive down to Raleigh and turn right back. He would have tomorrow and Wednesday to finish up his research. He also wanted to check the pawn-shops to see if anyone had hocked a two-carat engagement ring.

There was one last detail. ''Okay. We'll leave after breakfast, as soon as we take care of something. You don't have to do it, but it might help your case.''

''What?'' she asked suspiciously.

''I want to go to an independent medical lab and have your blood drawn. Whatever drug the kidnappers gave you, traces of it might still be in your system. A blood test would also prove you weren't on any other types of illegal drugs.'' He held his breath, fully expecting her to refuse.

To his surprise, she smiled. ''Why, Ryan, that's a *brilliant* idea. I wish I'd thought of it yesterday.''

Chapter 10

Ryan's relentless questions extracted any pleasure Christine might have taken from the sumptuous breakfast. She'd had no idea how gentle he'd been with her before until this morning, when he started shooting rapid-fire questions at her. There was little sympathy shown now; Ryan Mulvaney was pure, unadulterated unbiased journalist.

Whenever she hesitated, even for a few seconds, he looked up from his computer where he was taking notes, his eyes boring into hers, as if searching for a weakness.

She tried not to take it personally. This was Ryan at work, showing her a different persona from the man who'd held her last night, gently coaxing responses from her. This was how he made his living. He wasn't nasty or unfair, just direct.

They went over the specifics of the kidnapping again, minute by minute. He prompted her to remember details she never would have thought of—the color of the paint on the walls of the apartment where she was held, for instance. She remembered now that it had been a nauseating pea green.

When he asked what kind of bush she'd fallen into, she drew the line. "I wasn't on a first-name basis with the bush, okay?" she said impatiently. "How am I supposed to know what kind of bush it was? I'm not a horticulture expert." She had long since given up on breakfast, and was now stretched out on the bed, staring at the ceiling so that she wouldn't have to look at him.

"Then what did it look like?"

"Like a bush!"

"Try to remember."

She sighed in defeat. He wasn't going to give her an inch. "Okay, if it's that important. Um, let's see…it had long, straight, spiky branches, sort of all coming from a middle trunk." She closed her eyes, trying to picture the darn thing. "No leaves. I think maybe it was getting ready to bloom, because there were little bumpy bud things on the branches." She was amazed at the sensory detail Ryan was able to pull out of her.

"Good, that's good!" he said as he typed furiously. "A lot of this is to protect you, you know. If we do locate the place you were held, and all of these details are verified, no one can doubt your story."

"They'll just think I was in collusion with the environmentalists," she said glumly. "That's what my father thinks." And with that statement, she opened up the can of worms she and Ryan had been tap-dancing around all morning. She supposed she couldn't avoid it any longer.

"Let's explore that more deeply," he said, sounding much like the shrink she'd seen after her mother's death. "You've only spoken with your father once since the kidnapping, right?"

"Yes. When I called him from Costello's. We talked for maybe a couple of minutes. The other time I called him, he was asleep. I talked to his personal secretary, and to our housekeeper."

"You weren't allowed to talk to him while you were a hostage?"

"They had me say hello into the phone once, just to

prove to him they really had me, but that was all.'' She told him about the one-sided conversations she'd heard between the terrorists and her father. She had never doubted—still didn't—that they'd made a clear demand for one million dollars, and that they'd identified their organization to her father.

"I did some research on your father last night, on the Internet,'' Ryan said cautiously. "He not only voted against environmental issues on several occasions, but he introduced a controversial bit of legislation that passed recently, allowing certain kinds of legal chemical dumping.''

Christine sat up and stared at him. She'd forgotten that part. "Yes, that's it! That's what they were talking about. They're blaming Dad for the destruction of a waterbird habitat, and they wanted the million bucks to restore it. I can't believe I forgot that part.''

"I can't, either,'' Ryan said, shaking his head, dutifully typing in what she'd said.

Oh, dear. It did sound as if she were making things up off the top of her head. "Really, Ryan, I think it was the drug. It killed off some short-term-memory brain cells or something. They told me all this when I was under the influence of that drug.''

"It's okay, Chrissy. I believe you.''

Did he? she wondered. Did he really? She was anxious to go to the medical lab and have her blood tested, but that wasn't going to happen until she answered all Ryan's questions. She decided to get on with it, to blurt out the rest. He'd pull it out of her eventually, anyway.

"Let's get back to this phone call to your father, the one from Costello's,'' Ryan said. "I'd like you to go over it word for word, as closely as you can remember.''

She did. Humiliated, she repeated every hurtful word she and her father had exchanged. She didn't even have to try that hard to remember. The conversation was etched into her brain.

"So...let me get this straight,'' Ryan said. "Your fa-

ther's story is that he was trying to pull the money together?''

"That's what he tried to tell me," Christine said. "But
it's not true. My father is a very wealthy man, and I know
everything about his finances. He could have had twice that
amount in unmarked bills in the blink of an eye.''

Ryan didn't seem shocked. He just continued typing. "It
staggers me to think about that much money," he said,
more to himself than to her. Then, like a bird of prey, he
went for the kill. "You know, when faced with a kidnapped
child and a ransom demand, people usually do two things.
They pay it, or they call the police. Your father didn't do
either, or at least not right away. Why? You mentioned the
word *collusion* a few minutes ago.''

She was prepared for this one. "There are two possible
reasons for my father's behavior. The first is because he
thought I was in cahoots with these environmentalists, so I
wasn't really in danger.''

"Any particular reason he would believe that?" Ryan
wanted to know.

"Dad and I have had frequent arguments about environ-
mentalism. It's the one issue we're diametrically opposed
on. But I've never openly contradicted his views, and I've
certainly never gone out of my way to make friends with
the environmental lobbies or anything like that. So it makes
only minimal sense he would believe I could do such a
thing as fake my own kidnapping in order to extort money
from him. But it's what I want to believe.''

"Uh-huh. And what's the second reason?''

Christine took a deep breath. "That he didn't want me
back. That he didn't care if the kidnappers killed me.''

Ryan was very good at hiding his reactions, but this time
he couldn't disguise his shock. His mouth hung open, his
fingers stilled on the keyboard, and he stared.

"What are you saying?" he asked.

"I'm saying that, for various reasons, I'd become a liability to him, and I was worth more to him dead than alive, Think of all those sympathy votes.''

Ryan swallowed, his throat suddenly dry. Stan Greenlow was no choirboy, but only a monster would stand by and do nothing when his daughter's life was in danger. ''You are going to elaborate, I hope,'' he said. ''What 'various reasons'?''

Ryan sensed he was at the heart of the matter—the real raison d'être for his story. Kidnapping, threatened rape, daring escapes, those were all window dressing. The emotional part—the part people would salivate to read about—was about to be revealed.

Christine got up and started pacing. ''I don't want to tell you this,'' she said. ''It could destroy my father's entire political future. But the whole story doesn't make sense unless I do tell you. I'm just hoping you'll find some way not to reveal it to everybody who can read.''

''I've already told you I'm committed to telling this story in as fair a way as possible. Facts only, no conjecture, everybody gets to tell their fair story—including your father, if he'll talk to me. That's the only assurance I can give you. Everything you tell me now is on the record.''

''I know. Okay, here's the deal.''

Ryan listened as Chrissy outlined her father's ten-year downward spiral into prescription drug addiction. He dutifully took notes, but he wondered how he would ever communicate the pain in Chrissy's voice, the agony of a young woman faced with too much responsibility too early in life, watching as her father disintegrated before her eyes.

''So far we've always managed to cover for him,'' she said.

''Who's 'we'?''

''Gerald, me, and our family doctor. No one's ever suspected. But there's another doctor in the picture now. I don't know where Dad found him. He's one of these Dr. Feelgoods—you know, the kind that passes out pills like candy. So in the past few months things have gotten much, much worse. I was beginning to worry that Dad would accidentally kill himself with those damn pills, or send himself into a coma. So I laid down an ultimatum. I told him he had to check into Betty Ford…or I would go public with his problem.''

Damn, that was gutsy, Ryan thought. "Did you mean it?''

She seemed to think about his question. "Yes, I did. I'd made threats before, but this time I was serious. I didn't want to lose him, especially not by slow, painful degrees.''

"And when did this confrontation take place?''

"About a week ago, I guess.''

Mere days before the kidnapping, Ryan thought. Perhaps, in Stan's mind, his daughter's anger was motive enough for her to try and extort money from him. "Were you angry?'' he asked. "Did you raise your voice?''

"I did raise my voice,'' she admitted. "But I wasn't exactly angry, more like desperate. He has an illness. I was desperate, and I used the only leverage I could think of to force him to get help.''

Ryan could see why Chrissy had become a liability to Stan Greenlow. Drug addiction in any form made people do horrible things they wouldn't consider otherwise. But to sacrifice his beloved daughter? To turn a blind eye and a deaf ear to the possibility of her being raped, beaten, tortured to death?

"You see why I prefer the collusion theory,'' she said softly.

He nodded, feeling a little sick.

"And you understand why I didn't call the police right away? I read the article in your paper. Dad was quoted as saying he had no idea what had happened to me, that no ransom demands had been made, and I knew he was lying.''

She flopped back down on the bed. "I just couldn't deal with it. All I wanted to do was push it from my mind, pretend I was some other person, without all these problems and decisions to make. It was almost like I had a mini-breakdown or something.''

"You'll have to face your dad eventually, you know."

"Yeah. But not for a few days. I want to talk to Michelle first. She has a real practical way of looking at things. Sometimes she can see whole new angles that I never dreamed of."

Ryan clicked off his tape recorder, closed down his computer files. For some reason, he felt incredibly crummy. Chrissy had volunteered this information without much prompting from him, yet he felt that he'd somehow violated her.

"You're done?" she asked.

"For now. We need a break. How about that fun trip to the medical lab I promised you?"

"Okay. I guess I'm about tapped out, anyway." She yawned. "I'd better call Michelle and tell her I've been delayed." She picked up the phone by the bed and dialed the number from memory. Again, Ryan listened. Apparently Michelle had heard about her half sister's disappearance, because this conversation involved some lengthy explanations.

"I'll arrive sometime this evening," Chrissy said. "Then I can tell you the whole story. Please don't worry." She hung up, then disappeared into the bathroom without a word.

When they'd both dressed, they packed up their few belongings and headed downstairs. Ryan checked out, and they took the elevators down to the garage. His car was exactly where he'd left it. Why he'd thought anyone would bother with it was beyond him. The terrorists were after Chrissy, not his car.

He supposed he was a little paranoid where his Vette was concerned. He'd already lost his custom hubcaps.

Chrissy, once again incognito with her hat and sunglasses, seemed to have more of a spring in her step this morning. "I really think this lab idea is so smart," she said. "Have you thought of any other ideas that might help verify my story?"

He unlocked and opened her door. "Well, you said they took your engagement ring and earrings, right?"

"Uh-huh."

"Did they mention what they planned to do with the jewelry?" He let Chrissy think about her answer while he walked around to the other side of the car and got in.

"I don't think they said, at least not to me," Chrissy said. "Maybe one of the women wanted the jewelry."

"It seems more likely to me they would want to get rid of it—fence it, pawn it. I contacted a buddy on the police force who works in the theft division. He's going to lean on some of the fences he knows, see if he can get some info. Meanwhile—"

"We could try the pawnshops," she finished for him, almost bouncing with excitement. "I can't believe I didn't think of that. Two-carat diamond rings don't get pawned every day. If some pawnbroker saw it, he'd remember it."

"I thought you were in a hurry to get out of town."

"Oh, what's a few more hours?"

"Great." He had no idea how many pawnshops there were in D.C.—fifty or five hundred. But with two pairs of hands and two telephones, they could at least make a dent in the list. It wasn't that Ryan truly believed they'd find the ring just sitting around in a pawnshop window. A professional fence would pay more for the jewelry. But who knew how savvy these environmental jerks were? Maybe they didn't have good criminal contacts. They sure were piss-poor kidnappers—couldn't get the ransom, couldn't hold on to their hostage, couldn't even get any publicity.

Anyway, even if their pawnshop search yielded nothing, at least he'd succeeded in getting Chrissy to hang around a few more hours. He told himself he was just protecting his story, his source. But the reasons went deeper than that. He just plain liked having her around. She was nothing like he'd expected Stan Greenlow's heiress daughter to be.

Ryan knew right where one of those independent medical labs was. They'd sprung up everywhere since the demand for confidential AIDS testing skyrocketed. People didn't like going to their family doctors for something like that. Chrissy gave her name as Dawn White—an alias Ryan had chosen for her, a bit more anonymous than Chrissy Green would have been. They ordered a comprehensive drug screening, and then Chrissy disappeared through a door marked Patients and Medical Personnel Only.

He paid the fee while he waited for her—another blow to his credit card, but who was counting these days? He was amazed the charge went through.

She reappeared a few minutes later, holding a wad of gauze in the crook of her arm. "Okay, I'm done. How long will it take to get the results?"

"They said three to five days." And no amount of wheedling or bribery would make it happen any faster, Ryan had discovered.

"Oh." She frowned. "That won't even be in time to make your deadline."

"No, but it's the best we can do."

She shrugged. "Okay. What next?"

"We need phones and a yellow pages. I called Fran while I was waiting. She said we can work at her studio as long as we don't bring any terrorists with us."

Chrissy shivered. "You don't think they know where we are, do you?"

Without thinking much about it, he put his arm around her. "I think we shook off your friend Denny last night. He was working alone, it seemed to me, maybe trying to redeem himself for letting you escape. I'm hoping he's given up."

"For now." She shivered again. "I hate having to be constantly afraid. If the police don't catch these guys, I'll be looking over my shoulder for a long time to come. And I won't have the benefit of my father's security, either."

He gave her shoulders a squeeze and released her. "You won't be alone. You'll have your sister—"

"Living hundreds of miles away."

"What about friends?"

"I doubt any of them will even speak to me after this

fiasco. My so-called friends avoid scandal like the plague. I only realized it recently, but I don't have a single close girlfriend I can call.''

"And your fiancé?" He hated to even ask.

"Ha! Are you kidding? I tried calling him for help. I might as well have told him I had leprosy and several STDs.''

They stopped in front of Ryan's car. "And you're still going to marry the jerk?"

She peeked out from behind her sunglasses. "Did I say that?'' She climbed into the car before he could respond, but that was just as well. Better that she didn't see the silly grin that was undoubtedly lighting up his face. His step was a little bit lighter as he sprinted around to the driver's side.

"So, you're giving Roberto the boot?" he asked as he started the engine.

"Absolutely. I realized I was about to settle for a luke-warm situation. Robert and I were...comfortable together. I used to think that was appropriate—desirable, even. No messy emotions getting in the way of day-to-day harmony. But I was wrong.''

"I should hope so," Ryan murmured. A passionate, exciting woman like Chrissy locked in a bloodless marriage would be a colossal waste. "Anything in particular make you change your mind?" He wasn't holding his breath for any specific answer to that question, he told himself sternly. Perhaps she didn't see him as the enemy anymore. In fact, they were uneasy allies now. But that was a long way from...well, it was a long way.

"I think it's just that, for the last couple of days, I've been feeling everything very intensely—fear, anger...passion.'' Her voice dropped on the last word. "I realized that I've been living in this emotional vacuum. All these feelings I had were blocked up somewhere in my brain, and now they're pouring out of me. I think that's why I've been crying and shouting and laughing so much, not to mention the bad dreams.''

"And the kissing," he added, flashing her a mischievous wink. "Don't forget that."

Her face turned a charming shade of pink. "Ryan, please."

"Is the memory that unpleasant?"

"It's embarrassing that I fell all over you like that. And that picture! I hyperventilate every time I think about it. I would just die if that picture went into *Primus* magazine."

"It won't." The pictures belonged to Fran, of course, and she could do whatever she pleased with them, but he was confident he could sway her to his way of thinking on this. If anyone even suspected he was on intimate terms with Chrissy—whether it was true or not—the integrity of his story would be shot to hell.

As for Chrissy falling all over him, he seemed to remember some mutual falling going on.

"This is Fran's studio?" Chrissy asked when Ryan pulled into an alley a few minutes later. "This looks almost as bad as that street where the Pit Bulls hang out."

"It's a warehouse district, Princess," he said. "The rent's cheap, and there's plenty of space. Lots of photographers are located down here. Don't worry, it's safe, at least during the daytime."

Chrissy's nose was wrinkled in distaste as he led her up a flight of crumbling concrete stairs to a steel door. He rang the buzzer. Moments later, Fran answered. "Come on in, guys. My partners are both out today, so we have the place to ourselves. How's the story coming, Rye?"

"It's coming," he said. "I'll let you read what I've got."

"Can I read it, too?" Chrissy asked.

"No!" Fran and Ryan said together.

Chrissy stopped. Her body went tense, her eyes sparkling dangerously. "Why not?"

Ryan put a hand on her shoulder, soothing, calming. He really liked touching her, and he was glad to find excuses to do so. "Reporters never let their sources read their stories until they're in print," he explained.

"Why not?"

"Because they always start screaming for changes if they don't come out looking squeaky-clean," Fran said.

"But I wouldn't do that," Chrissy argued as they all walked across the cavernous studio's wooden plank flooring. "Maybe I could help you fill in the holes."

"Every source does it," Ryan said. "And if there are any holes, I'll find them and fill them myself, thank you."

"Well," Chrissy said huffily. "I'm only trying to help."

Fran laughed uproarously at this, and Ryan kept his own smile under control only with the utmost willpower. For a woman in her position, Chrissy was surprisingly ingenuous, even naive. And he enjoyed the hell out of her. A lot.

Chrissy's back was hurting, and her bottom was asleep. She and Ryan had been on the phone for hours in Fran's office, checking out dozens and dozens of D.C.'s hundreds of pawnshops. They were concentrating on the ones closest to Peak Street, and it seemed there was one on every corner in that neighborhood.

Most of the people she talked to were nice, some were indifferent, a few were downright rude, as if she'd just called and asked if they had Prince Albert in a can.

She punched in yet another number. "Good morning…er, afternoon. I'm looking to buy a high-quality diamond solitaire, and I was wondering if you might have something in the neighborhood of, oh, one and a half carats." This was the ruse Ryan had devised. Posing as customers, he'd said, would get them a lot more information than mentioning right off the bat that the jewelry was hot.

"As a matter of fact, miss, I do have something in that range. It's actually about two carats, but I can work with you on the price, you know what I'm saying?"

Chrissy gestured frantically toward Ryan. "Well, that's very accommodating of you. Can you tell me more about the ring?"

"A guy brought it in just last week. It's pear-shaped. Good-quality diamond, real clear, no occlusions. It's set in white gold."

Ryan had his ear pressed up against the phone, listening in. His nearness distracted her. She closed her eyes, willing her thoughts to come together. "Um, are you sure it's white gold? Not platinum?"

"I'm sure. I got some earrings, too, real knockouts. A carat apiece. I could cut you a real good deal if you bought the ring and earrings together."

"Hmm…I might be interested," she said, trying to contain her excitement. This had to be it! "Can I come by and see the pieces this afternoon? Will you hold them for me?"

"They aren't going nowhere. You need directions?"

"No, I see there's a map in the yellow pages." She concluded the call, then gave a war whoop. "I found them! Ryan, you're a genius!" Impulsively she threw her arms around him, her feeling of triumph bubbling over into something more, something visceral and earthy that made her want to do more than kiss Ryan.

But kiss him she did, long and slowly and thoroughly.

Ryan didn't take long to pick up the ball. His surprise over her exuberance turned quickly to an enthusiastic response. He kissed her back, with a fervor equal to her own, invading her mouth with his tongue, burying his fingers in her hair. He pulled her closer, leaning against a work table, snugging her body between his legs.

"I know this is crazy," she murmured against his lips between kisses.

"Mmm-hmm…" Ryan agreed complacently as he trailed damp, satiny kisses along her jaw, then her neck.

"I just threw myself at you," she whispered, as if confessing some terrible sin to a priest. "That's not like me." But she didn't regret it, not for an instant. Ryan's kisses had migrated to her collarbone while his hands roamed up and down the sides of her hips, then encircled her waist and imprisoned her so that she couldn't move—not that she wanted to.

"It's those blocked-up emotions you mentioned earlier," he murmured, still kissing, still teasing with his tongue.

He'd nuzzled aside her shirt, trying to gain better access to her breast.

She wasn't wearing a bra. She didn't have one, and she hadn't thought it mattered that much, since she was wearing Ryan's thick cotton shirt. Now she felt suddenly vulnerable. If he even came close to touching her nipple…

He did, and fire shot through her, turning her knees to jelly and the rest of her to quivering acquiescence. No kisses had ever produced such results, not even with Doug. She felt helpless against the roaring tide of passion washing over her.

"Ryan?" His name on her lips was both a plea and a caress.

He raised his head and met her gaze with desire-glazed eyes. His breath came in short gasps. "Lord, Chrissy, what's happening? I suddenly want you so bad I could take you right here on this table."

"It's my fault," she said immediately. "I was so excited about finding my ring, and so grateful for all the trouble you've gone to dig up the truth, and I—"

He silenced her with another kiss. "I wasn't exactly looking to assess blame."

"I wish we hadn't checked out of the Sheraton." She could hardly believe she'd dared to whisper that, but it was true. She wanted him. She was crazy about him—Ryan Mulvaney, the man who was going to destroy her father's reputation.

But he was also going to salvage hers, she reminded herself. If he didn't publish his story, everyone would think she was a liar or a lunatic, or both.

"Don't say that," he said sharply. "Don't tempt me." He tensed. "This has gone far enough. I'm a reporter. You're a source. I can't sleep with you, don't you see?"

She was afraid she did.

"How do you think people would view the story if they found out I was your lover? Every word I wrote about you would be suspect. They would think you slept with me so I wouldn't write bad things about you."

She nodded, deflated. Why did he have to be so damn right? She was appalled that her eyes had filled with tears.

"Oh, Chrissy, I'm sorry." He wrapped his arms around her and hugged her, but the embrace was meant to comfort, not to excite. "Your life has taken a traumatic turn," he said. "Don't make crazy decisions you might regret."

Chapter 11

"I've already made some crazy decisions," Chrissy said with a crooked smile. "Why stop now?"

Ryan had to make her understand. If she came on to him again, there was no way he'd be able to turn away from her. It would take a stronger man than him. "Chrissy—"

"No, really, Ryan, I know you're right." She sniffed and blinked. Her eyes were shiny with tears, but they didn't spill over, thank God. He'd have done *anything* to stop her from crying, but it looked like he wouldn't have to this time.

She took a deep breath and pulled away from him. "Let's go to the pawnshop, okay?"

He nodded, not meeting her gaze. He had to force his mind back to business. "I need to call my cop friend and see if he can go with us. As an independent witness, he can verify our story about where the jewelry turned up, and he can get a warrant to seize the stuff as evidence, or stolen merchandise, or something. That way we'll make sure the diamonds don't go for a hike once the dealer figures out you're not a real customer."

Christine finger-combed her mussed hair, her hands
ying to undo the damage his had done moments ago.
Mmm-hmm, yes, that sounds smart.'' She refastened her
irt, which Ryan had managed to unbutton. She had in-
edible breasts, not large, but round and firm and lus-
ous—

Stop it! He would drive himself crazy if he didn't stop
inking about it. This wasn't like turning down a call girl
r some guy's wife. This required restraint like he'd never
ad to call on before. The realization that he could never
ave her, no matter how much mutual desire smoldered
etween them, made him want to throw his computer in
e Potomac and forget about this whole stupid story.

This possibly career-making, extremely lucrative story.
amn.

The sound of boot heels on wood floor made him jump,
noothing his own hair, positive that although he and
hrissy were standing several feet apart, Fran would know
hat they'd been up to. But she said nothing as she entered
e office area where he and Chrissy had been holed up,
aking their phone calls. Fran was carrying Ryan's laptop,
hich probably meant she'd read his notes and the embry-
nic story he was forming.

''Any luck?'' she asked, handing the computer back to
im.

''Yes!'' The word nearly exploded out of Chrissy. ''This
ace called Easy Duzzit Pawn has my jewelry. We're get-
ng ready to check it out. Thanks, Fran, for letting us use
our phones and all. You've been a big help.'' She threw
er arms around a surprised Fran, who stood there like a
ee trunk, her mouth opening and closing like a landed
sh's.

''Um, you're welcome, Prin—'' She stopped herself.
Christine.''

''May I use your rest room?'' Chrissy asked.

''Sure. It's around that corner, on your right.''

''Thanks.'' She practically skipped her way around the
orner.

When Ryan and Fran were alone, she looked at him lon
and hard. "Why's she so nice to me? Why does she lik
us? We're a public figure's worst nightmare."

"Because we believe her," Ryan said simply.

"The story you're writing isn't particularly flattering, e:
pecially to Stan Greenlow."

"I know. The story's evolving, though. The first versio
was scathing. I toned it down a lot. Did I tell you sh
submitted to a drug screening?"

"Really?"

"And we did find her engagement ring at a pawnsho]
like she said. The pawnshop angle was my idea, not her
so I couldn't possibly believe she set this up as some so
of fake evidence. Fran, she really was kidnapped by te
rorists. I firmly believe that now, and I want to prove it.

"Watch out, Rye," Fran cautioned. "You're soundin
suspiciously biased."

He shrugged. "Yeah, well, who wouldn't be? I can't n
like her. You can't, either."

"Hmm." Fran shuffled her feet, then admitted, "She
not what I expected. So, are you sleeping with her (
what?"

The question startled him, but it shouldn't have. Fra
never minced words. "No. And that's all I'm saying c
that subject, all right?"

Fran rolled her eyes. "Yeah, yeah. Well, if you're plar
ning to, better hurry. 'Cause you can sugarcoat the facts a
you want, but this story will *not* make her happy with yo
Maybe she'll come out sounding okay, just a little flak;
But women don't like it when you trash their daddies."

"I know," Ryan said on a sigh. Did he want journalist
infamy, or momentary sexual bliss? He didn't kid himsel
That was what she represented. Good sex had come an
gone in his life, but stories like this came along once in
lifetime. Yet the decision was surprisingly tough.

"It's going to be a great story," Fran said, maybe sen
ing his vacillation. "It's the best thing you've ever writte

Don't mess it up by getting your feelings all wrapped up in it, okay?''

He couldn't answer her.

Ryan phoned his friend at the police department, who agreed to meet them in two hours at the pawnshop. That would give him time to get a warrant. It would also give him and Chrissy time to kill, and that worried him. Without something constructive to keep his hands busy, he was afraid they might wander.

''Are we ready?'' Chrissy asked brightly when she reappeared. She had her cap on, her sunglasses perched on top of it.

''We meet my friend at the pawnshop at around two-thirty,'' he said.

''Oh. Rats. I wanted to go now.''

''Yeah, me too. Want to catch some lunch?''

That brightened her, as he'd figured it would. She'd only picked at the fourteen-dollar breakfast he ordered for her earlier. ''Sure, I'm starved. Want to come with us, Fran?''

''No, I've got work to do. Besides, three's a crowd. But thanks. You guys can let yourselves out the back. I'm heading for the darkroom.''

''Oh, Fran, what about the pictures?'' Ryan asked. ''I can fax my story at the last minute, but you'll have to overnight the photos if you want to make deadline.''

She fidgeted. ''Oh, um, it's taken care of. I Fed Exed them yesterday.''

''*All* of them?'' he asked suspiciously. ''Before you showed them to me?''

''Well, yeah. Don't get all weird on me, Rye. I'm sure the editors will pick and choose, anyway, and you can tell them to ax any you…um, don't like.''

Great, just great. *Primus* magazine now had in their possession a picture of him and Chrissy kissing like a couple of randy teenagers. His credibility had probably just gone right out the window.

''You sent them *that* picture?'' Chrissy wailed.

"I didn't know it would be so controversial," Fran said. "I'm sorry. It doesn't really fit in with the story you're writing—you were right about that. So I doubt they'll run it."

Ryan wasn't so sure. Maybe it wasn't just Chrissy's reputation on the line here, or her father's. Maybe it was his.

Well, he'd asked for it by kissing her when he knew there was a camera close by. A lot of people's lives get screwed up by hormones running amok. Suddenly he knew what it felt like to be on the other side of the fence.

He was sure Fran hadn't sent the picture maliciously. She was excited about the story, like he'd been in the beginning.

"It's okay, Fran," he said, aiming for sincerity. "We'll work something out."

Chrissy stood by, arms folded, her sunny mood having evaporated.

Suddenly Fran smiled. "I know. I'll have to sign an agreement of some form, right? A release or something? I could refuse to sign one for that one picture."

Chrissy looked hopefully at Ryan.

It was generous of Fran to offer, but he didn't want her to hurt *her* reputation with the magazine. "We'll work something out," he said again.

Chrissy, her face falling again, followed him silently out the back door.

Christine's elation over locating her ring had left her. For a while, she'd forgotten about the photos, about Fran's role in taking them. Heavens, had she actually hugged the woman and thanked her? Her earlier anger toward Ryan had reasserted itself, too. She wasn't one to hold a grudge, but she couldn't completely put aside the fact that he'd deceived her about his intentions, allowing Fran to secretly tag along and record her admittedly odd behavior.

"I will do something about that picture," Ryan said as they got back into his car. "I never intended for that moment between us to be anything but private. I hope you believe that."

"I do. I think," she said on a sigh. "Instead of lunch, can we go for a walk? I'm used to working out almost every day. All this sitting around has made me antsy." Not to mention a few residual hormones she needed to chase off, or wear out, or something. What did hormones do when they weren't needed, anyway? Did they disappear? Go dormant? Did they reproduce, like viruses? She was beginning to think that was what hers were doing.

"Sure. We'll go to the Mall. Since it's a weekday, it won't be too crowded. We can grab some hot dogs or pizza afterward, if you want."

She nodded. She'd never felt so torn in her life—crazy about Ryan one minute, despising him the next. Maybe she was falling in love with him. She'd always heard, though she'd never believed it, that falling in love entailed a lot of highs and lows, lots of extremes.

It hadn't been that way with Doug. She'd been sort of obsessive about him, and then it had been over suddenly and that was that.

She chuckled at the idea that she was falling in love. So what if she was? Talk about a doomed relationship.

"If there's anything to laugh about, I wish you'd share it," Ryan said. "I could use a good laugh."

"No, nothing," she said hastily, realizing she must have once again let her feelings out into the open. "Just more of those crazy, pent-up emotions escaping. It's nice to feel things so…so fully, but enough is enough. I'm going to need a therapist if this keeps up."

"I'll go with you. I'm feeling a little crazy myself— Oh, look, a parking place right on the street. How lucky could we get?" He expertly whipped the Vette into a parking place that a Volkswagen Bug had just vacated. It was a tight fit, but he managed.

They were several blocks from the Mall, but Chrissy didn't care. The air was brisk with a hint of drizzle, almost jacket weather, so she walked quickly, hoping to warm her blood. Of course, she could just look at Ryan. He tended to heat her blood right up.

They walked without talking for about twenty minute
By then, Ryan was breathing hard, though Chrissy wa
barely winded. Normally she did aerobics four or five time
a week with a personal trainer, so this was literally a stro
in the park for her.

"You really are in shape," Ryan said. "I'm at least
weekend athlete, and I'm eating your dust."

She found the compliment enormously pleasing. The
she was irritated. No matter how hard she tried to dislik
Ryan, she couldn't, at least not for any length of time. Sh
slowed her pace. If she walked much farther in the flims
canvas shoes, her feet would regret it. "You said somethin
about grabbing a hot dog?"

"I knew that appetite of yours would kick in sooner c
later." He scanned all around him. "Ah, there's a vendo
truck. Hot dogs, pizzas, submarine sandwiches, take you
pick."

"I'll take pizza," she said. The brisk walk had improve
her mood. She vowed to work on the aspects of her lif
that she could change, and ignore the rest. The photos wer
out of her control.

After the pizza, Chrissy talked Ryan into stopping at
bank branch. She had her account number memorized, s
she could get a few hundred dollars with a draft to tide he
over. She carefully wrote out the draft while Ryan pace
the lobby. It occurred to her that she might need ID, whic
she didn't have. Sometimes they asked for it, sometime
they remembered her and didn't ask.

"You're Christine Greenlow?" the young teller said i
an overloud voice, fluttering her fingers nervously. He
two-inch green fingernails glittered under the bank's fluo
rescent lights. "The one in the paper?"

"Shh! You don't have to tell the whole city. Yes, that'
me."

"Cool. Everybody's been wondering where you are."

"Well, they won't wonder much longer, if you don
give me my money and let me get out of here." Her fee

ould root to the floor and she would become a tourist
traction.

"Oh, sure. Sorry." The woman punched in Christine's
ccount number with her nails, then frowned. "Um, there
eems to be a problem. That account is closed."

"Closed? You mean…I can't get to my money?"

"Yes. Your cosigner—that would be Stanley Green-
ow—closed the account because the checkbook was sto-
n."

It took a few moments for this news to sink in. She'd
ad this account since she was in college. Her father's name
as on the account for convenience's sake, but he hadn't
othered with it, or even looked at it, in years.

Now, suddenly, he'd taken it away from her. She had a
eeling she would discover the same thing with her credit
ards—that all the accounts would be closed or frozen.

"All right," she said to the teller. "Thank you. And I
elieve that this bank protects the privacy of its patrons,
es?"

"Huh? Oh, yes, ma'am. Christine who?" She winked
onspiratorially.

"I think we understand one another." Christine walked
ack to where Ryan had found a chair to perch on. "I can't
et my money," she groused. "Dad fixed it so I can't. He's
ying to force me to come home."

"How can he do that?" Ryan wanted to know.

"His name is on everything of mine, even my trust fund.
don't get full control of that till I'm thirty."

"You've never established credit in your own name? No
ainy-day fund tucked away that your dad doesn't know
bout?"

"No. It never occurred to me to do that. All my financial
tuff was set up when I first went away to college, and I've
ever had reason to change it."

"Well…I guess that means you'll have to go home."

"No way," she said flatly. "He's playing dirty pool, and
at makes me even more determined not to knuckle under
him. I mean, I knew he could be underhanded and

sneaky, but not with me!'' But that wasn't strictly tru
He'd been lying to her for years about the drugs, mo
blatantly in recent months. He would tell her that he hadn
taken any pills in weeks, or that he'd lost the bottle
tranquilizers, left them in a hotel room, whatever.

She'd always seen through the lies, but she'd seldo
confronted him. He'd been trying to protect himself, h
addiction, which was what addicts did. What he was doi
to her now, however, was different. It was nasty, almo
malicious. He was trying to slap her down, bring her
heel, and he didn't care if he hurt her in the process.

At least that was how it seemed to her.

Ryan was studying her, his expression a mixture of co
cern, compassion, and something more, something sh
couldn't name. It was as if he were trying to put togeth
a puzzle, solve a brainteaser.

''Don't worry,'' she said. ''I won't be out on the stre
My sister will take me in until I figure out what to do.
won't keep sponging off you.''

''I wasn't worried about that. Come on, let's get out
this bank. I don't trust Miss Green Fingernails not to ca
everyone she knows and tell them you're here.''

Christine shivered. ''Is it almost time to go to the paw
shop?''

''Yeah, we can start heading over there.''

Easy Duzzit Pawn was only a few blocks from Pea
Street, where she'd been the last time Denny tried to acco
her. It was the same type of neighborhood, with boarde
up windows and not much activity. The few people wh
were walking around had the dead-eyed, hopeless look
the eternally impoverished. Even the children showed
excitement about life.

Ryan parked in front of the shop. ''We're a few minut
early. We can go in and browse, but don't ask about yo
jewelry until my friend Larry gets here.''

''Okay.''

She found the pawnshop fascinating—she'd never bee
inside one before. Here, you could buy every manner

electronic device, bicycles, household items, even movie videos, for what seemed like ridiculously low prices. She spotted an ultraexpensive vacuum cleaner. Her father had bought one for Connie, privately complaining that no vacuum cleaner should cost over a thousand dollars. The one here was priced at a hundred and seventy-five dollars.

"Where does all this stuff come from?" she asked Ryan.

"People bring it in as collateral for small loans. When they don't return with the money after a certain period of time, the stuff comes out on the floor with a price tag."

She wandered close to the jewelry cases, trying not to look too interested. "Oh, look at all the old wedding sets. How sad. Once upon a time, each of those rings belonged to some blushing bride-to-be. Do you think they come from divorces?"

"Mostly, I guess. I've heard a lot of merchandise at pawnshops is stolen, though."

"That's even sadder." At least she'd realized the huge mistake she was about to make with Robert *before* the wedding.

The bells on the pawnshop door jingled, and a tall, pale man with thinning hair entered, looking around. Ryan waved. "Hey, Larry. Over here." Then he motioned to the pawnshop's sole employee.

"Help you folks?" the clerk asked.

Chrissy knew the minute he opened his mouth that he was the one she'd talked to. "Yes, I spoke with you earlier about a two-carat engagement ring?"

The man looked down at the floor. "Ah. Funny thing about jewelry. It gets hot all of a sudden. Someone looks at a piece that's been sitting around in the case for months, gathering dust. If they don't buy it right then, everyone who comes in the shop wants to see it. It'll sell within twenty-four hours. You put a vibration on it—"

"Excuse me," Ryan said, "but what are you trying to tell us here?"

"I sold that set!" he said, his unlit cigar bobbing up and down with every word. "Not twenty minutes after I got off the phone with you, lady, a couple came in here, saw the ring and bought it right off. I couldn't exactly turn them down. I'd be crazy to turn away a sure sale of that much money. But, now, I have another ring you might like. The diamond's not quite so big, only a carat, but it's really special." He started going through his keys, trying to find the right one.

"I don't want another ring," Chrissy said hotly. "I wanted that one."

The broker looked at her quizzically. "How could you? You never even saw it!"

Larry broke in. "We have reason to believe the ring and earrings were stolen merchandise, originally belonging to this woman. I'm with the Metropolitan Police, theft division. Could I ask you a few questions about the jewelry?"

The man nearly dropped his cigar. "You're a cop? Honest, Officer, I didn't know that stuff was hot. A guy came in here with a sob story about his sick granny—you know the kind of thing I hear every day."

Ryan's friend Larry held up his hand. "We're not interested in prosecuting you, Mr., um…"

"Franklin, Deke Franklin."

"Mr. Franklin." The detective pulled a notebook from his jacket pocket. Ryan did, too. Christine knew she should stay and listen, but she didn't have the heart. Her jewelry had taken a hike, as Ryan had feared it might. There went her evidence. Maybe this Franklin character had smelled a fishy story and hidden the jewelry. If so, maybe Larry could get the guy to cough up her diamonds.

She wandered around the shop. There was a beat-up piano in the far corner. She sat down to play. Fumbling at first, because she hadn't played in years, she suddenly picked up the thread of a haunting melody she couldn't remember the name of. Some Bach thing, probably. It matched her mood.

She'd forgotten how pleasurable playing the piano could be. She closed her eyes, able to play by feel, and let the music wash over her.

When she finished, she found Ryan sitting beside her on the edge of the bench, watching her with acute intensity.

"How many years did you take lessons?" he asked.

"Nine, maybe ten. A long time."

He reached for the keyboard and struck a series of chords. "I took them for six. My mother made me. I was never as good as you are, though."

"I'm not good," she protested. "I'm rusty as an old barn-door hinge."

"Maybe so, but you have a feel for the music. You don't just play the notes, you…express them."

She laughed. "My teacher never said that. She said I was lazy and I didn't practice enough, that I abused my God-given talent by neglecting it." She wrinkled her nose. "I couldn't stand my teacher. Mrs. Toffler. I quit piano lessons as soon as I was allowed. But I did enjoy the playing," she said wistfully.

"Interest you folks in a piano?"

Christine jumped. Mr. Franklin, obviously none the worse for wear, even though Larry and Ryan had no doubt questioned him to within an inch of his life, stood behind them. "This one here has a wonderful sound. Stays tuned, too. Make a nice wedding present, Mr. Mulvaney, and it costs less than that two-carat ring. Bring you a lot of pleasure, especially given that the lady plays like an angel."

Christine found herself blushing—not due to the compliment, but because of the reference to her and Ryan and wedding presents all in one breath. Surely he hadn't jumped to the conclusion that she and Ryan were engaged, but then, she supposed they hadn't exactly explained why they were hanging around together.

"Thank you," she said, "but we're not really in the market for a piano."

"Well, if you ever are, come see me. Best prices in town."

They both thanked the pawnbroker, then headed out.

''Can you think of any more leads we can follow up?'' she asked as soon as they were in the car, seat belts fastened.

''I've about blown my wad. Unless—I really hate to ask you this, but is there any way you can get me in to see your father?''

Chapter 12

Christine's stomach churned. She didn't want to see or talk to her father until her feelings weren't so raw. She might do or say something she'd regret, something she couldn't ever take back. "Why don't you just call him?" she suggested hopefully.

"I tried that. At his office, at his home."

"You have his unlisted home number?" she asked in disbelief.

"Yup. Getting unlisted numbers is a snap if you know who to ask. Anyway, I didn't even get past the first line of defense. His policy is, he's not talking to reporters. He gave his official statement to the *Guardian* and one TV station, and that's all us vultures are getting."

Oh, why was her father being so obstinate? Was it because he had something to hide? Because he was afraid of what he might inadvertently reveal to a sharp reporter? Why didn't he come up with a reasonable story and stick to it, something he was eminently good at? By hiding under a rock like a snake, he was giving rise to all kinds of speculation. Christine had avoided looking at any TVs or newspapers since she saw her dad on the news last night, but from the way people reacted to her, she figured the coverage was massive and unflattering.

"I'll call Gerald, his secretary, and try and get you an appointment," she said.

"That'd be great."

"You don't have to be grateful," she said. "Chances are, if he refused once, he'll refuse again. Anyhow, I'm doing it for him, not you. I want him to explain himself in some fashion that won't make him sound like a coldhearted political machine."

"I'm afraid he sounds worse than that. You might tell him that he can't do himself much harm by talking to me. It's already pretty bad."

"Even without mentioning Michelle?" she asked cautiously.

"I didn't write about Michelle, because you were right—an illegitimate child from thirty years ago doesn't have anything to do with the current story. I didn't even mention it to Fran."

"Thank you, Ryan." Her personal pendulum was swinging toward adoration again. He could charm the socks off an earthworm. "What about Dad's drug problem? Is that in the story?"

He worried his lower lip with his teeth. "I haven't decided about that one, yet. It seems to fit into the big picture, though. Without it, some things don't make sense."

Christine sighed. She supposed she'd known all along that the drug-addiction problem would come out sooner or later. Maybe she'd even secretly hoped Ryan would be the one to reveal it. She was tired of carrying the burden of such a secret on her shoulders.

"Where's your cell phone?" she asked abruptly. Might as well get this over with.

"Right here." He reached under his seat and retrieved a leather case, which he handed to her.

She pulled the phone out of the case, switched it on, dialed her father's private number...and put the call through. Her hand was shaking. It was just Dad, she tried to tell herself, but that didn't work. "Dad" had become someone she didn't know.

"Greenlow residence," Gerald's wary voice announced.

"Gerald? Hi, it's Christine."

"Christine." He sounded cool. Gerald had always been friendly toward her, if a bit reserved. Had her father turned him against her? "Your father's not here. He's at his office."

"That's all right. It's you I wanted to speak to, anyway."

"Me?"

"Yes. There's a reporter who wants to interview Dad—"

"Senator Greenlow isn't speaking with reporters," Gerald said in a way that made Christine think he'd repeated the same sentence a dozen times that day.

"Let me explain," Christine said patiently. "I think Dad will want to talk to this particular reporter. He's been working on an in-depth story about my kidnapping and Dad's role in it, and things look pretty bad for the senator. If he hides behind his no-comment smoke screen, it'll look as if he really does have something to hide."

She paused, letting Gerald digest her request.

"Did it ever occur to you, Christine, that he might just *have* some things to hide? This little stunt of yours will ruin his whole career—"

"No, Gerald, listen to me. This was no stunt. I was kidnapped by these radical environmental guys. Dad chose to believe the kidnapping was a fake. I'm sure he had valid reasons, but he needs to explain to the public what those reasons were. Otherwise, people are going to think he didn't even care whether I lived or died." She said this as casually as she dared—as if *she* didn't doubt his love, but others might.

There was another pause. Christine crossed her fingers, hoping that Gerald would see reason. If he agreed to schedule an interview, her father would probably go along with it. Gerald had been his secretary for more than ten years, and her father trusted him implicitly.

"What exactly does this reporter want to ask? Could I approve the questions ahead of time?"

"Um, I don't know. Let me ask." She turned to Ryan. "Can Gerald approve the questions ahead of time?"

Ryan seemed to be thinking hard about that. Was this one of those things that reporters didn't do, she wondered, like allowing a source to read a story before it was published?

"All right," he finally said. "I'll give him a list of my questions. I reserve the right to ask all of them, but if there are any the senator doesn't want to address, he can simply say, 'No comment,' and I'll move on."

Christine relayed Ryan's answer to Gerald.

"I suppose there's no way out of this," Gerald finally said. "I can give this reporter fifteen minutes, either Thursday morning at seven, or Friday—"

"Oh, no, Gerald, it has to be tonight," she said. "He's got a deadline."

"There is absolutely no way—"

"Then the story will go to press as it is," she said. "Come on, Gerald, you can always fit fifteen minutes in here or there."

"Then have the jerk here at six tonight," he said, with very un-Gerald-like rudeness. "He might have to interview the senator while he's dressing for the opera this evening." He hung up with a haughty sniff.

"Six o'clock tonight," she told Ryan.

He smiled. "Great. You'll come with me?"

"No. I'll get you through the front gates. The rest is up to you. And, Ryan..."

"Yes?"

"Give him a chance to explain, to make you understand. I won you over. Maybe he can, too."

It was doubtful Senator Stan Greenlow could win him over, Ryan thought as he cooled his heels in an over-decorated anteroom in the Greenlow mansion, waiting for the great man to make an appearance. The man had ignored a ransom demand for his daughter, and that was impossible to justify, in Ryan's mind. Sure, he would claim he'd believed the whole thing was a hoax, but hadn't he considered the possibility that he could be wrong? Shouldn't he have notified the police, just in case? Instead, he'd just turned a deaf ear to the men who threatened to kill his daughter.

There had to be a reason. And Ryan was determined to find out what it was.

Finally the senator made an appearance, resplendent in evening wear. He was still a handsome man at fifty-two, one of those guys who had eased into middle age gracefully, with thick, silvering hair and laugh lines around his eyes.

But there were subtle signs of dissipation, too—a certain floridness in his face, a slight paunch, not quite masked by his cummerbund, a nervous tic on the right side of his face.

He appeared clear, though, and plenty alert—not tranquilized.

"Good evening, Senator Greenlow," Ryan said, with all the politeness he could muster. "Thank you for seeing me."

"Apparently my daughter convinced my secretary that I should," Stan said, quickly shaking Ryan's proffered hand, then dropping it as if it were a snake that might bite. "You're…in contact with her? Is she really all right?"

Ryan resisted making the bruising comeback that was on his lips. Like, Why are you showing concern *now?* "She's alive and healthy," Ryan said. "But she's having to rely on strangers. For some reason, the assets in her bank accounts have been frozen."

"Oh, I did that," Greenlow said dismissively. "There are few ways a man has control over his grown-up daughter. Money is one of them."

"It hasn't changed her mind, you know. She's still not coming home."

"Is this what you're here for?" Stan said suspiciously. "To torment me with groundless threats from Christine?"

"No. I'm here to get some answers to a few questions.

You saw the questions earlier. Is there any area you'd like to start with?''

"Yeah. Where'd you get your information?"

"You should know better than to ask a reporter that question. But I will tell you that Christine supplied me with a lot of the facts, and I have every reason to believe she's been telling me the truth."

"That girl wouldn't know the truth if it bit her in the butt. She's lied to you, just like she has to everyone else."

Ryan hadn't expected such open animosity from Greenlow. "So you're denying you have a problem with abusing prescription tranquilizers?"

"Unequivocally. I don't even take tranquilizers."

Okay. Ryan would return to that question later. "Let's just work our way down the list of questions, then." Without waiting for agreement, he added, "Why didn't you pay the ransom that was demanded for the safe return of your daughter?"

"There was no ransom demand."

"The phone company verifies that three phone calls from a cellular phone were made to your private line—one on the evening your daughter disappeared, two the next day. Can you explain who made the calls?"

"I don't remember. It could have been anyone. I don't keep a phone log for that line, as it's used for personal calls only. But almost everybody has a cell phone these days."

Fair enough, Ryan thought. A nice, pat answer. And he didn't believe it for a second. Ryan switched tactics. He took out his notes and read from them, detailing seven separate occasions in recent history when Stan Greenlow had voted against environmental concerns. "Can you sum up your views on protecting the environment?"

"I'm a probusiness person," he said. "Like everyone else, I think it would be nice to clean up the air and water and leave the spotted owls alone, but not at the expense of business. American business is what makes this country strong, it's what keeps food on our tables. I believe in letting business self-regulate. Americans need less government interference.''

Good answer, Ryan thought. What clever PR person thought that one up? ''When your daughter called you around noon yesterday, what did she tell you?''

''She told me she was safe, that there'd been no kidnapping, that it was all a mistake and not to worry.''

''And your response?''

''I was angry with her for trying to manipulate me, naturally. I'm afraid I lost my temper. Do you have children, Mr. Mulvaney?''

An image flashed through his mind of golden-haired babies who looked like their mother. Like Chrissy. Alarmed at his turn of thoughts, he shook his head to clear it. Where had *that* come from? ''No, sir, I don't.''

''Well, if you did, you'd know that they try your patience sometimes, even after they're grown. Christine has always had me wrapped around her little finger. I've been that way since she was born. She uses it to her advantage sometimes, but this will not be one of those times. You can tell her that, since you're apparently…close to her.''

''She doesn't want anything from you, except the truth,'' Ryan said slowly, succinctly. ''Those ransom demands were made. I know that's true. *Why didn't you respond?*''

''I've already answered that question. You're violating our agreement by harping on the same question. So either we move on to a new subject, or this interview is over.'' He said this with little emotion, not even raising his voice—as if he knew he had the advantage here.

So far he did, Ryan thought as he struggled to get his temper under control. But he wasn't done yet.

He went through a few more routine questions, double-checking small but significant things Chrissy had told him. Greenlow answered, looking at his watch more and more frequently. Ryan decided he'd better go for the jugular before he was kicked out and missed his chance.

''About those tranquilizers. I interviewed a certain pharmacist who swears—anonymously, of course—that you have a long-standing prescription for a drug called Sulvenaze, which you have refilled every couple of weeks, fifty tablets at a time. Do you still want to stick by your story that you don't take tranquilizers?''

Finally, Ryan had silenced the senator. He stood there swallowing, licking his lips, his eyes darting around as if he expected his guardian angel to swoop down and save him. Eventually he found some words.

"If a pharmacist told you that, he was lying. And if you print one word about tranquilizers, I will sue—you and whatever rag you write for. I have very deep pockets, Mr. Mulvaney. Even if you believe you're correct, even if you think you can beat me, defending such a suit costs a lot of money. You'll run out before I do. Think about it.'' With that parting shot, he swept out of the room.

The threat made Ryan break out in a cold sweat. No reporter wanted to face a libel suit. But he wouldn't back down now. He'd seen the fear in Stan Greenlow's eyes; he'd even smelled it. Thank goodness he'd thought to ask Chrissy the name of the pharmacy her family used, and lucky for him there'd been a chatty pharmacist on duty. The pharmacist had been all too willing to dish with him, sling a little mud on the senator, so long as she could remain anonymous.

Greenlow had stood strong with his story about there being no ransom demand. The story sounded feasible—until such time as the kidnappers were caught and they revealed that they had, in fact, called the senator from a stolen cellular phone, using the number extracted from Christine.

Then ol' Stan would look like the lying son of a bitch he was. Ryan only wished he could figure out why Stan had been so eager to keep the kidnappers' identities a secret from the rest of the world. What was he hiding?

Ryan gathered his things, preparing to leave. The door to the anteroom opened a crack, and he expected to see Gerald, nose in the air, ready to throw him out into the street. Instead, a tiny woman appeared in the doorway, looking roughly the same age as his great-grandmother Donnelly. She had snow-white hair pinned into a tight bun on the very top of her skull, pulling tight the wrinkles that would otherwise have been in her forehead. She had wrinkles everywhere else, very thick glasses, and a stoop to her walk that made Ryan believe she'd spent too many years leaned over, scrubbing floors or toilets.

Behind the glasses, however, her unblinking blue eyes appeared sharp. "Mr. Mulvaney?"

"Yes?"

"I'm Connie, Christine's maid. She called a while ago and asked me to pass along a few things for her."

Ryan had been there when Christine called. He'd been so consumed with thoughts of the senator and his come-uppance that he'd forgotten all about seeking out Connie. Thank goodness the wizened little maid had decided to find him instead. She held out a brocade-patterned traveling bag.

Ryan took it. "Thank you, Connie. Do you have a few minutes to talk to me?"

Christine had said not to bother, that the staff was trained never to talk to the press, under penalty of termination.

"Oh, yes, I'd love to talk to you," Connie said eagerly, coming fully inside the room and closing the door.

Ryan could only hope Gerald was occupied elsewhere and wouldn't find them here.

"Can you tell me about Christine?" Connie asked. "Is she really all right? She sounds so...so strange on the phone, almost like a completely different person. This isn't like her at all, you know. She's never gone against the wishes of her father, though sometimes I wish she would."

"She's really fine," Ryan reassured Connie, his heart going out to the older woman. From what Chrissy had told him, Connie had been like a grandmother to her, serving as her nanny from the time she was a newborn just home from the hospital. "Staying away from home right now is something she feels she has to do."

"I understand. Ties that are too tight can strangle. I've tried to tell Senator Greenlow that many a time."

"Then you feel like his control over her has been too tight?"

"Oh, much. They clung to each other after the missus passed on, and that was good. But while she recovered from her grief and got back on her feet, the senator never quite recovered. He continued to…to *need* Christine long after he should have encouraged her to live her own life. He never should have made her come home from college. She was thriving so during that brief time. She would come home for breaks from school looking so happy, singing like a bird, hugging everyone."

She'd been in love, Ryan thought. Chrissy had told him about her brief, intense affair with somebody named Doug. Someone Ryan despised sight unseen. The oaf probably hadn't properly appreciated the gift he'd been given, not the way Ryan would if he and Chrissy—

There he went again, fantasizing about something he could never have. He'd missed Connie's last few words, and she was possibly the best source he would talk to.

"She was so sad, like a little wet sparrow," Connie was saying.

"I'm sorry, what?"

"Just that she wasn't the same after she came home from college for good. That's when I knew things were wrong, but no one would listen to me, not His Majesty, not my princess, either. Who am I, after all? Just the maid."

Princess, Ryan thought with a smile. So he and Fran weren't the only ones to use that nickname. "Some people can't learn things by having people tell them," he said. "They have to discover things through experience, make their own mistakes. I think Chrissy—Christine—has figured things out now."

"I hope so. But she's so inexperienced. Being completely on her own for the first time ever will be so hard for her. Could she even get a job?"

"She said she would go to her cousin Michelle's for help and support," Ryan said, still trying to reassure the older woman.

"Oh, I should have known," Connie said. "Of course Michelle would be the one to help her." She smiled fondly. "You shoulda seen those two when they were little girls, as alike as two peas in a pod, though of course there are quite a few years' difference in age."

"Seven, I think Christine told me."

"You must be close to her, then, if she told you about Michelle."

He wanted to answer in the affirmative. But he could hardly call his and Chrissy's relationship "close," despite the fact that they'd spent the past two days together. He was spending time with her out of professional necessity. She was spending time with him because she needed him temporarily.

It occurred to him then that perhaps Connie didn't even know he was a reporter. She was being awfully forthcoming. A few days ago, he might have readily taken advantage of the situation. But now he thought of Chrissy, and what she would think when she read quotes from her maid, quotes acquired through deception.

"Connie, did you know I'm a reporter?"

Her eyebrows flew up. "Why, no. I figured if the senator was talking to you, you couldn't be."

"I am. I'll consider your previous comments off the record. But if there's anything you'd like to add...?" he asked hopefully.

She pursed her lips, folded her arms. "I've said too much already. But I will add one thing. What you people are putting on the news isn't right. I might lose my job over this, and heaven knows what a woman my age would do out on the street, but Christine *was* kidnapped. I saw out the window—two men, putting a large object into their truck. I didn't think much of it until later, when we all realized Christine was missing." Connie covered her face. "Oh, now I've stepped in it. I can see why the senator doesn't like us talking to reporters. Sometimes things just fly out of my mouth without any forethought."

"I appreciate your candidness, Connie," Ryan said, flipping off his recorder. He already knew that if he used Connie's information, he would do it in such a way that she wouldn't get into trouble.

The door flew open. Gerald stood there, almost snorting. "What are you still doing here? I thought the senator escorted you out." His gaze narrowed when he saw the little maid, who was trying to make herself invisible. "Connie! You know better than to speak to—"

"Oh, pipe down, Gerald," she said, straightening to her full four-foot-eleven or thereabouts. "This young man is trying to help our Christine get out of the pickle she's in."

"He's trying to hang the senator!"

"Perhaps he can't do one without the other," Connie sniffed, slipping by an outraged Gerald.

And that, Ryan thought as he left the Greenlow residence, was the crux of the matter. No matter what he wrote, he would hurt Christine. He was almost tempted to give some other reporter the information he had, let some other schmuck make Greenlow look like a criminal. But the story was his. It had fallen into his lap. He almost felt like it was his solemn duty to follow through.

Christine awoke the next morning cranky and sore. An old recliner in Fran's living room had served as her bed. Not only had she been hideously uncomfortable from the chair's lumps and bumps and the odd spring poking out, but she'd had to deal with Ryan sleeping on the couch, not six feet from her. His every movement, his every sigh in his sleep, had made her keenly aware of his manly presence and the fact that she wanted, more than anything, to curl up next to him.

She might have, too, if it hadn't been for the knowledge that Fran could walk in on them anytime. And maybe that was a good thing.

They'd opted for Fran's living room instead of a hotel. It had just seemed easier, since Christine had been hiding out there during Ryan's interview with her father, and it saved Ryan money, too. This story, he'd said, would end up costing him, instead of paying off, if he wasn't careful.

At least she had her things. Bless Connie for packing up a bag for her. She had her toiletries, her purse and wallet, which contained her driver's license, credit cards, and more than a hundred dollars in cash, several changes of clothes—separated with tissue paper in the old-fashioned way Connie liked to pack—and a modest white ruffled nightgown.

Ryan's clothes had served their purpose, but Christine looked forward to returning them to him. Today her association with him would terminate. He would take her to Michelle's and finish his story, and that would be that.

Ryan was still sleeping. He'd stayed up late last night, polishing his story, making phone calls to double-check facts. He'd even gotten Lieutenant Brich on the line. Apparently she'd taken some heat for her cavalier treatment of Christine, and she was eager to tell her side of the story.

Fran had stayed up, also, reading copy, offering suggestions. The familiarity between them, the gentle teasing, had placed them in a club that Christine had felt excluded from. She'd gone to bed early.

Now she stretched and climbed out of the recliner, her gaze never leaving Ryan. He had a blanket thrown over him, but in his sleep he'd twisted it around until it didn't cover much but his knees. He was wearing nothing but a skimpy pair of gym shorts. Christine stared, unabashedly drinking in the sight of his almost naked form.

She would miss him. She'd never known anyone quite like him. She remembered the way he'd faced that scumbag with the gun to save her, and she grew warm all over. Of course, he'd done a few less honorable things, too—lied to her, manipulated her. But she couldn't seem to hold a grudge against him. After all, she'd lied to him, too. Everybody lied once in a while—not maliciously, but to suit their own purposes.

She fervently hoped that would prove to be the case with

her father. Ryan had been annoyingly tight-lipped last night, when he returned from the interview.

Apparently Fran wasn't up yet, either, so Christine grabbed a shower. Since she had time to kill, she reveled in using her own things—lotions, powders, scent. She even put on a touch of makeup, then her favorite pair of faded jeans and a crisp long-sleeved cotton shirt with a pattern of pale roses on it. She dried her hair and curled the ends with the curling iron, feeling more feminine than she had in a long time.

Someone banged on the door. "Hurry up, Princess. There might be other people who need the bathroom."

Christine refused to let Fran ruffle her feathers. She stuffed her things into her bag, taking her time, then opened the door. "If you needed to get in here earlier," she said mildly to a bedraggled Fran, "you could have knocked. I thought everyone was still asleep."

"Yeah, well, I'm awake. You might go in there and wake Prince Charming, if you two want to get on the road at any reasonable hour." She brushed past Christine into the bathroom and slammed the door.

"Fran's not a morning person," Ryan explained. He was standing by the sofa, the blanket wrapped carelessly around him.

And he would know, wouldn't he? "Oh, she doesn't bother me," Christine said breezily, determined not to let any petty jealousies spoil her mood. Today she was going to see Michelle. Her sister would help her through this mess. No matter what awful things Ryan decided to put in his story, Michelle wouldn't judge Christine for it. She probably wouldn't judge their father, either. She'd always been completely accepting of the fact that her biological father didn't publicly claim her. She'd seemed to understand, and they'd always shared a cordial, if not a close, relationship.

Maybe Michelle would be able to help Christine forgive.

"I started some coffee," Ryan said, "and the paper's on the kitchen table, but I'll warn you it's not pretty."

Ryan seemed to feel completely at home here, Christine thought, again battling her jealousy. It was irrational. She could not have Ryan Mulvaney, so jealousy was a useless emotion.

And why can't you have him? a little voice inside her asked.

"Because," she murmured. They had nothing in common other than raging physical attraction. He was a working-class reporter living on the edge, and she was an heiress. They had no possible use for one another once this article was finished.

Chapter 13

"Did you say something?" Ryan asked.

"No," she snapped, wondering why she suddenly felt so antagonistic, so irritated.

"Did I say something wrong?" He held out his arms in a helpless entreaty.

"No," she repeated, her voice carefully modulated, as she went into the kitchen. She sat down at the table and searched the front page for the story she knew would be there. There: Greenlow Denies Kidnapping. Then, in the subhead: Police Can't Confirm Daughter's Hostage Claims.

She read the first few paragraphs, then shoved the paper away, unable to stomach the rest of the story. It wasn't as if she'd expected anything more complimentary to surface in the *Guardian*.

"Don't worry," Ryan said as he poured himself a cup of coffee. "You'll be vindicated."

"And my father will be toast," she said glumly. "What if I told you now that Dad was right? It was all a hoax?"

Ryan froze, and stared at her for long enough that she knew she'd startled him with an intriguing possibility. Then he relaxed. "I'd think you were trying to protect your old man. Noble, but in no way believable. I talked to Connie last night."

"Connie? She actually spoke with you?"

"At length."

"Oh, Ryan, you didn't trick her into talking, did you? She can be so naive—"

"Relax. I told her exactly who I was. She wanted to talk, even if it meant jeopardizing her job. She cares for you a great deal, and she can't stand the thought that everybody thinks you played a great big practical joke."

"Oh, Ryan, you won't quote her, will you? If Dad finds out she talked to you, he will fire her, never mind that she's been on our payroll for almost sixty years."

"I won't get her fired," he said, sounding absolutely certain. He sipped his coffee. "Mmm…good Colombian."

Christine realized she'd unconsciously been waiting for someone to serve her. She got up, searched the cabinets until she found a mug with a film company logo on it and poured herself a cup. It was good.

She saw the lipstick prints she left on the cup and realized Ryan hadn't even noticed the care she'd taken with her appearance this morning. Well, heck, what did men know, anyway? "How soon can we leave for Raleigh?"

He rubbed his face. "I'm going to fax my story this morning."

"You mean you're done?"

"Yeah." He continued, but seemed reluctant. "I found the missing link last night, Chrissy. While you were asleep. I'd been fooling around with some Internet stuff yesterday. A guy e-mailed me 'cause he heard I was wanting information about NATURE. This guy is a member of the group—not one of your kidnappers, apparently, but he'd heard all about it. And he told me why you and your father were targets."

She was afraid to ask, but she had to know. "Why?"

"The senator was taking kickbacks from chemical companies. NATURE had already tried blackmail to get money from him. When that didn't work, they decided to up the ante.''

Ryan hated what he'd just done. But better that she hear it from him, someone who cared for her, than from some newspaper or on television.

Chrissy looked utterly crushed. ''Are you sure about this? I mean, he accepts PAC money from big-business interests, and they're often antienvironmental, but—''

''This was a lot of money, Chrissy. And it was from one chemical company in particular, not a PAC. It's no wonder he didn't want to advertise that NATURE had kidnapped you. He couldn't afford for anyone to look too closely into his campaign accounting.''

''Have you verified this information?'' Chrissy asked. ''I mean, let's face it, these NATURE guys aren't exactly the souls of honesty, not from my experience.''

''I'll be making some phone calls this morning,'' he said. But he knew in his gut what he would find out. The story had the ring of truth about it. It was the last detail that made sense of everything else. So simple he should have guessed it.

Kickbacks. Blackmail.

''Chrissy,'' he said, standing behind her, with both hands on her shoulders, ''there's nothing you can do to save him. All you can do is save yourself.''

''I should be with him,'' she said. ''No matter what he's done, I still love him.''

''Of course you do.'' No one should expect Chrissy to forever turn her back on the man who'd raised her, who'd given her everything, made her what she was. But it nauseated him to think of a man like Greenlow being the recipient of Chrissy's continued moral support, her unconditional love. He didn't deserve that, not after he tried to sacrifice her in the name of saving his political career.

''I'll take you back to him, anytime you want,'' he said, praying she wouldn't accept his offer. She ought to go to er sister's and chill out, at least until she'd had time to assimilate all that had happened.

Her face turned hard. "Oh, sure. Our reunion would make a touching epilogue to your story."

Her unfounded suspicions cut him to the heart. He hadn't even been thinking about his story. He had enough to win him a goddamn Pulitzer without milking Christine for any more emotional punch. "Call a cab, then," he said bitterly. "I'll even pay for it."

Silence. Then: "No, I think not. I'll stick to our original agreement. That is, unless you've decided to welsh."

"No, I'll do my part." He ground out the words, dumping the rest of his coffee down the sink. It had lost its appeal. "I have to make my calls first, though. Why don't you make yourself useful and go out and buy us some bagels? There's a bakery around the corner."

Chrissy stared at him like a wounded fawn. "I can't."

"Why not?" He was feeling the first prickles of guilt over his treatment of her.

"I'm afraid." She barely mumbled the words. Then she looked up at him, her eyes blazing. "Look, I know we haven't seen Denny in a while, but he's still out there somewhere. What if someone from NATURE was watching my dad's house? They could have followed you, and now they're just waiting for a chance to—"

"Oh, Chrissy." How could he have forgotten the danger? Before he knew what he was doing, he'd tugged her out of her chair and into his arms. "I wouldn't purposely put you at risk, ever. I'm sorry. I'd forgotten about Denny. Of course you can't go out alone, not till those bastards are behind bars."

He hugged her to him. She was stiff and unyielding at first, but her wiggles of attempted escape only made him hold on to her more tightly. He wasn't letting her go until she believed him. He did care for her. He didn't want to hurt her.

Eventually she stopped struggling and relaxed.

"There, that's better," he said. "I...I don't want anything to happen to you, ever." Lord, she smelled good this morning, like freshly cut roses and rain. Her skin, her hair, even her breath—

No, he wouldn't kiss her again. Hadn't he used her enough?

Apparently he wasn't getting through to her. "You can let me go now, Ryan. Please."

He did, though reluctantly.

She reclaimed her chair, straightened her blouse, took a sip of her coffee, all without looking at him. "I don't think you're a bad person, Ryan. You're performing a job. You've treated me very decently, even kindly most of the time, and for that I'm grateful. I don't know what would have become of me if you hadn't interceded. But I don't kid myself that you actually *like* me. People like you and Fran, you laugh at people like me, and maybe rightly so. I can see now that it was probably silly of me to get all gussied up with makeup and perfume, when I have no place to go, nobody to impress."

"There's me," he said, aching for her, wondering if her wealth and status in life had always put people off, separated her from her peers. "I noticed, and I'm impressed."

"Yeah, sure," she said dejectedly. "I feel like everything I do, I'm just giving you more ammunition for your story. 'Princess Christine couldn't wait to get her hands on her makeup case. Even when she's sleeping in a recliner, she wears a prissy nightgown that someone starched and ironed.'"

He'd noticed the nightgown, all right, but he hadn't thought of it as prissy. More like sexy, in a virginal sort of way. He'd fantasized for hours about how he would get underneath all those ruffles and flounces.

How could he make her understand that he wasn't out to exploit her? In the story's latest evolution, he'd taken out almost all the personal details that didn't relate strictly to the kidnapping or her dealings with her father.

He could let her read it, of course, and see for herself that he wasn't taking advantage of the fact that they'd been practically on top of each other for the past couple of days. But he resisted the temptation. When he'd faxed the story off and it was gone—then, maybe, he would show it to her.

The phone rang. He tensed as the sound was cut off midway through the second ring. Apparently Fran had caught it on another extension. That meant she was out of the bathroom, he hoped. He felt grubby next to the pristine Chrissy, and he desperately needed a shower.

"Ryan?" Fran called from the bedroom. "Can you pick up the extension, please? It's the managing editor from *Primus*. He wants to talk to you about the story."

Ryan swallowed. He wished he could talk without Chrissy sitting two feet from him.

"I'll step outside," Chrissy said, as if he'd broadcast his wishes over a loudspeaker. A door from the kitchen led to a back staircase with a roomy landing. She went out and closed the door firmly.

Ryan picked up the kitchen phone, though in his mind he'd followed Chrissy outside. "Ryan Mulvaney."

"Ryan! Bruce Garlock, *Primus*. Holy cow, those pictures are dynamite! How did you do it? Where is she now? Who's that guy she's kissing?"

Fran broke in. "Ryan, I told him there was a problem with that particular photo."

"Problem? What problem?" Bruce asked in a manic voice.

"You can't use it," Ryan said, praying Fran would back him up. "It was sent by mistake. It has nothing to do with the story I'm writing. As for the guy, it's me."

"Oh." Bruce sounded suddenly deflated. "That does shed a different light on things. So? What about this story?"

"It's a different sort of dynamite."

"Christine Greenlow on a plate?" Bruce asked hopefully.

"Better. Senator Stan Greenlow on a plate."

"Oooh, I like the sound of that. Bad enough to lose him the election?"

"Bad enough to lose him *any* election, for the rest of his life." He could almost see Garlock, the opportunistic little rodent, licking his lips.

"So, what's the E.T.A. of this little gem?"

"Late this afternoon. I was given a juicy tidbit late last night, and I need to confirm the details this morning."

"That's cutting it a little close, Mulvaney."

"Believe me, it'll be worth a late night."

"All right. I want to see it by four o'clock. And I'm faxing you both our brief contract. Sign it, fax it, then over-night-mail the original. First North American rights, and as far as the money goes—"

"I want twice the original figure you quoted," Ryan said without blinking.

"Ryan!" Fran scolded, an edge of panic in her voice.

"It's a much more valuable story than the one we first discussed," Ryan continued calmly. "And there are expenses. Hotel rooms, gas, not to mention a new lock for my back door after the terrorist broke in." That ought to whet ol' Garlock's appetite.

"If I can get that amount approved," Garlock said, slightly more cool than before, "you'll both have contracts within the hour." He hung up.

"Damn, Mulvaney!" Fran called to him from the other room. "You trying to put the kibosh on the whole deal, or not?"

"I'll get what I asked for," he called back. And at least he had some good news to tell Chrissy. He opened the kitchen door. She was leaning against the balcony railing, her face to the morning sun. For a moment, he just drank in her beauty, hesitant to disturb her.

Fran came up behind Ryan and opened the door wider. "Hey, Princess," she called, jarring Chrissy from her reverie. "We got semigood news."

"What?"

Instead of calling her inside, Ryan went out to stand with her in her patch of sunlight. "*Primus* isn't going to run the kiss picture."

She brightened slightly. "That's something, at least, though I suppose at this point the fact that I kissed some guy at the zoo is the least of my worries."

Ryan inwardly bristled at being referred to as "some guy." Was that all it meant to her? "I have a deadline of four o'clock for the story, but I'll be done before then, and we can leave for Raleigh," he said coolly.

"Okay." She looked over at Fran. "Will you come with me to buy some bagels?"

"No," Ryan said. He looked at Fran. "I don't think she should leave the apartment."

"No problem," Fran said. "The grocery store down the block delivers. I'll call and order us some provisions, including bagels."

Chrissy smiled at Fran, a little sadly. "Thanks, Fran. I'll pay for the groceries. I have a little money now."

Fran waved away the offer. "Keep it. You might need it."

As Ryan made his calls and put the finishing touches on his masterpiece, Christine sat in the living room and pondered her fate. First she would take shelter with Michelle; then, she decided, her first priority would be to force her father into treatment for his drug addiction. Now would be her best chance to get him to agree, when he no longer had a reputation to protect, and thus had nothing to lose.

She would have to deal with Robert, too, but that could be accomplished with a succinct phone call. He didn't even deserve a face-to-face meeting.

Then would come the really hard part—deciding what to do with her life. She would like to finish school but had no idea where she would get the tuition. Realistically, she supposed, she would have to find a job and save money for college.

"Hey, maybe I could join the army," she said to Ryan as he walked by her, toward the kitchen, with his empty coffee cup. "I could learn a useful skill, and they'd give me money for college, just like it says on the TV ads."

Ryan gave her an indulgent smile. "You wouldn't look good in camouflage."

She frowned back at him. This princess image of her had to go. She was *not* some delicate hothouse flower. She was strong and brave and intelligent and capable, and soon she would also be self-sufficient. Then she would show Ryan that she wasn't so different from him, other than in the obvious male-female ways.

She realized, then, that she was contemplating some kind of future in Washington, a future that included Ryan. And why not? Once this nasty business was over and people had stopped talking about it, both of their lives would have to resume some sort of normalcy. They could start over, pretend none of this had ever happened.

Except it had, and it would forever mark them.

"I'm done," Ryan announced.

"Hmm?" Christine had been so deep in her thoughts she hadn't realized how much time had passed. It was early afternoon.

"I just faxed the story off. We can start out for Raleigh now."

"Oh. Oh, good." Should she congratulate him or something? She decided that wasn't necessary. "My things are packed. We can leave whenever."

He looked at her quizzically. "You're not curious about the story? I'll let you read it now, if you want, as long as you promise not to call *Primus* and threaten to sue or anything."

She shook her head. She was sick to death of thinking about this story, and now she was simply relieved that it was done. She could move on to something else. "Let's just go, okay?"

Chrissy made yet another call to her half sister. Ryan didn't even bother to listen in this time. Then he and Chrissy said their goodbyes to Fran and thanked her for her hospitality.

"You're easy houseguests," she said. "And, Christine, despite all my teasing, I think you're a pretty good sport

Don't hold a grudge, okay? Come back and visit any time. You can show me how you do that funky braid.''

Christine reached up and touched her hair self-consciously. While she was sitting around with nothing to do, she'd done a four-stranded French braid to her hair—something she'd learned in the dorm at college.

"Okay, I will," Christine replied, lifting her chin a notch. She didn't think Fran was making fun of her this time. "As soon as I get settled someplace, I'll give you a call."

Ryan, she noticed, did not issue any similar invitation. She decided she might have to work a little harder where he was concerned.

"Oh, Ryan, the contract from *Primus*," Fran said. "You haven't faxed yours in yet. Want me to do it for you? I can fax it, then overnight it with mine."

"Um, no, that's okay," he said. "It's mixed up here with my notes and stuff. I'll stop at the first post office I see and overnight it."

She shrugged. "Okay. If you say so." She closed the door, giving Ryan one last, speculative stare.

"I talked to your father again this morning," Ryan said to Christine as they walked to the car.

"Really? Did you confront him with the kickback stuff?"

"Yeah. I had to at least attempt to get his side."

"And what did he say?"

Ryan sighed. "He denied it, of course. Threatened all kinds of ugly things, but no threats I haven't faced before."

"Oh, dear." She wondered again whether she ought to give in to her father's manipulation and go home. Someone would need to be with him when the manure hit the fan. She could always leave later. Before, she'd worried about whether she would have the strength to leave when she was facing him head-on. Now she was sure she would. She'd grown stronger in the past few days, more confident.

"Maybe I should see him," she ventured.

"Um, I don't think that would be such a good idea."

"Really?" Earlier, he'd been all for Christine and he father making a reconciliation. "Why not?"

"He's looking for a scapegoat to blame his problems or Right now, it's you."

"Really?" she said again.

"He's very angry at you for cooperating with the polic with the press. He's still convinced you somehow orche trated this whole series of events. But if it's any consola tion, there's no doubt in my mind that he still doesn't be lieve you were really kidnapped. He thinks it was a hoa one you instigated. So he wasn't willing to risk your li for the sake of protecting his secrets."

That was something, at least. But having her own fath believe she would do something this hurtful was painfu enough.

"To Raleigh, then."

Soon they were on I-95, heading south out of town, an a heady sense of anticipation overtook Christine. The sta of turgidity she'd been in for the past three days was givin way to action, and it felt good. The miles flew by wit incredible speed. They would reach Raleigh before dark.

And then she would say goodbye to Ryan.

She tried not to be depressed by the thought. She sti had some things to look forward to, even if the next fe days would not be very pretty.

"When does *Primus* come out?" she asked Ryan.

"Friday."

She had two days before all hell broke loose. "What ar you going to do?" she couldn't help asking.

He shrugged. "I think I'll visit my sister. We've bee sort of out of touch lately. Then, I don't know, I'll do wh. I always do. Try to hustle some work."

"What will you do with the money you get from *Pr mus?*"

"Mmm… Live on it. Pay bills. Buy some new hubcaps.

"You'll let me know how my blood test came out? gave you Michelle's phone number, right?"

"Yes, on both counts. Garlock has said he'll publish the results as an addendum. You getting hungry?"

"Always," she said, smiling. Her appetite was their private joke.

"We're not too far from Emporia, where Josette lives. I know this really good café—it's called Southern Fried Hospitality. Great catfish, hush puppies. It's a little bit out of our way. You game?"

"Sure." She'd vote for anything that would give her a few more minutes with him. Oh, Lord, was she really that besotted? She was afraid she was.

They'd already come through Richmond, nearing the North Carolina border. Ryan took an exit off the interstate, onto a much smaller highway. The countryside was more accessible, and Christine drank in the soothing sights of grazing sheep on rolling green hills. The traffic had disappeared.

All except for one car, behind them.

Christine turned around to have a better look. "Ryan?" That was all the warning she was able to get out before the Corvette's back window shattered in an explosion of broken glass.

"Get down!" Ryan's first instinct was to protect Chrissy. He grabbed her by the back of the neck and pushed her down with one hand, desperately trying to keep his car on the road and slam down on the accelerator all at the same time.

He could see the car clearly now through the gaping hole that used to be his back window. It was the red Firebird, nearly bumper-to-bumper with him, an assault rifle aimed out the driver's window.

He wasn't sure how Denny had found them. Maybe he'd been following them all along, waiting for an opportunity to get them isolated. At any rate, he'd raised the odds in his favor considerably with the big gun. Either he planned to take out Ryan and grab Chrissy, or he meant to kill them both. Maybe he was a total loose cannon, and the frustration of his failure to recapture Chrissy had sent him off th deep end.

Ryan began to widen the gap between the two cars b virtue of the Vette's superior horsepower. Another sho rang out. By the sound of it, the bullet had struck metal.

"Let go! You're about to break my neck!" Chriss yelled, though her words were muffled. Her face wa pressed against his thigh, his hand clamped on the back o her neck and pressing far too hard.

He loosened his grip, though he didn't release her. "Sta down."

She turned her head to the side. "Is someone shootin at us?"

"Yes." He swerved from side to side as he drove a close to a hundred miles per hour down the country roac giving Denny a more randomly moving target to aim a Since he was doing both the driving and the shooting, Rya suspected he was alone. And his aim probably wouldn't b too good with his left hand.

"What are you doing?" Cold wind roared in from th back window, almost drowning out her words.

"Trying to keep us alive."

"Is there something I can do to help?"

He had to admire her. Any lesser woman would hav dissolved into hysterics by now. He wished there wa something handy she could do to help the situation—lik throwing a box full of tacks out the window. It worked i old movies.

"Get the map," he said. "It's to the left of my seat. D it without raising your head."

"What about the cell phone?" she asked as she unfas tened her seat belt and crawled over his lap to look for th map. Any other time, he might have enjoyed the experi ence.

"I, um, left it at Fran's."

She groaned. "What a time for you to get forgetful Okay, I have the map."

"Find Highway 608 near Emporia, going due east, an

find me the shortest route back to the interstate." He figured the big highway was his safest way to find civilization, or at least other cars. Out here in the country, they were sitting ducks.

Another shot sounded. Chrissy squeaked. "He's still there?"

"He's dropping back. This car can outrun his Firebird any day."

Still lying half in his lap, Chrissy studied the map. "Are we east or west of 619?"

"Hell, I don't know."

"Six-nineteen south will take you right to the Interstate. Otherwise you'll have to go through a town called Callaville—"

"There's something up ahead." It wasn't much of a road. It wasn't even marked. But since Ryan had left the Firebird on the backside of a hill, he decided to risk it. He slammed on the brakes, sending a screaming Chrissy rolling onto the floor, and made a left turn on two wheels.

The road wound through a copse of trees, seeming vaguely familiar. At any rate, Ryan hoped, his car would be out of sight before the Firebird topped the hill and Denny realized the Vette had made a turn. If they were lucky, Denny would scream right on by the turnoff.

The car hesitated, and Ryan punched the accelerator again. Nothing happened. From reflex, he glanced at the gas gauge, then did a double take. It was flat-out empty, and they'd filled up in Richmond.

"What's happening?" Chrissy said, peering up at him from the floor, where she'd fallen. The car was sputtering, gradually losing speed.

"A bullet must've hit the gas tank," he said matter-of-factly. "We're out of juice."

"Oh, my God!" Chrissy was showing the first signs of true panic, and he didn't blame her. If Denny was behind them, they were doomed, or at least he was. She might yet survive to draw a ransom, though he didn't hold out a lot of hope for that.

She raised up and peered between the bucket seats, out the back window. "Where is he?"

"I don't know. I might have lost him."

"Please, let's hope so."

With the last bit of oomph the Vette had, Ryan drove off the road and into the dense vegetation, hoping to hide the car. Even if he'd fooled Denny momentarily, the jerk would eventually figure out what had happened and come this way. If he saw the disabled car and figured out Ryan and Chrissy were on foot, they would be easy targets.

With a scraping of branches against the Vette's once sparkling blue paint job, the car came to an abrupt halt. Ryan looked behind him. They would still be visible from the road to someone looking, and they'd left tire tracks in the soft shoulder. Damn.

"Now what?" Chrissy asked. She'd recovered somewhat from her momentary burst of panic.

"We hoof it."

"To where?"

"I know the area, vaguely. We're only about three or four miles from my sister's house. We'll go there and call the cops." If Josette had a phone. The one and only time he visited his sister since she moved out here last year, he remembered, things had been pretty primitive.

"I wish we had some way to defend ourselves," Chrissy said with a shiver as she opened the passenger door.

"Wait a minute. I think we do." Ryan opened the glove box. There was the blue steel pistol he'd taken away from Denny two days ago. He'd forgotten about it until now.

"Do you know how to use that thing?"

"No, but it couldn't be all that complicated." He examined the pistol, trying to figure out if he was supposed to cock it, wondering how many bullets were still in it. Denny had fired off one shot, he remembered.

"Here, give it to me," Christine said impatiently.

"Excuse me?"

"I know guns. My father taught me how to shoot."

He stared at her in disbelief. When he didn't immediately hand her the gun, she took it from him.

"This is a Glock nine-millimeter automatic." She expertly popped out the magazine and examined it. "Terrific, we have four bullets."

"Make 'em count," he said ominously, deferring to her obvious expertise. Who'd have thought pretty, feminine Chrissy could be a gun-totin' mama?

She tested the weight of the gun in her hand, adopted a shooting stance, peered down the gun's sight at an imaginary target. "Okay, I'm ready. Should we wait here for him and use the car as a barricade, or…?" Her voice trailed off as she stared at Ryan. Or rather, at Ryan's shoulder.

"What?"

"There's blood on your jacket."

He looked down, only then noticing the dull pain in his shoulder, the tingling in his arm. There was not only blood, but a large hole, as well. And one to match it on his back.

He pulled the jacket aside. Chrissy made a gurgling noise of obvious distress. His pale blue shirt was soaked with blood.

"Well, I'll be damned," he said, really noticing the pain now. "I've been shot."

Chapter 14

Christine felt every drop of blood drain from her head to her feet. Ryan had been shot! He was standing there in front of her with a gaping hole in him and blood dripping down him like some horror-movie special effect.

She felt dizzy.

"C'mon, Chrissy," he cajoled, "now is not the time to turn into a Victorian maiden and faint on me. I need you."

"B-but... Hospital. We have to get you to a hospital!"

"Yes. And that means finding a phone. And we might want to get out of the middle of the road before Denny comes back."

The reminder of the danger they were in, aside from Ryan's injury, galvanized her into action. He was right. Of all times, right now she most needed a clear head.

"We need to stop the bleeding, or at least slow it down," she said practically. She was already pawing through her suitcase, looking for something with which to make a suitable bandage. She came up with a T-shirt and a scarf. "Take off your jacket. Hold this shirt against the wound, and I'll tie it on with the scarf."

"Never mind the scarf," he said. "I'll just hold the T-shirt in place. The bleeding has already slowed down a lot. The bullet must have come through clean, and I don't think anything's broken." He wiped up some of the blood with the T-shirt, then flipped the folded shirt over and pressed it against the wound. "It'll be okay," he said gently, touching her arm. "Let's just go. The sooner we're away from here, the better."

They kept near the road at first, ready to leap for cover in the woods if they heard a car coming. But then the trees thinned out, and they found themselves in a crop field of some sort. Beans, maybe. Christine wasn't sure. But they decided to veer farther from the road. If a car came by, they would have to drop down and lie flat, hoping the scrubby little plants concealed them.

That eventuality happened not once, but three times, during the next few minutes. Each time, they would fall to the ground, flattening themselves as much as possible. Christine would ready the gun, just in case. Each time, the car that passed by was not Denny's. Each time, Ryan was slower to get up.

"Let's go back to the road and try and flag down the next car," Christine said.

Ryan shook his head. "The next one might be a red Firebird. Come on, we'll make it."

"Then let's not worry about finding your sister's house. The first place we see, okay?"

"Yeah, okay."

They decided to get away from the road altogether and cut across the countryside. Christine kept hoping they would stumble across a farmhouse, a gas station… something. But they didn't.

After about twenty minutes, they hit another road, this one dirt. "I know where I am now," Ryan said. His speech was slightly slurred, and he had become increasingly unsteady on his feet.

Chrissy worried that he might pass out. She didn't know how much blood he'd lost, but it looked like a lot. What would she do if he suddenly stumbled and fell, unable to continue? She would have to drag him, she supposed. She couldn't just leave him on the side of the road while she went for help.

After the next fifteen minutes, he was leaning on her shoulder, breathing as if he'd just run a marathon. "How much farther?" she asked, having given up hope of simply stumbling upon civilization.

"Not…far," he answered, almost panting. "Mail-box…up ahead. See?"

She did see! Oh, thank God, it couldn't be more than another eighth of a mile. She put her arm around Ryan as he stumbled along beside her.

The rusty mailbox, it turned out, was at the end of a long, winding driveway. Chrissy was beginning to think there was no Josette, no house, indeed no people anywhere in this godforsaken part of the country. But finally she saw it—and a pitiful thing it was, listing to one side, paint peeling, two windows boarded up.

"Your sister lives *here?*" she asked, almost hoping they had the wrong house.

"This's the place," Ryan said. "There should be dogs barking."

Chrissy didn't hear any dogs.

"She has hunting dogs," he insisted.

Oh, Lord, was he delusional? Had the blood loss made him so disoriented he'd led them to the wrong house? It didn't matter, she supposed, as long as someone lived here, someone who could help them. But she had her doubts. She didn't see any cars or lights. More importantly, she didn't see any telephone or electrical lines leading to the house.

Ryan took the creaking porch steps one at a time, slowly, leaning on the banister on one side, Christine supporting him on the other. When he reached the porch. he took a series of deep breaths and seemed to draw strength from them. "I'm okay now. I can make it." He walked up to the door and knocked loudly.

No one answered. Christine wasn't surprised.

"Are you sure this is the right house?"

"Yes." He knocked again. "Josette? Josie? Honey, if you're in there open up, it's Rye." He turned to Christine and whispered, "She's kind of reclusive. Sometimes she doesn't come to the door."

Ryan's explanation gave Christine a chill. Sounded as if Ryan's sister were a bit of a strange bird, living by herself in this hovel, refusing to answer the door. But after repeated knocking and calling, it became apparent that Josette, if she lived here, was not home.

Christine didn't hesitate. Ryan was weaving on his feet. If she didn't get him somewhere safe, and fast, he was going to pass out on her. She took the gun from the waistband of her jeans and used the butt to break a window.

"Chrissy, careful!" Ryan said.

She punched out the rest of the glass, reached inside and flipped the stiff lock. In moments she was climbing through the window into the house's dim interior. She ran to the door, opened it and pulled Ryan inside.

Finally she felt safe. At least Denny wouldn't have a clear shot at them.

But her optimism didn't last long. This house was obviously abandoned. What little furniture was left was covered with sheets. The light switch, when she flipped it on, produced no results.

Christine whisked a sheet off a chair by the window and guided Ryan to it. He sank down with a sigh.

"Oh, that feels good. Is there a phone?"

She knew without even looking. "No. But we can rest, and clean that wound properly, and then figure out what to do next. If you'll keep an eye out that window, I'll take inventory here, see what we can make use of."

Surprisingly, the house was clean. Not much dust. Whoever had lived here must have vacated fairly recently. The pantry contained a few foodstuffs. The primitive gas stove hissed when she turned it on, and a match safe hanging on the wall was full of matches.

The first thing Christine did was fill an old pot up with water from the sink—hand-pumped well water—and set it on the stove to boil. Then she ran upstairs to have a look. There was a bed, a sorry old thing, to be sure, but it would have to do. A linen cupboard yielded a pile of old sheets, clean, if a bit musty, and a wool blanket. No pillows, though. She quickly made up the bed, then grabbed another sheet and brought it downstairs.

The water was just beginning to boil. She tore the sheet into strips and dropped them into the bubbling water. Sort of like cooking pasta, she thought.

"You look like you know what you're doing," Ryan said from the kitchen doorway.

"I assure you, that is strictly an illusion. I've read in historical novels about people boiling sheets for bandages, that's all. Thought I'd give it a try. Here, sit down before you fall down." She pulled a rickety chair out from an old formica kitchen table.

"How will you dry the bandages?" he wanted to know.

"Hmm, I hadn't thought of that." It would take hours to air-dry the wet strips of cotton. "Well, I'll use these boiled ones to clean the wound. I don't have to, like, re move any bullets, do I?"

"No. The bullet is lodged in the Vette's dashboard."

"Phew... Good, okay. Then I'll use this other part of the sheet that I didn't boil for the bandage. It's a clean sheet."

"Maybe we should just leave it alone," Ryan said. He pulled the blood-soaked T-shirt away from the wound and looked down at it. "Blech."

"Is it still bleeding?" she asked, steeling herself as she came closer to have a better look. "Take off your shirt, for heaven's sake, so we can see what we've got."

"Are you sure you want to know?" But he followed her orders.

Christine turned off the stove. The sheet scraps had boiled long enough, she decided. After carrying the whole pot over to the table, she plucked one strip of cotton out with her fingernails, held it out of the water until it had cooled enough that she could handle it, then used it to scrub her hands.

"You *do* know what you're doing," Ryan said.

"I wish I did."

She cast the first strip aside, then used the remaining strips to wash away the blood. Ryan winced every so often, but he didn't make a sound.

"I'm sorry if I'm hurting you," she said. Every time she wiped blood off the wound itself, it oozed more, though Ryan had been right about its not bleeding a lot. The bullet must not have severed any major blood vessels.

"Amazingly, it doesn't hurt that much." he said. "You'd think a bullet wound would really, really hurt." Despite that reassurance, perspiration had popped out on his forehead and upper lip.

"If only I had some kind of disinfectant. Alcohol or peroxide or something."

"Now *that* would hurt," he said.

"I found a bottle with a few drops of cooking sherry in it," she said. "Do you suppose—"

"No way. You're not basting me with cooking sherry. Just bandage it. As soon as we get to a hospital, they'll fix it up right. All I want right now is to not bleed all over everything."

"Okay. One bandage coming up." She tore off another section of sheet and folded it to make a thick pad. The small entrance wound in his back wasn't bleeding, so she placed a smaller pad on it. She had Ryan hold the bandages in place while she used longer, thinner strips to tie them down. She wrapped them across his shoulder at a diagonal, around the other side of his neck, under his arm. Then she wrapped more strips straight across, under both arms.

By the time she was done, he looked like a half-baked mummy.

"Are you sure all this is really necessary?" The complaint lacked any real bite. Instead, he was looking at her with definite amusement, and something else. There was a sudden heaviness between them, like they'd both been immersed in warm honey.

She shook off the feeling. She must be imagining things. "The bleeding won't stop unless the bandage is pressed tightly against the wound," she argued reasonably. "And I don't think you should use your right arm, either." She was already fashioning a sling from the last bit of the sheet.

She was leaning over him, fumbling with a knot at his left shoulder, when she felt something on her ear—something warm and sensual. Startled to realize Ryan was kissing her, she could think of no reasonable way to respond except to go perfectly still…and enjoy it. Of all the strange times to find pleasure, this had to be the strangest.

"Mmm, sorry, Chrissy," he murmured drowsily, kissing her neck now. "After all that touching, and you being so near, I couldn't resist."

"Uhhh… Ohhh, Ryan, stop."

"Really?"

All right, so only an idiot wouldn't have read the reluctance in her request. "At least until I finish this stupid knot."

"Deal."

She pulled back so that she could see his face. Was this part of his delirium? She still wasn't sure whether he was thinking straight. She wasn't even sure this was really his sister's house, and not some stranger's.

He smiled, a little bleary-eyed, then grew serious. "You're being so good to me, Chrissy. It's a lot more than I deserve."

"What was I supposed to do, let you bleed to death on the side of the road?"

"I dunno. But all this seems above and beyond."

"Maybe I like you, okay?" she snapped. "Though God knows why. You can be real annoying."

Ryan submitted to her ministrations, but only grudgingly. Her touch was incredibly gentle and soothing, not to mention arousing. He wouldn't have thought it possible, but even with this gaping wound in his shoulder, he was more fixated on her touch and his reaction to it than on the pain.

He'd probably taken advantage of her kindness by kissing her, but he hadn't been able to help himself. She was so close, and she smelled so good. But it was the look of concern in her green eyes that went right to his soul.

Despite her denial, there was something more going on here than just kindness, or responsibility. She was... protecting him. Caring for him. During that seemingly endless hike from the car to this house, she'd looked at him with such worry, such anxiety, that he'd begun to wonder who was in more pain.

No one had ever looked at him like that before. Of course, he'd never been shot before, either. New experiences were abounding.

She finished the knot, then straightened up and put a couple of feet of distance between them, as if she were afraid he would make good on his promise to stop kissing her *only* until she finished the sling. It was probably a good thing his reflexes were a little bit dulled, because he would have made a grab for her. His judgment—if he'd ever had any where Chrissy was concerned—was dulled, too.

He couldn't stop looking at her. She was flushed and disheveled, her hair was coming out of her braid, her lipstick was long gone, she had a gun stuck in the waistband of her jeans, like some desperado—and she'd never looked more beautiful, or sexier.

Mostly sexier.

"I think you should go upstairs and rest," she said. "I'll make us something to eat. Then maybe we can figure out our next move."

Ryan knew what he wanted *his* next move to be. Hmm. Maybe when his shoulder didn't hurt so bad. Now that the immediate danger was at bay and his adrenaline rush had diminished, a throbbing pain had set in.

She helped him to his feet. It was humiliating how weak he was, how wobbly. Gratefully he put his arm around her. She was strong, so much stronger than she looked at first glance. She'd tackled the gore of his bullet wound without blinking. He might be dead if not for her actions.

"Got any aspirin?" he asked, without much hope.

"Hurts, huh?"

"Yeah."

"I'll check my purse as soon as I get you to bed."

They'd reached the stairs. He positioned himself between her and the wobbly banister and began his laborious path upward.

"Oh, Ryan, I'm sorry I got you into this. You could have been killed."

He laughed. "Sweetheart, I definitely got myself into this. Don't take the credit."

"I'm the one who insisted you drive me to Raleigh."

"I wanted to do it. Anyway, it was my idea to leave the interstate. I'm sure that's what Denny was waiting for—a chance to isolate us, do his thing with no witnesses. He might have been following us from the time we were at my place."

Chrissy shivered against him. "It's so creepy having this guy fixated on me. I think he must be beyond trying to get me back to redeem himself. By firing at the car, he could have just as easily shot me in the head as you in the shoulder. I think he's gone off the deep end, and he just wants me dead because I humiliated him."

Ryan hated to agree with her, so he said nothing. But he suspected she was right. Their enemy was a whole lot more dangerous than he had originally suspected.

When Ryan saw the bed neatly made with faded floral sheets, turned down like a bed in a hotel, he had to smile. "What, no mint on the pillow?"

"Not even a pillow. Are you sure this is Josette's house?"

"Yeah. I remember it. I think I slept in this room, on this bed, when I visited."

"And when was that?"

"Oh, about a year ago."

"That long?"

He sat down on the edge of the bed and started to lean down to untie his shoes, then thought better of it. He was so dizzy he could easily have toppled over onto the floor.

"Here, I'll do that," Chrissy said, kneeling down.

She was only touching his feet, he told himself. Don't get excited. But it was too late to tell his body that. The only thing that was going to unexcite him at this point was unconsciousness…or satisfaction. He found himself fervently wishing for the latter.

"Josette and I aren't close. She isn't close to anyone in the family," he explained. "She had a terrible time as a teenager."

"Don't we all?" Chrissy asked wryly. She slipped off first one of his shoes, then the other, seeming to linger over the task.

"Hers was more terrible than most. She took up with a gang—the Pit Bulls, as a matter of fact."

Chrissy looked up sharply at that.

"Drugs, crime, jail, you name it, she was involved with it. She thought it was great fun to be a rebel. Until she was gang-raped and pregnant."

Chrissy gasped. She sat down beside him on the bed. "Oh, Ryan, that's awful. I'm sorry I was flippant about it. What happened?"

"She had the baby and gave it up for adoption. She ended up having another one three years later, when she was eighteen. She married the father, but he was a slimebag. He beat her and my nephew. We eventually got rid of him, but it wasn't easy."

Chrissy was listening with rapt attention. He couldn't blame her. It was a horror story. Sometimes he was amazed that his own sweet sister had lived such a nightmare. She'd had the same upbringing as him, but something had gone wrong.

"What happened then?" Chrissy asked.

"She moved to Richmond, then Emporia. She lived with a lot of different guys."

"And did she ever straighten herself out?"

"Well, not really. She's always done right by her kid, I'll give her that. She's a devoted, concerned mother. But she's not too stable herself."

"I'm not surprised, after what she's been through," Chrissy said with another shiver. "You don't have any idea where she's gone?"

"No. I never thought she would just move and not tell anyone. It's kind of spooky."

"You have to find her. She might be in trouble. She might need help. And her little boy…how old is he?"

"Seven, I think. Yeah, that would be right."

"It must be so hard. When you find her, maybe I could talk to her," she said. "I'm about her age, right? And I wasn't gang-raped or anything like that, but I did go through a similar experience. Maybe just having a friend to talk to would help."

"Chrissy, you're too nice for your own good." He made good on his promise then, wrapping his good arm around her and kissing the heck out of her.

She didn't resist, not even a tiny bit. In fact, he got the distinct impression that she'd been waiting for him to kiss her. She kissed him back, fiercely, moving her lips against his with an insistent pressure, boldly meeting the thrusts of his tongue with her own. She slid her arms around his neck, but even in the throes of passion he could tell she was being careful not to jar him.

Her total selflessness—especially after the opportunistic way he'd treated her—bowled him over.

He broke the kiss, reeling from its effects. Much more of this and he would end up face first on the floor. "You know what I'd like to do right now?" he whispered into her hair, close to her ear, almost hoping she wouldn't hear the improper suggestion about to pour out of him. He couldn't hold his desire in any longer. He wanted her, and he needed to express that wanting, even if he couldn't act on it just yet.

"Mmm, I have a pretty good idea. But I couldn't possibly allow it."

"Why not?" he asked, nuzzling her neck.

"You need rest, not sex."

"Can't I have both?"

They both knew that was merely wishful thinking. He was too weakened by his injury to even sustain a good hard-on, though his body was trying.

"Get under the covers," she said. "I'll fix us something to eat and bring it up here."

"You think there's actually enough in the pantry to fix a meal?" he asked dubiously, unbuttoning his jeans. He was having trouble accomplishing the task with his left hand.

"It might not be gourmet fare, but it'll have to do." She started to turn away, then changed her mind and walked over to him. She quickly, efficiently, unfastened the last two buttons of his jeans, then headed for the door.

"Chrissy?"

She halted. "What?" she asked, looking everywhere but at him.

"If there's any sign of Denny, you call out good and loud. I'll wake up. And keep that gun handy."

She slumped a little bit at the reminder of the danger they were still in. "Okay."

Downstairs, Christine found some rice, soy sauce, a can of mushrooms, a can of diced tomatoes, and a little packet of cajun seasoning from some fast-food place. She threw it all together in a sort of meatless jambalaya and hoped for the best. Her snobby French cooking classes hadn't prepared her for this seat-of-your-pants-style cuisine.

When she tasted the concoction, it wasn't half-bad. The bad news was that there weren't any individual serving dishes of any kind, and there was no silverware. On the top shelf of a cabinet she found one cracked tumbler, which she filled with water from the pump. Not too fancy, but at least it was cold.

She carried everything upstairs, only to find Ryan fast

asleep. She wasn't surprised. He'd been up most of the night working on his blasted story.

She decided not to wake him. Hopefully, the rest would help him regain some strength, and he could eat when he woke up. That is, if she didn't eat their whole dinner first. It smelled pretty good.

She perched herself on a derelict wooden rocking chair with peeling paint and dug into the pot of rice, using the only utensil she'd found, an old wooden spoon, to shovel the food into her mouth.

She'd come a long way, she thought, from the formal dining room, bone china and sterling flatware of her father's house. If Connie could see her now, she would faint from the shock.

While she ate, she watched Ryan. He slept fitfully, shivering every now and then, making Christine wish she had more blankets. But she'd scoured the house, and other than the dusty sheets covering the furniture downstairs, this was it.

She very carefully rationed the rice dish, leaving more than half for Ryan, despite her ravenous hunger. He needed it more than she would. She finished the water. Then she took the leftovers downstairs, covered the pot, and set it on the back porch, where it was cooler. She checked around outside, front and back, to reassure herself that no terrorists were lurking about, then returned upstairs.

Ryan was still shivering. The obvious answer, of course, was body heat. With a mischievous smile, she removed her clothes, laid the gun on the floor by the bed within easy reach and climbed under the covers. She plastered her body against his, tucked her head against his good shoulder, and closed her eyes.

She'd never behaved this brazenly with any man before, not even Doug. But something had happened between her and Ryan during the past few hours. Coming within a hair's breadth of death had created a bond between them. Although her behavior seemed rash, something only a loose, immoral woman would do, it seemed right somehow. She knew that when Ryan found her there, he would be pleased. He would not find her sluttish or too forward. He would welcome her with open arms.

She was counting on that. If she was wrong, the incident would be terrifically embarrassing.

Chapter 15

Ryan thought this had to be a dream. He'd been drifting in and out of sleep, his throbbing wound and the uncomfortably cold room making deeper sleep impossible. But this was the first time he'd awakened feeling toasty-warm, and he soon figured out why: A naked woman was pressed up against him.

He was on his back, and Chrissy was flesh-to-flesh with him, all along his left side. Her head rested on his shoulder, her silky hair, now liberated from its braid, tickling his neck. One tendril of her hair lay across his chest. He could feel her warm breath along his collarbone.

He was instantly hard, and the pain in his shoulder was forgotten. "Chrissy?" he whispered.

"Yes?"

So, she was awake. "What the heck are you doing in bed with me? Not that I'm complaining," he hastily added.

"You were cold," she said. "I was tired. It seemed like a reasonable solution to both problems."

In his more logical mind, he knew that this wasn't reasonable at all. Yet nothing had ever felt more right.

"Are you feeling any better?" she asked.

"Mmm-hmm, much better," he said, though *better* wasn't the word. He couldn't recall ever feeling this spectacular in his life. He pulled his left arm out from between them and eased it around her shoulders. If she got it into her head to make an escape, he wasn't going to let her go easily.

It was dark outside, but a bright moon shone through the room's single window. "How long have I been out?"

"About three hours. I fixed some dinner for you, but you fell asleep before it was ready. I saved some for you. Do you want me to go downstairs and heat it up?"

"No," he answered quickly. He had his own ideas about heating up, and they didn't involve food. He felt so helpless, though. How was he supposed to seduce a woman when he was flat on his back, with only one good hand?

"You're not hungry?" she asked.

He ought to be, he supposed. But he didn't have room in his brain to acknowledge hunger. His head was too full of Chrissy—the feel of her warm skin against his, the scent of her hair, the soothing sound of her voice. Surely she hadn't gotten into bed with him naked just to keep him warm. She couldn't be that naive.

"I had in mind satisfying an appetite, all right," he said, then held his breath.

"Ah." She didn't tense up, the way he'd half expected. Instead she snuggled closer. Her hand wandered to his chest and began toying with the hair that grew there, moving gradually lower and...lower. "I was afraid I'd done the wrong thing by joining you like this."

"No, sweetheart, it was the completely right thing."

"Good." She reached lower still, then clasped his erection through his briefs.

He groaned with the pure, white-hot pleasure her touch evoked. "I can't... Oh, yes, that feels good."

"You can't what?"

"I'm handicapped with this bum shoulder. I can't do this

the way it ought to be done. You'll have to do most of the work.''

"Mmm, you call this work?"

"I don't know about you, but it's making me break out in a sweat. Why don't you kiss me?"

"Gladly." She released him, causing momentary disappointment, but then she was draping her body half over his, covering his face with soft, damp kisses. "I'm sure you've…" *Kiss.* "…made love to a lot…" *Kiss.* "…of women before." *Kiss.* "But have you ever…" *Kiss.* "…had one make love…" *Kiss.* "…to you?"

"Not like this." He was almost past being verbal. She was focusing on his mouth now, her teasing kisses outlining his lips, finally settling warmly over them. Oh, how this woman could kiss. No, he'd experienced nothing like this before.

"I've never done anything quite like this, either," she said, her voice husky, as she moved her attention to his jaw, his ear, his neck. Her hair brushed against him, creating a new wave of sensations every time she moved her head even a fraction of an inch. "Tell me what you want me to do."

"You're doing fine, Princess."

"Don't call me that." Despite the scolding, she continued her tender ministrations. "I hate that image. It's not me, and I think I've proved that."

Oh, yeah. She was proving it right now, as she invaded his ear with her clever tongue. No icy princess could ever be this hot. "Sorry. I meant it as a term of affection." And he did feel affection for her. More than that. Stronger. He suddenly couldn't bear the thought of being separated from her, saying goodbye to her. Not after all they'd been through.

Easy, he cautioned himself. She was here now. That was what was important.

"S'okay," she said.

He wrapped his good arm around her, then ran his hand down her back, her firm flanks, her thigh. "Think you could finish undressing me?'' His cotton briefs had become incredibly constricting.

"Sure I can. I knew you wouldn't be able to resist giving me instructions.'' With an admirable economy of movement, she flicked back the blanket, then slowly slid his briefs down his legs. She managed to touch him liberally during the process, and he suspected she was torturing him on purpose.

"While you're down there, think you can—" Wait. That would really be taking advantage. His idea of heaven was Chrissy's tight little mouth wrapped around his member, but the last thing he wanted to do was turn her off with his more earthy desires. She was a lady, worthy of respect and dignity, even in a situation like this.

"What?"

"Nothing.'' He reached out and encircled her wrist, then gently tugged. "Come back up here. Lie next to me.''

"Okay. In a minute.'' She was staring at him, or rather at the obvious evidence of his total arousal. Before he knew what was happening, she was kissing him there, just as he'd been about to ask her to do. And it was ten times better than anything he could have imagined, like he had a million nerve endings he hadn't previously known about.

He squirmed in pure ecstasy. "Chr-Chrissy, you have to —stop.''

She did so, abruptly. "I'm doing something wrong?'' she asked, her voice fraught with insecurities.

"No, Prin—I mean, darling. You're doing everything fine. I'm the one who's lost control.'' He was actually gasping for each breath. The woman was incredible, no doubt about it. He was about to explode, and he would prefer to do that when they were joined in that perfect way only men and women could be.

Was she ready? he wondered. He felt like such a klutz. If he wasn't crippled, he would make damn sure she was writhing and just as hot for him as he was for her.

"I'm yours, Chrissy,'' he said, meaning it with all his heart. "You do with me whatever you want.''

"But I... Like this?"

He found her naïveté endearing. "Exactly like that," he said as she swung her leg over him, straddling him. "I don't know about you, but I've been waiting a long time for this."

"Yes, me too." With those words, she sheathed him, in one swift, elegant movement. She closed her eyes, hand on his chest, biting her lower lip.

All Ryan could do was groan. This was good. Incredibly good. If he died tomorrow, his life would have been complete.

But he didn't want to think about death, as close as he'd come to it today. He wanted to think about living life to the fullest. Life with Chrissy.

She began to move against him, and he thought maybe this was a dream after all. It was certainly otherworldly. He lightly touched her thigh, her waist, her flat belly and her breasts as she rode him, memorizing the feel of her, knowing he would want to savor the memory later.

An exquisite pressure built inside him, familiar in some ways, unique in others. He felt oddly in balance with her, with himself and with the universe, as if his whole life had been building up to this moment, every aspect mysteriously oriented to bring him together with this woman.

He opened his eyes and found her gazing at him, her eyes so full of love for him that it was spilling over. He realized it then, that she did love him. She didn't have to say it. He could feel it, like a concrete thing. It had weight, a texture, a firmness, a color, a scent. He could have painted a picture of it, it was so clear to him.

Her love surrounded him with warmth and joy.

The scary part was, he loved her back. He didn't know how it had happened, but she'd gotten under her skin with her strength, her gentleness, her caring. Her Chrissyness.

She smiled, her teeth glowing white in the moonlight, then closed her eyes and breathed deep. Her movement became more dramatic, faster, more intense, and his previous sense of control vanished. He was at her mercy now.

Just when he thought he couldn't hold on another second, his name was torn from her throat. She went rigid; he exploded, emptying himself into her in wave after wave of the most indescribable delight.

She slumped forward, laughing and crying at the same time. Ryan felt like doing the same, but he settled for putting his good arm around her and burying his face in her hair.

"I'd forgotten," she murmured. A thin sheen of perspiration glossed her back, making it slick where he caressed her.

Did her comment mean she'd had sex this good before? he wondered. He sure hadn't. He decided it was better not to delve into the subject of comparisons. He was afraid he might become jealous, and that was such an alien emotion to him, he wasn't sure how he would handle it.

It was enough that she was with him now, united with him body and soul. He trusted the future to take care of itself—if they both survived to see it.

Christine didn't want to move. She'd found the most perfect corner of heaven she could ever have imagined, and she was loath to let it slip away.

She'd forgotten how good it could be—only really, nothing had ever been *this* good. She shivered to think of what Ryan could do when he was whole, when he could actually move.

"Are you cold?" he asked solicitously.

"No, I'm perfect."

"I'll say."

"I mean it. I've never felt happier. I know that sounds silly."

"Huh-uh. It's like there's a big ball of sunshine and flowers all around us."

She couldn't tell whether he was serious, or making fun of her. She decided to pretend he was on the level. "That's very poetic, but it describes exactly how I feel."

He chuckled. "I used to write bad poetry in high schoo
It made the girls think I was deep and mysterious."

"You are deep and mysterious," she said, rubbing he
cheek against his beard-roughened chin. It felt good. "
could know you a lifetime and still not figure you out."
And that, she was afraid, was hitting a little too close t
the truth. She wanted to spend the rest of her life gettin
to know him.

Was it a girlish fantasy? Men liked sex. Men rarel
turned down sex. This meant everything to her, but it migh
be nothing to Ryan. It wasn't as if he'd pursued her. She'
given him little choice in the matter.

He said nothing more, but he continued to hold her ter
derly. She contented herself with that. Now wasn't the tim
to dissect what tonight meant, if anything. Lately, she'
been living moment to moment, so she might as well con
tinue.

Eventually she eased away from him, carefully maneu
vering herself to lie beside him so that she didn't jar hi
arm. "How does your shoulder feel?"

"Mmm…could be better."

"What about dinner? Do you want something now?"

"I'm starved. No, don't get up," he said when sh
started to move. "Lie here with me a little longer. I'll ge
up in a while and find the leftovers." He pulled the cover
back up over both of them.

"After that, will we leave here?" she asked. "In th
dark, it would be easier to move around without bein
seen."

"You're right, but—I'm sorry to say—I don't think
could walk fifteen feet in my current state. Maybe by morn
ing."

His weakness, and the fact that he readily admitted to i
worried her. How much blood had he actually lost? Ho
long would it take for his body to replenish what he'd lost
Would he really have made any progress by morning?

"I could go on my own and bring back help," she sug
gested.

"No way," he said flatly. "We have to stick together. I would worry myself into a coma if you left here without me."

"And I guess I would worry about leaving you here alone," she admitted. All this mutual worrying gave her a warm feeling inside. "All right. We'll stay together."

"We can take turns sleeping tonight," Ryan said. "At least one of us should be awake, in case Denny makes an appearance."

"You think he might? I figured that if he was going to find us, he'd have done it by now."

"Hate to burst your bubble, but we're a long way from safe. Denny could be hanging out in town, talking to people, asking questions, finding out if either one of us has relatives in the area."

Christine shivered. "I hadn't thought of that. If he's determined, it's only a matter of time before he shows up here."

"Yeah."

After that cheery realization, neither one of them could sleep. Christine went downstairs and reheated the rice dish, despite Ryan's protests that she needn't wait on him. She wanted him to conserve his strength. He would need it tomorrow.

After Ryan ate, they lay in bed, talking quietly, listening for the sound of a car engine through the cracked window, jumping at every animal noise outside.

Eventually Christine drifted off, secure in the circle of Ryan's arm. She awoke maybe a couple of hours later to find Ryan lying on his side, watching her.

"What, was I snoring?" she asked drowsily.

"No. You're just so pretty I can't stop staring at you."

She felt self-conscious about that. What if she'd drooled in her sleep or something? She flipped over and turned her head to look out the window so that he couldn't see her face. "You must be tired," she said. "Why don't you try to get some sleep? I'm awake now."

"Sleep is the last thing on my mind." He leaned forward

and kissed her ear, her jaw, until she felt compelled to turn her head and meet his lips with her own. He kissed her—not with burning passion, but with a reverence that shook her to her core. She hadn't known it was possible to communicate anything except lust with a kiss, but Ryan's kiss had spoken of something far deeper than mere physical longing.

Oh, did she dare hope? What if this was just wishful thinking on her part? Or some new game he was playing? She'd just realized that when it came to love, there were a lot more things that could go wrong than could go right.

"I want to make love with you again," he murmured. "Once wasn't enough—not that twice would be."

She was sorely tempted. Her body clamored for more of the pleasure she'd taken from him earlier. But every bit of exertion she put him through now would translate into less energy he would have by morning. "No, Ryan," she said firmly. "Please sleep. I'm getting up and getting dressed. I'll watch for Denny, don't worry." She slid from the bed before he could stop her.

He sighed. "I couldn't possibly sleep."

She remembered giving a similar argument when she was a little girl and her father was trying to get her to take her nap. And her father would say, "Just try. If you can't sleep, think of something pleasant—like riding your pony." She would take his advice, and before she knew it she would be waking up, her nap over.

"Just try," she said now to Ryan as she pulled on her jeans. "Think of something pleasant, like… What's your favorite thing to do?"

"Mmm, I think we just established that."

Oh, dear, they were back to *that* subject again. It was nice to envision him falling asleep thinking of her, though. "Visualize a long, hot bath," she suggested. He couldn't possibly find any more appealing image. She longed for a good soak herself.

As soon as she was dressed, she grabbed the gun, stuck it in her waistband and slipped out of the room. Ryan didn't offer any further protest. She lit an oil lamp she'd found earlier in her rummagings, then washed the rice pan and straightened up what little there was to straighten in the kitchen. When she checked on Ryan a few minutes later, he was sleeping. Thank God.

She watched him for a few minutes, her heart so full it ached, then withdrew and returned to the living room. With nothing to occupy herself with, she simply sat in a chair by the window, watched, and waited for Denny to come.

The sound of a car engine startled her, and she realized she'd been dozing. The gun was still clutched in her hand, though, so she couldn't have been too far gone.

A car was coming along the dirt road toward her at a faster-than-safe speed. She saw the lights bouncing up and down with each bump and pothole it hit, heard the whine of the engine.

The car slowed as it neared the driveway. The lights flashed to bright. Was the driver trying to find an address, perhaps? Oh, please, don't let it be him! she prayed.

Her prayers were dashed when the car turned into the driveway. Only someone looking for them would come here. And only one person she knew was looking for them.

She thought about calling upstairs for Ryan, then decided not to. This fight was between her and Denny. Ryan had nearly gotten himself killed during the last confrontation. He would be safer where he was. She still held out hope that Denny didn't mean to kill her, that he wanted the million-dollar ransom—the ransom that didn't exist and, in all likelihood, never would.

She flipped the safety off the Glock, raised the window, knelt in front of it and braced the gun on the sill, ready to fire. The wall might provide her with some cover.

Her hopes for a reprieve evaporated when the car stopped in front of the house with a neat little fishtail that set it at a ninety-degree angle to the driveway, facing right. It was a red Firebird, all right. The right front fender was badly crumpled, causing Christine to wonder what the car had been through since she first saw it, two-and-a-half days ago.

The driver climbed out, hitched up his pants and strolle around the car, as confident as a bulldog approaching helpless kitten—or at least that was the way it appeared t Christine.

She decided she'd show him helpless. The best defens was a good offense, right? She waited for him to wal around the car, then aimed for the ground right in front o his feet. She squeezed off bullet number one.

The man did a frantic little dance, then raced for th protection of his car, diving behind it.

Christine congratulated herself. She'd made that bulle count for something. But she had only three left now.

Ryan awoke to the sound of gunfire—a single gunsho to be precise, and it seemed to be very near. He raised u so suddenly that his head spun. His shoulder throbbec Then he remembered precisely where he was and what wa going on, and he nearly fainted from fear. Who had fire the gun, Chrissy or Denny? Was she even now lying in pool of blood downstairs?

Galvanized by those unpleasant thoughts, he forced him self out of bed, grabbed his jeans and walked—though h wanted to run—downstairs. "Chrissy!" he called as h cautiously descended each step. He wouldn't be any hel if he toppled head over heels down the stairs into a hea of broken bones.

"Here!" she called back. "Find a weapon. Our friend i back, just like you said he would be."

Ryan felt sick to his stomach, whether from fear or th food he'd eaten or general debilitation, he didn't know. Bu it gripped him like a vise in the gut.

When he reached the bottom of the stairs, he foun Chrissy kneeling by the window, gun poised.

"Are you okay?" he asked. She looked fine, but so ha he for a while after he was shot.

"For the time being. There might be an old knife in th kitchen. If not, I know there's a meat-tenderizing malle That will have to do."

Ryan's blood ran cold. This was it, then, kill or be killed. Was he up to it? Hell, yeah, of course he was! What was he thinking? To protect Chrissy, he would stab a rhinocerous to death with a toothpick. He gathered more strength than he thought possible and went to the kitchen to find a weapon.

He returned to the living room, having found two bricks, one very rusty knife, and the meat-tenderizing mallet Chrissy had mentioned. Chrissy hadn't moved. "What's happening?" he asked.

"Everything's status quo so far," she answered, keeping her voice low. "He's behind his car, probably trying to figure out what to do now that he knows we're not defense-ess."

Yeah, Ryan thought. Chicken-doo guys like Denny thrived on beating up on people who were weaker than him.

Ryan tried to figure out where his best vantage point would be—by the door, where he could attack Denny if he breached their walls, or at the window in the next room, ready to hurl bricks if the enemy got within twenty feet.

"Chrissy?"

"Yeah?" she answered, never taking her eyes away from the window.

"If you have to, can you kill him?"

"Yes," she said without hesitation. "I have three bullets left. I'll go for his knees with the second-to-last one. If that doesn't work, the last one is for his heart."

God, how had he ever believed she was a bored, spoiled rich girl? She had three times more guts than anybody he knew. But he also knew that she would never again submit herself to the indignities, the deprivations, those lunatic terrorists had put her through. She'd said the kidnapping had changed her, and now he saw what she meant.

"I'll use the gun if you want me to," he said.

She shook her head. "I'm the better marksman between us. You're better with knives and bricks, I'll bet."

Her answer made perfect sense. Still, he would spare her from killing, even in self-defense. With a nod, he moved into the next room, which had been Josette's never-used dining room. The window would afford him excellent access to anywhere on the front porch.

The eastern sky was just turning pink. As it gradually lightened, it appeared that Denny was going to wait it out, maybe see if his quarry would make a move first.

They could go out the kitchen door, he thought, and cut across the fields behind the house. Maybe Denny would never see them. Or maybe he was planning on a move like that, and he would cut them down like pop-up targets at a shooting gallery.

A flash of movement inside the car, now visible as morning dawned, made Ryan sharpen his focus. What was the man up to? That soon became apparent when the passenger window glided open, and Ryan found himself staring down the barrel of a rifle.

Instinctively Ryan backed away from the window. "Move aside, Chrissy," he called. "He's got a gun pointed at the—" He never finished his warning. Rapid gunfire shattered the silence of the morning. Bullets shattered glass, chipped plaster, splintered wood. As abruptly as the shooting had started, it stopped, and an eery silence reigned.

"Chrissy, you okay?"

"Yes. You?"

"No hits here." But they were lucky, damn lucky. There were bullets lodged in the walls, the ceiling, the furniture—everywhere but in them. "We can't afford to wait around anymore, Chrissy," he said. "Can you get a clear shot at him? If you can, take him out. The next round of bullets, we probably won't be so fortunate."

"I can't get a clear shot," she said. "Too much glass is in the way, too much car."

"Then do something to at least scare him. Shoot out a window. We know from experience how scary that is."

His order was no sooner issued than Ryan heard the sharp report from Chrissy's pistol and the instantaneous shattering of glass. The Firebird's rear window was gone except for a few pieces of glass clinging to the edges.

"Good job, Chrissy."

"Did I hit him?" she asked, sounding both hopeful and fearful.

Ryan peeked around the window casement. He could clearly see Denny moving around. It looked like maybe he was reloading his gun. "He's okay, still wiggling," Ryan said.

"Ryan?"

"Yes, Chrissy?"

"I love you."

Before he could react, the car's engine started up.

A surge of triumph roared through Ryan's blood—what little there was of it. "Hey, I think you did it! I think he's running like a dog with a tail between its—"

His words were cut off by another round of gunfire.

"Hit the floor!" he called just as he followed his own advice. He jarred his shoulder. Blinding pain flashed through him, like a million volts of electricity, and he wondered if he'd been hit again. But the shots ceased as abruptly as they'd started. The car roared, gravel popped under tires, and the Firebird careened away.

Ryan whooped. "All right, we did it. He's gone!"

There was no response from the other room.

"Chrissy?"

Still no response.

"Chrissy!" When he heard nothing, Ryan pushed himself up on his hands and knees. It took him a few moments to gain his feet. He half walked, half stumbled into the other room. And there he saw his worst nightmare. Chrissy was lying on her back, as white as the sheets draped over the furniture—except for the bright streak of crimson across her forehead, dripping blood into her golden hair.

Chapter 16

Ryan had scarcely let that horrifying image gel in his mind when another reality intruded—the sound of a police siren. Coming this way? How could the cops have been summoned?

He grabbed one of the sheets covering the furniture and dabbed at the blood on Chrissy's forehead. It didn't look all that bad—maybe just a graze from a bullet, or a cut from a flying piece of glass. He ripped a piece of sheet off, folded it several times and pressed it firmly to the bleeding area.

Chrissy was breathing, at least.

The siren got louder. Ryan looked up through the window and saw the flash of red and blue lights coming down the driveway. Thank God. His and Chrissy's ordeal was almost over, and they'd survived. At least he was feeling pretty hopeful that they would. Chrissy was still unconscious and he didn't know why.

The cop car bore a Virginia Highway Patrol logo on its door. A big-bellied officer squeezed his way out the driver's door, his hand on the gun at his hip, looking up and down, side to side. Ryan felt his first inkling of doubt.

Though he hated to do it, he left Chrissy for the moment and went to the door. He swung it open before the officer could knock and found the officer with his gun drawn, grinning.

"Hold on there, young man, what's the hurry?"

"Please," Ryan said, instinctively throwing his hands in the air, although he could get his right hand only partway up. His shoulder protested with screaming pain. "There's an injured woman in here. She's been shot or cut by flying glass, she's unconscious, and she needs to get to a hospital."

The cop's smile vanished. "You shot her?" He stepped inside to see for himself.

"Not me! Some maniac in a red Firebird drove up the driveway and opened fire on our house! Yesterday he shot out the back window of my car. I took a bullet in the—" He stopped. Chrissy was sitting up, her hand to her forehead, looking more than a little confused. But she was conscious, thank God.

"What happened?" she asked, staring at the blood on her hand. "Ryan?"

He was at her side in an instant. "You're hurt, honey. This officer is going to take you to a hospital. Right?" He looked at the cop, who had yet to identify himself.

"I guess that'd be the thing to do. Whose gun is that?" he asked, pointing to the blue Glock, which had dropped from Chrissy's hand.

"Mine," Chrissy and Ryan said together.

"Actually, it belongs to the guy in the Firebird. We took it from him when he tried to assault us with it on the street in Washington."

"Your friend in the Firebird is telling a different story," the cop said as he helped Chrissy to her feet. "Come on, young lady, can you walk to my car?"

"I think so. What did he say?" she asked, referring to Denny.

"He said he was lost, stopped by here to ask directions and someone started shooting at him. I nearly had a head on with him as he was tearing down the road, doing about seventy."

"He left out some of the story," Ryan said. "Like how he followed us all the way from D.C., then shot out the back window of my car."

"And he shot Ryan in the shoulder," Chrissy added. "It could have just as easily been his head. Oh, good heavens you aren't going to believe that scumbag's story over ours are you?"

The cop surveyed the damage done by Denny's gun, then shook his head, looking a bit confused himself. "We'll get everything straightened out sooner or later."

They started out the door, but the cop paused. "Maybe I just better radio for an ambulance."

"Am I that bad?" Chrissy asked fearfully.

"Nah, you'll live," he said, offering her a clean handkerchief, since the blood had soaked through the scrap of sheet Ryan had given her. "But I just realized I can't put all three of you—you two, and that fella from the Firebird—in my back seat. Might lead to some mayhem."

Christine's wound was superficial, though it had bled a lot. A bullet had grazed her forehead, but a few stitches was all she needed to patch it up. She had a concussion though, which her ER doctor in Richmond was a little more concerned about.

"Please, I'm sure it will be fine," she told the doctor for the fifth time. Ryan was at her side, and he absolutely refused to seek treatment for himself until he was certain she wasn't in any danger. "Will you tell him I'm not going anywhere?" She nodded toward Ryan. "He needs attention for his own wound."

"She's not in immediate danger," the doctor said gravely to Ryan.

"Well, what about unimmediate danger?" Ryan said.

"Ryan, the doctor isn't going to issue you a gold-plated

guarantee that I'll never, ever die, okay? Now stop being impossible and let him look at that hole in your shoulder.'' She hopped off the gurney and moved to a chair, indicating that he should take her place.

The doctor nearly had apoplexy. ''Please, we'll have to get clean linens. Have you checked in with the desk yet?'' he asked Ryan. ''We can't do anything around here without paperwork.''

''Please, just take a look?'' Christine beseeched him.

''Oh, all right.'' But first he leaned out the treatment room door. ''Rhonda, can you get one of the clerks to check this man in? He needs some immediate attention.''

Whoever he was talking to apparently answered in the affirmative, because when the doctor reentered the room, he looked a bit more relaxed. ''Now, let's see what we have here.'' He picked up a pair of scissors to cut off Ryan's bandage. ''Where did this dressing come from? It doesn't look too sanitary.''

''It was the best we could do at the time,'' Ryan answered sullenly. He clearly didn't like the idea of being poked and prodded.

The last of the bandage came away, and the doctor actually turned pale. ''Good Lord, man, how are you still walking around? What is this?''

''A bullet exit wound,'' Ryan said matter-of-factly. ''The entrance is on the other side.''

Suddenly the doctor became much more animated. Ryan was hustled into his own treatment room. Nurses were summoned. Even the cop who'd been standing guard over them was called in to have a look. Christine stuck determinedly by his side. He was x-rayed, aspirated, vacuumed, disinfected and stitched up, surgery being avoided only when Ryan howled such a protest that Christine wondered if he thought the doctors were suggesting amputation.

''I'd gladly take a second bullet if I could avoid this stuff,'' he whispered to Christine. ''The cure hurts a hell of a lot worse than the original injury.''

He couldn't afford to take the wound lightly, though.

Infection was a very real threat, and the doctor wanted to keep Ryan at least overnight for some intensive antibiotic therapy. He predictably refused, until Christine coerced him into cooperating, refusing to even speak to him until he fell in with the doctor's recommendations. She'd gotten him this far, and she damn sure wasn't going to lose him now to some germ.

"One day. I'll stay for one day," he groused. "And you better not leave me. People go into hospitals and don't come out, you know."

She had no intention of leaving him.

Unfortunately, she wasn't the only one who sought his company. There were detectives. The local police had checked out Christine's kidnapping story with D.C. law enforcement officials, and finally they believed her. It was kind of hard now for them to argue that she'd made up those bullet holes just to get publicity for her father.

When the police finished, hours later, a reporter weaseled his way into Ryan's room. Christine ejected him quickly enough, but it was obvious that news of their adventure with Denny the terrorist would be in the newspapers by tomorrow, and on TV that night.

Then, abruptly, they were alone. Christine was thinking about her ill-advised declaration of love when she'd thought they were about to die, and wishing fervently that she hadn't said those words. Not that they weren't true, but she wasn't ready for him to know about her true feelings. Everything had happened so fast, and she was so very afraid he didn't feel the same.

She sat in a chair several feet away from Ryan, far out of physical reach. Though they'd been clinging to each other for one reason or another for the past twenty-four hours, she now felt awkward about touching him. Whatever had to be said between them at this point, she didn't want it muddied up with hormones and whatnot.

"I wish the media hadn't found out about all this," Christine said glumly, breaking the silence that had so suddenly descended on the room.

"Why not?" Ryan asked. "You'll be vindicated. Isn't that what you want?"

"Yeah, but I wanted you to be the one to do it. This is your story, after all. You're the one who nearly got killed for it."

Ryan just stared at her. "I can't believe you just said that. You don't get it at all, do you?"

Of all the pain he'd been through in the past twenty-four hours, nothing compared to what Christine had just done to him. How could she think, after all they'd been through, after the intimacy they'd shared, after she'd saved his life, that he continued to want to profit from his relationship with her?

How could she love a person she thought would do that? Yet she'd claimed to love him. Her admission had been in the heat of battle, when they were outfirepowered four bullets to hundreds, but she'd said the words, and he'd believed them.

Then why couldn't she show a little more faith in him?

"I don't intend to write anything more about you or your father, Christine," he said stiffly, his throat thick with anger. He couldn't even bring himself to say aloud her nickname, the only name he'd ever called her by. It seemed to mock him, the intimacy between them.

"Why not?" she wanted to know. "You're the only one with the whole story. Who better than you to write the last chapter?"

Damn it! Because it wasn't the last chapter, not for him. He wanted his story with Chrissy to go on forever. If she'd ever loved him, even a little, she wouldn't, once she read the words he'd written about her.

Not that she necessarily ever would. He hadn't ever faxed or mailed the contract back to *Primus*. He'd forgotten about it, sort of accidentally on purpose. *Primus* might publish the story anyway, even without a contract. They had space reserved for it, and a verbal agreement. They might just risk a lawsuit from him for the scoop of the year.

"If you're so anxious to get your story to the public,"
he said, "I'm sure there are a million and one reporters
who would talk to you. They're probably roaming the hospital corridors as we speak, trying to figure out how to get
a crack at you. Why don't you go give them what they
want?"

Chrissy blinked at him, looking more confused than ever.
"I don't understand."

"I know."

"Well, fine, then!" She got up and stalked out of the
room.

When he was alone, his heart feeling like a chunk of
lead, he picked up the phone and dialed information for
New York City. "Yes, I need the number for *Primus* magazine, please."

A few minutes later, he had a ranting Bruce Garlock on
the line. "Where the hell are you?" Garlock shouted into
the phone. "And where the hell is our contract? I got four
blank pages to fill up, and legal won't let me use a word
of your story till I have the contract. You promised to fax
it and overnight it, and you haven't done either!"

Ryan let the editor wind down, finish his hissy fit. Then
he said, calmly, "I'm not sending the contract. I've
changed my mind. I don't want you to print that story."

"What? What are you talking about?"

Ryan decided to go for the truth. Nothing short of the
truth would explain his change of heart. "Bruce, I've fallen
in love with Christine Greenlow. I can't be responsible for
bringing this…this notoriety to her and her family."

"But she's not the one who looks bad! It's her old man."

"I know. And she loves her old man. I can't do it. Once
she reads that story, she would never speak to me again."

"It's a damn good story, man. You didn't pull any
punches but you didn't exactly eviscerate the woman, either. If you don't do this, some other reporter will."

"Exactly." Let her take out her anger and frustration on
some other reporter. Not him. The press was going to stomp
all over her and Stan Greenlow; some sharp journalist

would make the same connection Ryan had made between NATURE and the kickbacks. The news would get out without Ryan's contribution.

"Listen, Mulvaney," Garlock said, almost growling. "You pull this stunt with me and you'll never write for this magazine again."

Ryan didn't much care. He didn't write that much for *Primus,* anyway. "I'm sorry, Bruce. I know I'm creating a hell of a problem for you. I didn't plan it that way. I couldn't have known what would happen. The woman literally saved my life. She's been through so much. I can't cause her any more pain, I just can't."

Bruce heaved a defeated sigh. "Thanks a heap, Mulvaney." He hung up.

Boy, talk about burning bridges, Ryan thought. His career might never recover from this, if the story got around that he'd reneged on an agreement to sell an article.

Ah, hell, what career? He'd never thought much about how his stories affected the people he wrote about. But now that he'd been on the other side of the fence, he felt differently. He'd be rethinking his whole approach to journalism after this.

Someone tapped on his partially open door, and his heart leaped of its own accord at the thought that it might be Chrissy. But it was, instead, someone he hadn't expected to see, and he almost didn't recognize her.

"Josie!"

His sister smiled fondly. She was wearing a denim jumper, black lace-up boots and socks with little flowers—a very un-Josette-like getup. Her hair was short and styled into a puff all around her face, and she was wearing makeup. "Rye. And when I think of all the times you lectured me about the messes I got myself into…"

He had to laugh, even though it hurt. "I never lectured you," he argued.

"You did so, just like any big brother should." She claimed the room's only chair and set her purse down. "So, I hear there's a girl involved."

"How'd you know I was here?" he asked, sidestepping Josette's question. His feelings were still too raw for him to talk about Chrissy.

"The cops called me. I'm still the official owner of the house you broke into. They were trying to verify your story about it being your sister's house."

"And how did they find you? Where are you living, anyway?"

She hesitated. "Well…I got married. I'm sorry I didn't tell you, Rye. But things were just going so well for me, for the first time ever, that I didn't want to tell anyone for fear I might break the spell. You're not mad, are you?"

Mad? Nah, he could never be mad at Josie. He shook his head, then grinned. He'd certainly never expected this. "Who's the lucky guy?"

"He's an accountant, can you believe it? Me with a C.P.A.? I'd introduce you, but he's downstairs in the waiting room with Tad. He's so great, Rye, you wouldn't believe. He took to Tad right from the beginning, like he was his real son. He's going to adopt him."

"That's great, Josie!" He'd never seen his sister looking this perky. The smile on her face was so foreign, Ryan couldn't help staring. "I'm happy for you."

"I'm living right here in Richmond, can you believe it? So, never mind me, what's all this?" she asked, pointing to the IV lines and voluminous bandages. "You're okay, aren't you?"

He nodded. "This wasn't my idea." He'd checked into the hospital strictly to please Chrissy.

Josette pressed for details, so he gave her the bare essentials of the story. He stayed away from mentioning any kind of emotional ties to Chrissy and, thank God, Josette didn't ask about their relationship. She was curious, though—he could tell just by what she didn't say.

Josette left, promising to return in the morning when he was ready to check out. She would bring him to her place, she insisted, where he could recuperate and be babied for a few days before he returned to his own home. He went along with her idea. He wondered where Chrissy would go. Would she still try to stay with Michelle?

Alone again, Ryan had no choice but to relive scenes from the past few days and wallow in the fact that he'd driven Chrissy away from him. Hell, he shouldn't have gotten so snotty with her. He'd never told her how he felt about her. Without knowing he loved her, how could she understand that he would never exploit her for money or fame?

He had to find her. But when he tried to sit up, his shoulder protested so vehemently that he cried out with the pain. The stupid bullet wound hurt worse than ever. Besides, he was hooked up to all kinds of IVs—blood transfusions, pain drugs, antibiotics.

He slumped back on the bed, then pressed the button to summon a nurse. Maybe he could bribe her to find Chrissy and bring her back. He would lay it on the line with Chrissy. He would declare his feelings, his intention to spend the rest of his life with her, and see if that changed things.

It had better, or he was going to follow her around for the rest of her life until she understood. He'd make Denny look like an amateur when it came to persistence.

Christine wandered down to the first floor of the hospital, taking the stairs to avoid the reporters. She was so angry with Ryan that she could spit, and she wasn't even sure why. Talk to another reporter? As if she would do that! She was *his* story, and she liked it that way. He was the only one she trusted to relate the facts honestly.

So why didn't he want to write about her anymore? What had changed? *You fell in love with him, dummy.* He didn't want to involve himself any further in her life, for fear she would attach herself to him like a leech and never let go.

But wait, that didn't make sense. Why had he insisted she stay with him when he checked into the hospital? That didn't seem like the action of a man who was trying to get rid of a woman. So, what else had changed? Was he afraid of being the target of NATURE's crazed members? That didn't sound like the Ryan she knew. He wasn't afraid of anything.

She decided to call her sister again. The hospital staff had given her a small private waiting room where she could avoid the press and make phone calls if she liked. It seemed the Greenlow name wasn't without influence, after all. She returned to that room, settled into a soft chair, picked up the phone and placed a collect call.

"Michelle? Christine. I guess you figured out I've been delayed again."

"Christine, honey, where *are* you? I've been worried sick. Stan has called me about fifteen times, wantin' to know if I've heard from you again."

"Dad called?"

"Oh, Christine, I know he can be a jerk, but this whole thing has been one big misunderstanding. He really and truly didn't believe you were in danger."

"Then he thought I made it up?"

"He thought you were trying to start up a scandal to ruin his campaign so he wouldn't get reelected so he wouldn't have any more excuses not to seek treatment for the drug addiction."

Christine paused before answering to absorb everything Michelle had said. "You know about the drugs?" That was a very closely guarded secret.

"He told me everything. I really think you ought to talk to him," Michelle said. "Y'all got some serious air-clearing to do."

"Yeah, we do."

"And what about Robert?"

"He can fall down a well for all I care, the bastard."

"All right, Christine! I was wondering when you were going to see the light. I never could stand him."

"Why didn't you say so?"

"I would have, before you actually tied the knot. But I thought it would be better if you figured it out for yourself."

Where are you, anyway? Where's that guy you've been hanging out with?''

"I'm at a hospital in Richmond," she said. "I'm okay, don't throw a hissy. Ryan's here, too, but I...I think we're about to part company." For good.

"Oh, honey, do you want me to come get you? It's not that far."

"No. No, in fact, I think I'll do what I should have done in the first place. I'll go home."

"You don't mean it!"

"I'll go home, and I'll talk to Dad about getting my own place, getting a job, going back to school. I'll move out, but I won't do it like a little girl running away. I'll sit down and figure out my finances.''

"You can come stay with me if you want."

"Thanks, Michelle. Maybe I will. I'll let you know as soon as I make some decisions, okay?''

"Okay. You take care. Call me when you get home and talk to Stan. If he gives you any trouble, you turn him over to me."

Christine actually laughed. "I'll do that."

Now what? she wondered. She still had some of that hundred dollars. Could she take a bus back to D.C.? She couldn't, she realized. She couldn't just leave Ryan in the hospital. She'd promised to look after him while he was here. She had to at least keep that promise, even if he didn't want her to.

A shadow fell across her lap. She looked up to see a highway patrolman, his arms full. "Christine Greenlow?"

"Yes?"

"We found these things in Mr. Mulvaney's car when we had it towed. Thought you might need them."

Her suitcase! And some of Ryan's things, too. Another patrolman entered the waiting room with more stuff.

"Is that all of it?" the first officer asked.

"That's it."

"You can leave it here," Christine said. "I'll take care of it."

The officers seemed relieved to drop off their burdens and depart.

Christine began stacking up Ryan's things, intending to deliver them to his room. They would give her a good excuse to see him again and tell him of her plans. Maybe he would ask her to stay...maybe he would explain why he'd gotten so angry with her.

Then she saw the manilla folder, filled with neat typed pages. His story. He'd offered to let her read it after he sent it to *Primus,* and she'd declined. Now the temptation was too much. She closed the waiting room door, resumed her chair and began reading.

Fifteen minutes later, she was torn in two. Ryan hadn't lied. The story didn't contain a single untruth. And no reader who finished the story would be in doubt about Christine having, in fact, been kidnapped by environmental terrorists who tied her up, starved her and beat her.

Why, then, did she feel so negative after reading Ryan's composition? It wasn't just the horrid disclosures about her father's illegal campaign contributions. It was the way *she* sounded. Like a flake, a ditzy rich girl who had no idea what to do with herself when her father wasn't giving her minute-by-minute instructions.

Was that the way Ryan saw her? Was that the way she'd presented herself?

Was that what she really was? Well, regardless, that was how the rest of the world would see her. After this story came out, would anyone take her seriously again? Would anyone hire her as an employee? She couldn't help feeling angry at Ryan. Then again, she couldn't count herself blameless. She had said and done everything exactly as he'd portrayed it.

Again she began gathering up Ryan's things. She didn't want to delay talking with him. If they were really going to part ways for good, she didn't want anger between them. They'd come too far for that.

She opened the door and almost ran into someone standing on the other side, preparing to knock.

"Dad?"

"Christine, my God, are you all right?" The large man swept her into a warm hug. "Oh, Christine, I'm so sorry I didn't believe you, that I ignored— My God, I could have lost you. They said you were shot!"

Christine just stood there, stunned beyond words.

Chapter 17

Ryan's story nearly burned a hole through the manilla folder Christine clutched against her chest. She couldn't allow her father to see it, not yet. First she had to explain to him how Ryan had saved her life, not once but numerous times.

Stan Greenlow set his daughter away from him and studied her. He looked at the bandage on her forehead, the fading bruise on her jaw, her generally unkempt appearance. "Honey, tell me what happened. Did you really get shot?"

She gingerly touched the bandage. "They aren't sure if it was a bullet that grazed me, or just flying glass."

"We'll get you the best plastic surgeon money can buy," he said fervently.

Naturally, he would think of something like that, Christine thought impatiently. The possibility of a scar on her forehead hadn't even crossed her mind. "I'm sure that won't be necessary," she said. "It was a small cut. Come in the waiting room, Dad. We need to talk." It was then that she realized that Gerald was standing outside the room, along with a couple of her father's security guards. Behind them were two still photographers and a woman with a minicam. Had they recorded her reunion with her father?

The idea made her furious. If someone was going to invade their privacy, why couldn't it be Ryan? He'd earned the right, she figured.

Leaving everyone else outside, her father entered the room and closed the door. "You're sure you're all right? You just say the word and I'll fly you to the Mayo, get you a private suite—"

"I'm fine, really, just tired." They both sat down. Then, she couldn't resist saying, "It's a little late for you to be showing such devoted concern, don't you think?"

He closed his eyes. A tear escaped one, and Christine immediately regretted her harsh words. She hadn't seen her father cry since her mother's death.

"I'm so sorry, Christine, for doubting you. But you'd been so angry with me about the pills—"

"Concerned. I was worried sick, and you wouldn't listen to me."

"I know, I know."

"But how could you think that I would instigate something like that? That I would even associate with those terrorists? Do you know what I thought when I heard you refused to pay the ransom? I thought you didn't want me back. I thought you'd decided life would be less complicated with Christine dead than with Christine alive, and you'd get sympathy votes to boot."

"Christine! Good God, I may not be the soul of honesty and integrity, but I'm not a monster."

"I know. I realized that a little later. But the thought did cross my mind. I was confused. I'd been given this drug, and even after it mostly wore off, I was still a little disoriented, not thinking straight."

"So, will you tell me what happened? From the beginning."

Christine gave him an abbreviated version of her adventures, leaving out the romantic overtones. Her father frowned all the way through it. Even when she got to the part about Ryan's story and the kickbacks he'd learned about, her father's expression never changed.

"So, where is this story?"

"I've got it here," she said, handing him the folder. Better for him to read it here, in private, so that he could be prepared.

He scanned the pages briefly. "Well, this Mulvaney is a hell of a reporter, I'll give him that," he said. "He doesn't miss a trick."

Christine had expected a more dramatic reaction. "Dad, I thought you'd be bouncing off the walls. Aren't you mad?"

He shrugged. "Honey, it was all starting to fall apart long before the kidnapping. Some subcommittee was already starting to make inquiries. It was only a matter of time before this stuff came out."

"Then it's true?"

"Every word, I'm afraid."

She hesitated, then asked, "Why, Dad?"

"Why else? Ambition. After your mother died, that's all I had—my career. And you, of course. But you're grown up, ready to live your own life. I had one shot left at the presidency, and a damn good chance this time around of getting the Republican nomination. If I didn't get it, I was going to retire. I guess I lost all perspective." He sighed. "Anyway, it's over now."

"What's over?"

"The campaign, my career. I can't recover after a scandal like this. I have nothing left."

"You have me," she said, grabbing his hand. "I won't turn my back on you just because you've made some mistakes."

He nodded. "I guess I'll be checking into Betty Ford, too. I have nothing to hide, now. Besides, Dr. DeKalb got so rattled after that reporter tracked him down that he's cut off my prescription."

"Thank God for small favors," she said, but she put her

arms around her father's leathery neck and hugged him for all she was worth. "I'll help you through this."

"Now, honey, I don't want you to worry about me. You've got a wedding to think about, a new life with Robert."

Christine gasped. "Robert! I'm not marrying that scumbag. He left me stranded in this horrible neighborhood, wouldn't even come get me. Told me to take a cab. Ooh, wait till I see him. He's gonna be sorry he ever met me."

The senator cleared his throat. "Well, you'll get your chance, probably sooner than you thought. He's on his way here. He was about fifteen minutes behind me."

"Good. The sooner the better."

As if on cue, a tentative knock sounded on the door to the waiting room. "Christine, love, it's me, Robert."

Christine gathered up all of Ryan's things one last time. This was one confrontation she was actually looking forward to. She yanked open the door.

Robert smiled. "Darling!"

"You turkey." She slapped him hard enough that her hand stung like crazy. "I already told you, the engagement's off. And no, you can't have your ring back. It was stolen and fenced at a pawnshop." She turned to look at her astonished father. "Will you come with me to see the man I really want to marry?"

"Oh, Lord, not Mulvaney."

"He's the one."

Her father shook his head hopelessly. "I had a feeling this might be coming. Sure, take me to him. Let me chew on his butt a little bit, get it out of my system, before I give you my blessing."

Feeling inexplicably lighter of heart, Christine smiled and waved at the reporters and photographers who were now standing behind a barricade flanked by two hospital security guards.

"We're not exactly engaged," she said to her father once they were alone in the elevator. The bodyguards had stayed behind. "In fact, he might not even be speaking to me.

He's mad at me, I think because I suggested he might wan
to write a final chapter to his story, silly me. Apparently
insulted his integrity.''

''What, he's decided not to rip people to shreds with hi:
mighty typewriter?'' Stan asked derisively.

''Not everybody, just us,'' she replied as the elevato:
doors opened.

To her disappointment, she found Ryan asleep. Rathe
than wake him, she and her father retreated to a nearby
waiting area. ''You don't have to stay,'' she told Stan.

''What else do I have to do? Anyway, you've got me
curious. What are your plans?''

She shrugged. ''I don't know. He might just kick me
right out of his room.''

''Then you keep coming back. You know, I had to ask
your mother out four times before she finally accepted.
could have missed the whole boat if I hadn't been so per
sistent. You be persistent. Don't take no for an answer
Don't let misunderstandings get in the way.''

''No, I'm done with that,'' she said. She set Ryan':
things on the chair next to her, absently neatening the pile
That was when she saw a large white envelope she hadn'
paid much attention to before. Curious, she opened it and
pulled out the contents.

It was Ryan's contract with *Primus*. Unsigned. O
course! He'd told Fran he would overnight-mail it, bu
they'd never stopped at a post office. Had he forgotter
something so important? Somehow, she doubted it. He'
held the contract on purpose. Which meant…he intended
not to sell the story. But how could that be? He'd knocked
himself out for this story. It could bring him national at
tention, big-time job offers.

Something fluttered inside her chest, a tiny hope that had
sprung to life. He'd done it for her. Because he knew the
story would hurt her, even with the kid gloves he'd handled
her with. And he knew the story would be damaging to he
father.

That was what he'd meant when he accused her of no

'getting it." He loved her. The signs were there, she'd simply not seen them.

"What are you grinning about?" Stan asked.

"Oh, nothing." And everything.

Ryan stirred, then cracked his eyes open. At first he thought he was seeing things when the image of Stan Greenlow flashed through his brain. But no, the man was sitting a few feet from his bed, studying Ryan thoughtfully.

Was he here to kill him? Ryan thought blearily. Had *Primus* run his story anyway, and now Greenlow was here to exact his revenge? Then Ryan realized Chrissy was sitting next to her father, looking anxious.

He opened his eyes all the way. Was Chrissy actually smiling?

"Hey, sleepyhead, it's about time you woke up."

"Mmm. Pain drugs make me woozy," he managed. Then he remembered his earlier resolve to speak his mind to Chrissy, to let her know his feelings. He marshaled his thoughts together, intending to say something profound, but Chrissy beat him to it.

"You never sold that story to *Primus,* did you?" she asked without preamble. "I found the unsigned contract with your stuff the police pulled out of the car."

He shook his head. "No. I sent the story, but not the contract. I couldn't make myself do it, Chrissy. They might print it anyway, without my permission. I'm sorry. I should either have backed away from you or the story a lot sooner than I did. And I wasn't going to back away from you."

She surprised him with a huge grin. "I was hoping I'd read that right. Oh, Ryan, I'm past being hurt by all this publicity. Sell the story. Call that editor right now and tell him to print the story as it stands. It's good."

"You read it?" He cast a wary eye at the senator, who was being uncharacteristically quiet.

"We both read it," Chrissy said. "It's not exactly flattering, but it's as fair as anything that's likely to be printed about our family. Here, sign the contract. I'll take it down to the business office right now and fax it, and you can call the editor and tell him to print the story.'' She thrust the papers and a pen at him.

For a moment, he was tempted, but only for a moment. He shook his head. ''I can't do it. It would stand between us forever. Besides, I've become a part of the story. I'm nowhere near unbiased, if I ever was. No.'' He shook his head vehemently.

Chrissy exchanged a glance with her father. ''See, Dad, I told you he was a good guy. And he loves me. I think he fell in love with me the first time he saw me getting pawed by a bunch of hoodlums. Why else would he have risked his life rescuing me?''

Ryan didn't contradict her. He couldn't speak. He knew he probably had a silly grin on his face.

''Several times, apparently,'' the senator said dryly as he stood up and rubbed his hands together. ''Okay, I've had enough of this party. You two undoubtedly have things to talk about. I'm off to throw a press conference. Guess I'll have to tell everyone I'm going to Betty Ford.'' He was muttering to himself now. ''Guess I'll have to come up with some kind of clean-up plan for those wetlands, too. No, first I'll kick that worm Robert's butt from here all the way back to Washington.'' He left without saying goodbye.

''Mind telling me what that was all about?'' Ryan asked casually. ''Your father was looking me over like a prize-winning goat at the county fair.''

''He was checking you out for son-in-law potential.'' She looked up at the ceiling, down at her toes, anywhere but at him.

Ryan didn't know whether to take her seriously or not. ''And did he approve, or find me lacking?''

''Oh, he definitely approved.''

''Even after he read the story?'' Ryan could hardly believe that.

''I think the fact that you decided not to sell the story helped a lot, but he was already leaning toward approval

He likes the fact that you risked life and limb to take care of me. And he said you were a good reporter.''

"Well, there's just one question left, then. If I qualify as a son-in-law, do I make the cut as husband material?''

"Um, well, I might have been rushing things a bit. I said that about wanting to marry you as a parting shot to Robert.''

"So you don't want to marry me?'' he asked.

"I didn't say that. You're not…asking, are you? I mean, last time we talked, you told me to get out.''

He turned serious. "That was stupid of me. I got my nose out of joint because I thought you should read my mind, automatically have faith in me without my having proved I deserve it.''

"Oh, but you do deserve it,'' she said hastily, coming closer to the bed.

"You thought I would cash in on our relationship.''

"I thought—'' She stopped, seeming to choose her words carefully. "I'd hoped you would set the record straight—or keep it straight, that was all. You're in a unique position to tell the whole story, and I thought you would want to. I don't see anything wrong with that. But you can finish the story or not, print it or kill it, I don't care. I only care if you love me.''

She bit her lip. "Things haven't changed for me. Now that Denny is behind bars—and headed for Bellvue, I understand—and the rest of the group is being rounded up, and we're safe and sound, I feel exactly the same way as I did when I thought we were going to die. I love you.''

Ryan held out his hand. "Come closer, Chrissy.''

She hesitated, then took his hand.

"Closer.'' He reeled her in, then pulled her toward him until she realized his intent. She hesitated only a moment longer before leaning the rest of the way down and kissing him.

"Yes, I love you, too, sweet Chrissy,'' he murmured. 'And if I wasn't all trussed up like a Thanksgiving turkey, 'd show you how much.''

She produced a gratifying blush. "I don't know what t say. I'm afraid if I close my eyes, you'll disappear."

"No way. I'm a hostage here, remember? You're the on who can disappear in a puff of smoke."

"I'm here to stay."

"As for the marriage part…" His mouth was suddenl dry, so he took a swallow of ice water before continuing He wanted to get it right this time. "Chrissy, will yo marry me?"

She beamed at him. "Really? You mean it? I didn' guilt-trip you into it?"

"Of course I mean it. I haven't stayed a bachelor thi long by falling for guilt trips. So what's your answer? can't offer you anything like what Robert did—"

She pulled a face. "Oh, please."

"But I won't live off you, either."

"You wouldn't be able to. Surely you know by now ho\ little I have of my own. No reason we both can't work an earn money to live on like most people do, right?"

"I still haven't heard a yes."

"Yes," she said quickly.

"At the first opportunity, then. 'Cause, somehow, I douļ the senator will approve of his daughter living in sin fc long." He sealed their deal with another kiss.

*　*　*　*　*

♥™ SILHOUETTE
INTRIGUE™

AVAILABLE FROM 21ST JANUARY 2000

LOVER, STRANGER Amanda Stevens

Grace Donovan needed to get close to mysterious Ethan
Hunter; he was the one man who could identify her sister's
killer. He was the one man whose touch ignited in Grace a
burning fever of forbidden desire…

RELUCTANT WIFE Carla Cassidy

Lawyer Samantha Dark was coming home determined to
defend a friend accused of murder, determined to locate the
real killer, reluctantly prepared to work with Tyler Sinclair—
Mr Perfect himself. But at least her forbidden passion for him
was a thing of the past…or was it?

THE BODYGUARD Sheryl Lynn

JT McKennon was all man—loyal, strong and determined. As
a bodyguard he was the ultimate protector. But as Frankie
Forrest saw it, he was nothing but trouble—tall, dark and
broad-shouldered trouble. With her sister kidnapped, she had
to rely on his expertise, but protected in his arms, was it her
heart in real danger?

TO LANEY, WITH LOVE Joyce Sullivan

Laney Dobson needed to know if her missing husband was
alive. Turning to Ben Forbes, together they searched for
answers—finding unexpected desire… But when the body of
her husband was found, Ben feared Laney and her son were
still at risk. Determined to protect Laney at all costs, Ben
would even stop their wedding to catch the killer…

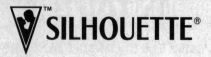

Look out in April 2000 for

A Fortune's Children Wedding

and the first book of a 5 part series

The Fortune's Children Brides

books and a surprise gift!

We would like to take this opportunity to thank you for reading this Silhouette® book by offering you the chance to take TWO more specially selected titles from the Intrigue™ series absolutely FREE! We're also making this offer to introduce you to the benefits of the Reader Service™—

- ★ FREE home delivery
- ★ FREE gifts and competitions
- ★ FREE monthly Newsletter
- ★ Exclusive Reader Service discounts
- ★ Books available before they're in the shops

Accepting these FREE books and gift places you under no obligation to buy, you may cancel at any time, even after receiving your free shipment. Simply complete your details below and return the entire page to the address below. *You don't even need a stamp!*

YES! Please send me 2 free Intrigue books and a surprise gift. I understand that unless you hear from me, I will receive 4 superb new titles every month for just £2.70 each, postage and packing free. I am under no obligation to purchase any books and may cancel my subscription at any time. The free books and gift will be mine to keep in any case.

10EA

Ms/Mrs/Miss/Mr ....Initials.................................
BLOCK CAPITALS PLEASE

Surname ....

Address ....

....

....Postcode.................................

Send this whole page to:
UK: FREEPOST CN81, Croydon, CR9 3WZ
EIRE: PO Box 4546, Kilcock, County Kildare (stamp required)

Offer valid in UK and Eire only and not available to current Reader Service subscribers to this series. We reserve the right to refuse an application and applicants must be aged 18 years or over. Only one application per household. Terms and prices subject to change without notice. Offer expires 30th June 2000. As a result of this application, you may receive further offers from Harlequin Mills & Boon and other carefully selected companies. If you would prefer not to share in this opportunity please write to The Data Manager at the address above.

Silhouette is a registered trademark used under license.
Intrigue is being used as a trademark.